STRONG
and
COURAGEOUS

Celeste Walsh

ISBN 979-8-88832-593-3 (paperback)
ISBN 979-8-88832-594-0 (digital)

Copyright © 2023 by Celeste Walsh

All rights reserved. No part of this publication may be reproduced, distributed, or transmitted in any form or by any means, including photocopying, recording, or other electronic or mechanical methods without the prior written permission of the publisher. For permission requests, solicit the publisher via the address below.

Christian Faith Publishing
832 Park Avenue
Meadville, PA 16335
www.christianfaithpublishing.com

Printed in the United States of America

PROLOGUE

My first conscious thought is, I am on a boat and being tossed at sea. I am bouncing side to side like a boat in a storm. But I'm dry, and I feel more like I am fighting my way up from a deep well, and my limbs are heavy and trying to drag me back to the depths of that well. Part of me wants to just sink back down to the cool, dark quiet, but then suddenly, a part of my brain screams at me to open my eyes. I blink away tears and try to shake my head but am rewarded with pain exploding below my left eye and cheek.

That's when I remember. That's when reality slams into me like a Mack truck, and I fight to push away the fog that was clouding my memory as I blink away more tears. "Wake up, Sarah!" I scream in my own head or maybe out loud. I don't really know. I just keep pushing upward for the surface. Bright light floods my vision as I remember fully where I am and how I got here.

I am on the dusty floorboard of a strange car in Egypt. My breath is coming in quick shallow gasps now, and I know I have to get it under control before I hyperventilate and pass out, again. I must have blacked out for a few minutes, and I don't want to do that again. I have to keep my wits about me and stay conscious if I'm going to make it out of this situation.

I'm having trouble slowing my breathing down, so I do the one thing I know to do, I pray. I ask God to help me stay calm and to give me strength to get out of this awful situation. I pray that I can find a way out of this on my own or that he would send someone to help me.

I take a few deep breaths and feel the Lord speak to me as I recall the verse in Joshua, "Be strong and courageous." I am feeling anything but strong as I've already been overpowered by two strange men. And as for courage, I've never been more terrified in my whole life. I can't see any possible way out, but I know I have to have faith anyway. I steady myself as I try to pull myself up from the floorboard but am rewarded for my efforts with a shove back down by a big meaty hand and words that are foreign to me.

Panic sets in again as I realize that I can't reason, negotiate, or even talk my way out of this if I can't communicate with my captors. I try to look out of the windows, but I can't see much from this angle. I know we are still in the city by the noise and traffic. I try to figure out the direction we are traveling, but it is still early, and the sun has not fully risen to its height in the sky.

As time passes, the traffic gets lighter and lighter. We are leaving the city. I estimate it's been at least forty-five minutes, but it feels like hours. I worry more as we leave the populated city and head for parts unknown and less populated. I close my eyes and save my strength because I know that I will have to fight for my life when the time comes. I try to pray again, but I just keep repeating myself over and over again like I'm caught in a loop. I whisper to myself, "Be strong and courageous." I decide to once again try to figure out the direction we are going and calculate the passing of time. I'm studying the interior of the car to see if there is anything I can use as a weapon. But my view is limited from my position on the floor, and I don't see anything of use.

I'm having a hard time trying to focus. I feel myself being pulled down by panic and despair. I keep asking myself, how did I get into this situation. I keep thinking why me. Tyler was right, I should have been more careful. This is all my fault.

I begin to despair and mentally have to kick myself again and say "be strong and courageous." I'm not sure if it is really working, but it helps give me something to focus on.

Time drags on and the day heats up. I can feel it through the floorboard. I try to shift and make myself more comfortable in the cramped space. I'm afraid to move too much as my captor keeps a close watch on me, and I don't really want my right cheek to match my left. It hurts but not nearly as bad. My top lip feels a little swollen as well, and I can taste a small amount of blood. I remember him hitting me to shut me up when they abducted me. They don't talk much, not that I could understand them anyway.

I keep flexing my legs and feet to keep the circulation going so that if the opportunity arises, I can run.

As the morning moves on, I am worried as to where I am being taken. It's been at least two hours now, and we seem to be somewhere in the countryside as I haven't seen any buildings in a while now. One positive is that I figured out that we are heading south. Not that it does me any good, as no one will know where I am or where I am headed, but I count it as a small win for me.

My brief moment of triumph is gone, and I am left feeling lost and alone. I sit thinking about how I got here. I retrace all the events that have led up to this one pivotal, horrible moment.

CHAPTER 1

The sun was just beginning to rise as we pulled into the loading zone at the airport. My best friend Lauren jumps out of my brother's SUV almost before we have come to a complete stop. I reach behind my seat to grab my backpack when my brother reaches over to touch my arm. "Promise me you will be careful." Holding his hand up to stop my reply, he says, "I know we've been through this before, but I still don't like you traveling to two different continents without any one to watch over you."

"I know you are concerned and I love you for it, but we will be fine. We've already agreed to stay together and watch each other's backs. No going off alone or with strange men. Now, stop worrying, give me a hug, and help me get our luggage out of the back."

I think about all the times my big brother has been there for me over the years since Mom and Dad died, and I'm reminded of how lucky I am to have him. As a twenty-one-year old, he never once complained about being stuck with the responsibility of raising a teenager when he could have been off enjoying college life with his friends. He never complained about doing housework or coming home early on Friday nights or helping me with algebra. Instead, he moved back home from the dorm so that I could stay in our family's home after Mom and Dad's car accident.

Tyler then petitioned the court to become my legal guardian. With the insurance money, he was able to pay off the house and set some money aside for monthly expenses and my college education. He graduated a year and a half later and married the year after that.

Six years later, Tyler and Lisa (that's his wife) still live in our childhood home where they are raising their two children—Danny, 3, and Eliza, 1. When I turned twenty-one, I decided it was time to move into an apartment. So, in my junior year of nursing school, Lauren and I found a two-bedroom apartment and moved in together. Tyler and Lisa were expecting baby number one and the house was getting a little cramped, so I decided it was time to move out on my own and give them some space. So Lauren and I have been sharing rent for the last three years.

Tyler tried to give me some of the insurance money, but I told him to hold on to it for me, and one day, when I'm ready to buy a house, we can negotiate then. He argued that it wasn't right that he and Lisa get the house while I paid rent and even offered to sell it and split the money with me, but I don't want him to sell our home. I reminded him that if Mom and Dad were still here, I would be moving out and paying my own rent anyway. I told him this would help me learn responsibility. (I'm no saint. I've thought many times over the past three years what I could do with that money. Like pay for this trip!)

All in all, I'm glad it's still in an account for me. It's not a lot of money, but it's enough for a small down payment. Maybe one day when I get married, I will use it to buy my own home. Since I'm not currently dating anyone and I don't know who, when, or where that might be, I'm content to share rent with Lauren. Besides, Tyler has put more blood, sweat, and tears into the upkeep of that home; he deserves to keep it.

When Lauren and I graduated college last year along with our two childhood friends Nicole and Stasia, we all agreed to work for a year and save up some money to treat ourselves to a graduation vacation. We decided it might be the only time that the four of us would be able to travel together before we ended up married with children or married to our jobs. So we spent an entire weekend mapping out the places on our bucket list that we wanted to visit. It only took two pizzas, a dozen chocolate chip cookies, two pints of ice cream, and too many gummy bears to count before we made our dream itinerary. We decided on two days in Paris, then a bus and train ride down to Italy where we would spend one day in Milan, one day in Florence, and two days in Rome. From there, we would hop another flight down to Egypt and spend our remaining time touring the pyramids and ancient temples of the pharaohs.

We worked with a travel agent who worked her magic and helped us find the best travel deals, hotels, and transportation. Once we had all the specifics worked out, we knew how much cash we would have to come up with. We've spent the last fifteen months working and saving for our trip, and we can barely contain our excitement!

I'm really proud of all the things Tyler and I have accomplished and how blessed I am to be able to take this trip with my friends. I'm so lost in my thoughts about how my life has turned out, that I lose my balance as Tyler nudges my shoulder with his. "You okay?" he asks.

"Yeah. Just thinking about how lucky I am to have you and Lisa and my friends."

"You're not going to get homesick and call me to come pick you up like you did at camp, are you?" he teases.

"Haha. No, I didn't get homesick, it was more like I got camp sick." I flash my best smile at him and reach for my suitcase. What I never did tell him was that I couldn't stand watching all my friends write letters home to their parents each day. I had already spent the previous year trying to adjust to the new normal. Eventually, everyone stopped asking how I was doing after I replied "fine" for the thousandth time.

Camp opened old wounds again. New girls, same old questions, and it just became too much, too claustrophobic for me. I didn't like answering the questions of what happened to my parents all over again. I didn't have anyone to write except Tyler, and one letter was all I could do. So, after three days, I called him up and faked severe menstrual cramps and home I went to the sanctuary of home and the people who knew me.

This trip will be the longest I've ever been away from my brother in my life. Even though we don't live in the same house anymore, we still get together at least once a week for dinner. Lisa does a great job of making sure we have family night each week. I couldn't ask for a better sister-in-law. I think Tyler needs this trip as much as I do. He checks in on me almost daily.

    I pull my suitcase up on the sidewalk and give Tyler one last hug and promise to check in with him every few days. I also make him promise to not obsess about his baby sister and take his wife out on a date while I'm gone. I make him promise it will be a grown-up date without the kids. He agrees, and we say goodbye as I run to catch up with Lauren who spotted Nicole and Stasia inside the terminal.

CHAPTER 2

September 10

We arrive in Paris at 12:45 p.m. after almost ten hours in the air. I've hardly slept, but the adrenaline running through me feels like I'm mainlining espresso. We check into our hotel and drop off our luggage and walk the surrounding streets until we find a quaint sidewalk café where we order an assortment of cheeses, baguettes, crepes, and fruit. We sip on French wine and sparkling water as we savor all the wonderful flavors that fill our table.

Nicole spends most of her time batting her eyelashes at all the handsome French men who pass our table. Several smile and send her a "bonjour" as they pass, but most are in too much of a hurry to notice. It's just as well, we've made a pact to keep this a girls' trip and no looking for potential husbands, for three of us anyway. Stasia is off the market as of the Fourth of July when her boyfriend of two years, Louis, proposed during the fireworks display out by the lake back home in Fort Worth, Texas. We promised to try to visit at least one bridal shop in each major city to see the current styles.

After our late afternoon lunch, we catch an open-air bus to see some of the sights of the city, Arc de Triomphe, Champs-Élysées, and ending with the Eiffel Tower. We've decided to leave the Eiffel Tower for tonight when it's all lit up. We spend time looking out over the most romantic city with its thousands of twinkling lights and busy streets filled with honking cars and people walking hand in hand. Stasia talks incessantly about how much she wishes Louis was here with her to experience this and take a moonlit boat ride down the Seine. We all threaten to toss her over the side of the tower if she doesn't stop acting like a lovesick ninny. (Of course, we can't do that, they have bars all around the top. I hear they were having too many jumpers, so they caged it off.)

We wind through the streets and enjoy the sights and sounds of Paris at night. There are street performers, and music flows out of several clubs along the way. Sometime after midnight, we fall into bed and sleep like the dead.

Lauren wakes everyone at 8:00 a.m. to groans and complaints that it's way too early. I don't mind so much because I don't want to waste one minute sleeping. I climb out of bed and head for the bathroom to get dressed. Nicole and Stasia agree to meet us in the lobby by ten. So Lauren and I head downstairs to ask the concierge to aim us in the direction of chocolate-filled croissants. He points us to a place named Au Petit Boulangerie where we indulge in chocolate croissants and rich, creamy French hot chocolate. Once we are well sated and quickly slipping into a chocolate coma, we decide to browse some of the area boutiques and shops. "A brisk walk will burn off some of the calories we just consumed," Lauren declares, as she sets off at almost a marching pace to see as much as we can in the next forty-five minutes before we meet the girls. Our plans today are to tour the Louvre and Notre Dame.

Lauren and I make a good pair. She is bubbly and outgoing and never meets a stranger, whereas I am more reserved and like to take things in slowly. I like to observe first before I act. That's not to say that I am meek or a pushover, because I'm far from it. Tyler made sure I was able to defend myself and with him being six years older than me, he never went easy on me when we were roughhousing. He always says that my laid-back demeanor is deceptive—that underneath, I am a powder keg with a short fuse. He encouraged me to use that to my advantage because people would not expect that out of me.

I've had to do a lot of self-discovery over the years. Not the drugs and alcohol type, but the deep, soul-searching type. I was pretty angry after my parents died, and my brother took me to talk to the pastor's wife one day after a pretty explosive exchange between the two of us. She was this sweet, quiet woman who taught me Sunday school in the second grade. She never raised her voice at us and always had a smile on her face. I couldn't imagine what "Mrs. Mary Sunshine" could say to help me. She had probably never had a bad day in her life. My narrow-minded, self-centered, fifteen-year-old world was about to be challenged by this unassuming lady.

We sat on the sofa in her living room where she offered me juice and cookies. As if I needed another reason not to like her. But I was raised to be respectful to my elders, so I told myself I could endure the rainbows and unicorns for at least one hour. (My attitude was pretty bad back then.)

She surprised me by asking me what made me most angry about my parents dying. Wow! No beating around the bush with her. I was so stunned that I just stared at her for several long seconds. "You know it's okay to be angry that your parents died, don't you?" she added. I was shocked that she would say such a thing. I thought for sure this had to be a trap, a trick question.

I considered my response carefully and responded with, "I thought it was a sin to be angry." Ha! Point for me.

She just smiled and answered, "Being angry is not a sin. It's when we act out in anger that our actions become a sin." Point for her.

A long silence stretched out between us as I considered what my next response should be. When words failed me, I reached for a cookie on the plate in front of me. To this day, I couldn't tell you what flavor it was. I just needed something to do while I sat there speechless.

Again, she asked, "What makes you the most angry about your parents dying?"

Right now, she is making me the angriest. I can't believe that she would continue with this line of questioning. Tears threaten the backs of my eyes. Who does she think she is? Why would she ask me such a painful question twice?

"The fact that they are not here!" I almost yell at her in frustration. "You don't know what it's like to not have them here to fix your breakfast or drive you to school or pick you up after a really bad day at school." I take a deep breath and continue to rattle off all the times that my parents aren't there. "Dinners, school plays, Christmas, Easter, birthdays, prom, my wedding…" my list ends with tears pouring down my face. "It just hurts so much knowing what they are missing, what I am missing. You don't understand how empty I feel."

"You're right that I don't know how you feel, but I know how I feel."

I'm still angry and interrupt her to scoff at what she thinks she could be feeling that comes close to how I feel. I know for a fact that her mother is still living. She plays the piano at our church every Sunday.

"What could you possibly think compares to how I feel?" I chew my words out between clenched teeth.

Nothing prepares me for the answer she gives. "Burying three babies in five years." I feel as though I've been punched in the gut. I can't believe what she just said. I thought she had the perfect little family with her husband Reverend Tom and their little boy Noah. I'm trying to remember how old Noah is. Is he four or five? She always seems so happy, so cheerful. How can this be?

After she gives me a few minutes to process what she just said, she continues on. "I lost all three babies before Noah. I would carry them for six to seven months and then lose them. After the first baby, I thought it was just a fluke and wasn't meant to be, so we quickly got pregnant again. When it happened again, I was pretty angry with God for making me go through that a second time. I said some pretty hurtful things to Him and the people around me who were just trying to help. It took me several months to realize that I didn't want their help or their sympathy. I wanted to be angry. It was the fuel that got me out of bed in the mornings and gave me a reason to keep breathing. All I could think about was how much I was missing: the birthdays, Christmas, Easter, holidays, first days of school."

I feel like a heel as she uses my same words, but she doesn't seem angry about it, just stating a fact.

"But you're not angry now. How…" I can't even finish my question as I choke back the tears.

"I spent a lot of time talking to God about all the things I was angry about, and He helped me to trust that there was a purpose in my loss. Romans 8:28 tells us 'that in all things, God works for the good of those who love him'—all things. I didn't understand at the time, but visiting with you and other mothers who have lost children helps me to understand that maybe my purpose was to help others through difficult times." She takes a deep breath and says, "And remember, I went through another loss before Noah."

Again, I can't answer, so I nod my head slowly to let her know that I do see how she might understand what I'm feeling.

"I would be happy to tell you how I stopped being angry all the time and started concentrating on all the good things I do have. It was hard work, but I'm happier now than I've ever been. Would you like to not be angry anymore?"

All I could manage was a nod of my head. She came and sat next to me on the sofa and placed her arm around my shoulders and just held me while I cried.

Over the next few months, we met a couple of times a week to talk, cry, pray, and remember all the good times and blessings that I still had. She had me tell her my favorite memories and bring picture albums to show her our family outings and vacations. She helped me to not be consumed by my loss but to remember the good times. She helped me realize that my parents would want me to be happy, and that Tyler and I are still here; we are still family. I still get sad and miss my parents, but I'm not angry about it anymore.

Lauren is one of those blessings that I still have. She helps me to be positive and reminds me how to embrace and enjoy life. When I'm in a bad mood, she does something totally unexpected that makes me laugh or at least laugh at her.

As we continue down this busy Parisian street, I'm overcome with feelings of gratefulness for everything I have. I decide right then and there that no more living in the past. I'm here in this beautiful city, and I'm going to make the most of it.

CHAPTER 3

September 13

We board an 8:00 a.m. train south to Italy. I'm exhausted from the past two days of visiting the Louvre, Notre Dame, museums, and dress shops (Stasia is getting married next year) and staying out dancing at a club until two o'clock this morning. I'm going to make the most of our train ride today. I spend the first two hours watching the countryside slide by before I drift off to sleep.

We arrive in Milan around three in the afternoon, and Stasia insists that we check into our hotel and find a bridal shop and browse before dinner. I convince her to stop and admire several cathedrals along the way. I'm amazed at the details and craftsmanship of all the architecture. The talent and commitment to spend their lives working on things that they may not live to see finished is inspiring. It's beautifully exhilarating.

The following day, we visit the Leonardo da Vinci museum, an opera house, and the Piazza del Duomo before catching a bus down to Florence, Italy. We make a short detour to Pisa to see the Leaning Tower of Pisa along the way. I check in with Tyler to let him know that all is well, and we are having a great time.

As much as I enjoyed Paris, I find that I really like the people of Italy. They are friendly and jovial. They seem to be more relaxed and less hurried. There is a timeless feel here with the cobblestone streets and architecture. It's almost like stepping back in time. I can almost imagine what it was like when horse-drawn carts and buggies clogged these streets.

We must walk ten to twelve miles a day trying to see as much of each city that we can. This is a good thing since we have consumed so much bread, cheese, pasta, and gelato.

Another aspect of Italy we have come to enjoy are the men. The Italian men have perfected the art of flirting and compliments. Nicole is spellbound by them all. We laugh as she is totally intoxicated by their flowery words and terms of endearment. It's fun to be told how beautiful you are by a complete stranger and to have compliments lavished on you. She could be easily enticed to run off with any one of them. But we girls must stick together and not fall for sweet words and a sexy accent. So we hook our arms through hers and steer her in the direction of our next stop.

Nicole is busy telling us why she is so taken with their dark, chocolate eyes, olive skin and godlike beauty, not to mention their great sense of style, when she nudges me and says, "We could find you a nice Italian man to marry. You said you wanted a beautiful, godlike man to marry someday."

I gape at her and say, "I said I wanted a godly man to marry, not godlike. Big difference, Nicole." We all laugh, and she continues to flood us with adjectives of all the wonderful attributes of Italian men.

September 16

We are one week into our trip with only four days left before we begin to make our way back home. I've managed to pick up French chocolates for Tyler, Lisa, and the kids and a cute pair of sandals for me in Milan. I also got a dress in Rome. So far, Rome has been my favorite city. I love all the fountains, cobblestone streets, and, of course, gelato on every other corner.

I'm reorganizing my suitcase and backpack as we prepare to head out to the airport for the last leg of our trip. I'm really excited because this is my bucket list portion of our trip. I can't wait to see the pyramids and ancient tombs, and hopefully, a mummy. Danny wants lots of pictures of a mummy, and I promised to send him one as soon as I can. I dress in light weight, white cotton capris and a light blue T-shirt. I make sure I have sunscreen, sunglasses, and a scarf in my backpack.

As we land in Cairo, I send off a quick text to Tyler to let him know that we arrived safely and I will call him tomorrow. It's late afternoon, and the air is hot and dry as we pile into a cab for the hotel. We make a quick stop to drop off our luggage and head out into the busy, littered streets of Cairo to find an early dinner. We have decided to eat and then go back to the hotel and lounge by the pool before we turn in for the night. It's been a busy week, and we all need a little downtime.

September 17

Early the next morning we meet up with a tour group of about six other people from several different countries to tour the Giza pyramid complex. We purchase our tickets and hire camels before passing through a security checkpoint to enter the complex. I'll have to let Tyler know how tight security is here. Hopefully he will be pleased to know that we went through a metal detector and had our bags searched. Then again, maybe I won't mention this as he might start worrying about who would smuggle guns or weapons into the pyramid complex.

We have camels and a guide to take us where we are going. It is hot, sandy, and totally exhilarating to be here in this place and experiencing the awe and wonder of just how massive these structures are. It's the most exciting thing I've ever gotten to experience, even if it is on the back of a smelly camel. I wrap my scarf around my neck to make it easier to get to if I should need it later as the temperature continues to rise.

We are scheduled to ride around the pyramids for the next two hours, so I take as many pictures as I can. I get several good shots of the Sphinx. We eventually stop at the great pyramid, and I pull out my ticket so that I can explore inside.

The tombs are long empty, and its former residents are probably housed in one of the many museums we plan to visit tomorrow. But today, I walk through the cool long tunnels that lead to the interior and enjoy the reverence that these tombs inspire. There is a sense of reverence even in their emptiness. It is a little haunting in its stark beauty and complexity. I can only imagine what it would have been like to be here when it was new and filled with worldly treasures.

By lunchtime, the camels are gone, and we are on foot again. After we stock up on water, we continue to mill around the ancient tombs and temples. It's obvious, from the amount of time and resources that went into the construction of each one, that their religious beliefs dominated their entire lives and society. We finish out the day with a cool walk through the Grand Egyptian Museum in Giza.

September 18

Today, we slowly make our way through the Cairo city streets, and we wade through the sea of people, vehicles, and, surprisingly, animals. There are several donkeys and other livestock scattered throughout the city streets. It's a far cry from the friendly, laid-back atmosphere of Italy. The Egyptians are more hurried and not as friendly as the Italians.

First, we will visit the Egyptian Antiquities Museum and then the Coptic Museum. We spend a couple of hours walking exhibit halls and taking in all the artifacts and mummies housed within these walls. I get a postcard with a mummy on it for Danny as the museum does not allow flash photography, and I'm not sure how well my pictures will come out.

As I examine each artifact, I imagine how it would have been displayed inside the pyramids and tombs we visited yesterday. It's so amazing to me how much gold was used in their art and jewelry—from the sarcophaguses filled with their mummified remains to the golden death masks that covered their wrapped, lifeless faces. Not to mention all the carved statues, jewelry, and Coptic art. The Coptic art dates back to Egypt's Christian era and includes a book of Psalms of David.

It's all so beautiful, and I am intrigued with each piece of art and the extravagance of that time period. Everything is so bold and colorful, even their written language is a form of art. True craftsmanship like this is rare in our age of machines and tools and instant access to just about anything you can imagine.

Before dinner, we decide to make our way to an open market to see what the merchants have to offer. We've been inside all day, and the dry heat takes some getting used to, but I know as the afternoon wears on that, the temperatures will cool. It was in the seventies yesterday evening, and we look forward to the welcome relief from this heat. The open desert around the pyramids had more of a breeze than these cramped city streets.

We visit many stands with pottery, textiles, and beautifully dyed scarves and cloth. There are also many food vendors in this area, so we decide to try some of the local cuisine. We feast on falafel balls and gyros with peppers and a creamy white sauce, and something sweet and doughy. The flavors are rich and spicy.

I ask the girls to help me be on the lookout for mummy souvenirs for Danny and maybe a doll for Lizzie. This market is located a little farther on the outskirts of town, but our cab driver assured us that it was the best one for purchasing souvenirs and experiencing the local culture. He was right, but the crowds are making me nervous, so I shift my backpack to the front in order to keep a better eye on it.

Lauren and Stasia are soon engrossed in negotiations over some colorful scarves and sandals, so Nicole and I move down the way to a table displaying replicas of mummies, falcons, and the Sphinx. As I ponder my choices, Nicole spots a small café across the street, which she is hoping will have a public restroom. She tells me to catch up to her after I make my purchases, but I'm distracted and mumble a quick okay. It's too late when I realize that we have just broken our agreement not to go off alone, but she is already across the street.

I quickly spin on my heel to make my way to the café without looking, and my sudden change of direction sends me crashing into a rather large man. He is obviously irritated by my collision with him and is speaking harshly to me in a language I don't understand (which is probably a good thing for me). He moves in closer as he raises his voice, and his eyes bore right through me. A tight knot forms in the pit of my stomach as I nod an apology and attempt to step around him. He mirrors my move and blocks my way. I once again tell him I am sorry, and this time I quickly step out of his reach and cross the street to the café.

I'm so flustered from the encounter that I run straight into Nicole as she emerges from the café.

"Where's the fire?" she jokes as she reaches out to steady me.

"You left me alone, and I was hurrying to catch up to you," I answer, half out of breath. I don't tell her about my encounter with the angry man that I bumped into. I would rather forget it, and I don't want it to ruin my day.

"I was just across the street, and Lauren and Stasia are headed this way," she says as she rolls her eyes at me.

Now I feel embarrassed that I overreacted. I probably blush down to my toes. Nicole reaches over and grabs my arm and teases, "Tyler still has his hooks into you halfway around the world. Relax and lighten up and stop worrying so much."

The loyal little sister in me bristles at her chiding. I want to tell her that Tyler only worries because he cares about me and after the loss of our parents, well, maybe he did develop an overinflated protectiveness. But I hold my tongue because any comment I make will make her feel guilty for talking bad about Tyler. I smile and decide not to make a big deal out of it.

We meet up with the girls and work our way back to the main thoroughfare loaded with our purchases. We will need to find a cab before dark, and nature's call has reminded me that I still need to find a restroom. I look around but don't see any promising places to stop.

As we walk down the street, the hair on the back of my neck raises, and I feel like someone is watching me. I turn around several times but don't spot anyone suspicious. Maybe I'm just tired and still rattled from my earlier encounter. I shake it off and try not to dwell on it anymore.

September 19

Today is our last day before we board our plane tomorrow morning to head home. I skipped my call home last night after Nicole's comment but decided to call Tyler this morning. I don't want him to worry, and I am still uneasy for reasons I can't explain. I decide talking to him might help put me at ease.

So, after breakfast, I excuse myself and walk around the hotel lobby to make my call. I have not taken into account the time difference until Tyler's groggy voice answers the phone. "Sarah, is everything okay?" I can hear the worry in his voice, and I realize what time it is so I hurriedly apologize and assure him everything is fine.

"Are you sure?" he asks. "You sound off or something."

"I'm fine, just tired and forgot what time it is there. I'm sorry I woke you. Go back to sleep. I'll call you when we get back to the States."

"Sarah," he prompts.

"Yea," I reply.

"Lisa says thank-you for the adult date."

That makes me smile, and I tell him to tell her she is very welcome. We say our goodbyes, and I promise to visit them when I get back. My tension is gone, and I'm glad I called. I feel silly that I let that one encounter spook me so badly yesterday. It's a bright sunny day, so I decide to walk outside to get some fresh air. I tell myself that I will only walk the sidewalk in front of the hotel.

I exit the building and walk a few steps down toward the corner when I realize that the doorman is not in his usual spot this morning. I decide maybe he is busy helping someone with their luggage and continue on my short walk. As I near the corner, I notice two men and a woman deep in conversation. They promptly stop as I approach and look at me as if I have intruded on a private conversation. I give them a faint smile and turn to change directions and head back the way I came. I hear footsteps and feel someone close behind me. I try to quicken my pace but am jerked backward as someone grabs both of my arms.

I try to pull away, but a hand snakes around and covers my mouth and prevents me from speaking. I can't see who has grabbed me either. I know it is a man by his size and the strength he is using to pull me quickly around the corner and out of site of the entrance. I'm beginning to panic and try to kick and fight, but my struggles only tighten his grip to the point of pain. I fight in earnest now knowing that whatever he has planned for me can't be good. My fingers are blindly seeking any soft tissue to sink into in hopes of causing some pain so that he will release me. I make contact with his face but can't reach his eyes. He gives a grunt as I drag my nails across his cheek.

The hand covering my mouth releases, and I think now's my chance to scream, but before I can utter a sound, that same hand smashes into the side of my head, stopping any sound I thought about making. It also knocks me off balance. As I get my feet squarely under me, he yells for someone else to grab my legs.

I buck with all my might. But for all my struggles, it is in vain. Tears begin to flow down my cheeks as I realize that I can't possibly fight off one attacker, let alone two. They carry me down the alley to a parked car and open the door to push me into the back seat. When the second man releases my legs, I kick out with all my might and catch him in the knee. He swears but doesn't go down and immediately strikes me across the face in retaliation.

The force of the blow to my cheek sends blinding pain through my head, and spots dance in my vision for a second. As the sting of the blow turns to pain, I am shoved onto the back seat of the car and pushed to the floorboard. The man who delivered the second blow jumps into the front seat and starts the car. My world goes black for a moment.

Terror threatens to cripple me, but I decide I'm not ready to give up yet. The farther this car goes, the lower my chances of survival are. I try to calm my breathing and decide in that moment I am not going to sit here quietly. I begin to beg them to let me go. I offer them money but quickly realize I left my backpack at the hotel. I start to look for my phone but realize that I lost it in the scuffle in the alley.

I again try to reason with my abductors and promise not to tell anyone if they will just let me out of the car. All my begging and pleading is rewarded with another blow. This time, it is a backhand to my other cheek that also grazes my upper lip, as I am told to stop talking. After the initial blinding pain, I sink into a dark abyss.

CHAPTER 4

This is how I ended up abducted and in a stranger's car, going God knows where, in Egypt.

We drive for what feels like hours, and from the lessening of sounds of the city, I know we have left Cairo far behind. The sun has risen high into the sky now, and my legs are asleep, but I don't dare move for fear of being struck again. The road feels curvy and less smooth than before. I worry that they are taking me to some remote location. The car suddenly lurches and starts making strange sounds. This new development is accompanied by some rapid and loud conversation in Arabic. I don't know what they are saying, but I do know that this new development has put a kink into their plans for me.

I begin to pray even harder. I pray for a window of opportunity to let me get safely away and for someone to offer me protection. At that moment, the car lurches again and makes a grinding noise. I take several deep breaths and shift my position slightly to try to restore some circulation to my legs. I need to be ready to act if this car breaks down. It might be the window I was praying for. "Strong and courageous," I remind myself again.

The car continues to lurch and sputter as we turn off the paved road onto what feels and sounds like a dirt road. I decipher that my backseat captor is giving the driver orders to turn this way and that by his hand gestures and loud speech. We travel for about ten more minutes, turning and twisting along this bumpy road when we finally come to a stop. I'm worried that they are going to get rid of me in some secluded area. I am wiggling my feet to help restore the blood flow faster when I'm suddenly shoved farther down onto the floor as the backseat guy barks orders to the driver once again.

I hear the front door open and think, *When the back door opens, I am going to fight my way out of here*, but the hand on my head pushes firmer and tells me to stay down. The back door opens, and the driver slides in and grabs a fistful of my hair as the other guy steps out of the car and firmly shuts the door behind him. My mind is racing trying to figure out why they traded places and what is going on. The fist in my hair tightens slightly as I'm told in broken English to stay down and be quiet. His grip loosens, and I blink away the tears threatening again.

We wait in the heat of the car for several minutes, and I am beginning to sweat. Finally, my other captor returns to the car and opens the back door. He says something, and the driver jerks my head upward so that I am looking at the captor standing in the open door. He tells me that when I get out of the car to walk calmly and quietly to the truck in the yard or he will break my knees. I don't reply, and the fist in my hair tightens, and I feel some strands give way. I nod as best as I can, afraid to speak for fear of crying. I have to keep it together now more than ever.

I slowly rise from the floor of the car and sit on the seat for a second as I try to get my bearings. I realize that we have stopped at a farm. The driver gives me a shove toward the door, and I stumble out of the car. The captor waiting outside firmly grabs me by the arm and begins directing me to a truck about twenty feet away. I start to struggle and am hit in the back of the left knee, and I go down hard in the dirt. Upon my emergence from the car and subsequent descent to the dirt, chaos breaks out in the yard near the house. An older woman begins yelling in unintelligible speech to me. She is obviously not happy about my appearance and my obvious unwillingness to get into another vehicle with these men. I get a surge of adrenaline and try to pull free of the hand around my arm and start screaming for help.

I try to push up to run, but blinding pain sears through me as the driver kicks me in the ribs, dropping me fully into the dirt. I can't breathe or move. I am gasping to get any air into my lungs, but the pain is too much, and I only succeed in making some mewling sounds. I try to lie very still and focus on getting some air into my lungs without having to take a deep breath. I'm pretty sure my ribs are fractured. I just hope they didn't puncture a lung.

The woman has ventured closer and is yelling and waving her arms, but the men only ignore her. The man who threatened to break my knees lifts me under my arms and begins to drag me to the truck. The movement sends white hot pain through my right side again, and my ears begin to roar as my vision is tunneling in. I know I'm going to pass out as, suddenly, the roaring gets louder. I hear a car door slam and realize someone else has driven up. I can hear at least one new voice, and he is yelling and coming closer. My torturer stops and drops me into the dirt where I land with a thud and a strangled cry. I am fighting to pull air into my lungs and remain conscious, but it's a struggle.

A heated debate rages around me, and I can barely make out that two men have actually arrived on the scene. I lie perfectly still and pray that they can help me because I no longer have the strength to help myself.

The voices have quieted, and I feel a hand touch my shoulder. I flinch out of reflex and groan from the fresh flash of pain in my side. One of the newcomers is talking to me, but I don't understand what he is saying. I take a few small breaths and whisper out, "Help me."

The man replies, "You are American." It is more of a statement than a question, but I nod to him.

"Can you stand?" he asks, as he places a hand on my elbow.

The tears flow freely now, and I shake my head in response. He calls for someone else to come close, and I see my captors step in my direction. The new man issues a warning for them to stay where they are. He then says something to the woman who quickly disappears into the house. The new man squats down so that he can look me in the eye as he speaks. I try to blink away the tears so that I can focus on the person who might be my only hope of survival. I look up into his dark sunglasses and plead for help with my eyes.

"My friend and I are going to help you stand. Where are you hurt?" Sunglasses asks.

"Ribs," is all I can utter. But I move my hand to indicate which side. He nods and tells me he will try not to hurt me.

I nod and work on steadying my breathing as I know that getting off the ground will be almost as painful as being dropped here.

Sunglasses and his friend slowly support and lift me to a semi-standing position. I'm not sure if I can walk, but the thought of being carried would probably be worse. I venture a look at my captors and can see the rage pouring off them as I gain my feet. I don't like them seeing how badly they have hurt me, so I defiantly force my feet to move.

With shaky baby steps, we make our way to the house. I notice that it is a stucco-like and stone structure. I will just be thankful to be out of this heat and able to sit down before I pass out. As we enter the house, I see an older man seated at a table with a younger girl applying pressure to a wound on his head. The bloody rag falls away as she watches us enter the house. I don't know what has her more spooked, the sight of me or the men entering behind us.

The older woman points us to a chair as she moves toward the older man and gestures for the girl to reapply pressure to his head wound. Sunglasses guy helps to seat me in a chair at the table and asks for a glass of water. The older lady hands him a glass, and he offers it to me. I am shaking, and I have to use both hands to steady the glass to bring it up to my mouth. I take a few small sips and set it down before I drop it.

My two captors have entered the room behind us and begin to speak loudly and are making gestures toward me. It is obvious they are not happy with this turn of events. They move to approach me, but Sunglasses's friend steps between them and me. It begins to get physical, but Sunglasses raises his voice and pushes them apart. He points to the door and after some hesitation, they go outside but leave the door open and watch me from a distance. I have no idea what they are saying as no one is speaking English. I don't trust anyone in this room, but between shallow breaths, I am trying to get a feel for what is going on. Plus, focusing on everyone else helps me not be so focused on the pain.

Sunglasses moves to speak to the older man and woman. They are deep in conversation as she is gesturing at the door and me and her husband. It's clear that she is explaining what all has happened since our arrival. The older man tries to rise from his seat, but Sunglasses gently places a hand on his shoulder.

Sunglasses removes some money from his wallet and tries to give it to the older man, but he pushes it away. He lays it on the table in front of him and puts his wallet back into his pocket.

My stomach grips tight again. Is he paying them off not to talk about me? Why is he giving them money?

He paces back and forth for a moment and stops in front of me. He asks me a question, but it's not in English, so I don't understand. I just say, "English please."

"My apologies. I forgot you do not understand Arabic." He sits in the chair next to me. "Who are you, and why are you here?"

I find the strength to try to plead for his help. "My name is Sarah. I'm nobody important. I just want to go home. Please. I won't tell anybody what happened here or about any of you."

He exhales deeply and stands and starts pacing again.

I try another tactic. "If you take me back to my hotel, I will pay you. I have some money in a bank account back home that I can wire to you."

"Did those men ask you for money?" he replies back.

"No. I don't know why they took me."

Sunglasses looks at me intently and says, "I have a pretty good idea what these men want with you, and it has nothing to do with your finances. I seem to have stepped into the middle of a hornet's nest, and we will have to tread very carefully to get you out."

I want to cry with relief that he wants to help me, but then a thought occurs to me. He didn't turn down the money. Maybe that's why he is willing to help. I don't care what the reason, he is my best option at the moment, and if it costs me the money in savings, so be it.

He turns to the older woman again and asks her a question. She takes my water glass and pours it into the sink and pours an amber-colored liquor into the bottom of the glass. She hands it back to Sunglasses.

He holds the glass out to me and urges me to take a sip. "It's brandy. Drink it. It will help with the pain."

I hesitantly take the glass and sniff it before I take a sip. Right now, I will take anything to ease the pain in my ribs. As I swallow, it tickles my throat and causes me to cough. I almost drop the glass as pain slices through my side. Sunglasses grabs my hand and the glass and waits until my breathing slows.

"Take small sips but try to get all of it down. I need you to walk outside with me." I nod and bring the glass up to my lips and gradually finish it off. Sunglasses takes it from me and sets it on the table and speaks to the woman in Arabic again. She nods understanding but says nothing.

"Are you ready to stand?" he asks. I slowly push myself into a semi-standing position and begin to sway. Sunglasses steadies me with a hand under my left elbow and leads me to the door. Before we step outside, he whispers to me, "I need you to trust me. I'm not making any promises, but I will try to help you."

When we step outside, my captors move to intercept us, but Sunglasses holds out his hand to stop them and begins to speak. The conversation goes back and forth. After a heated exchange, Sunglasses guides me to his car and opens the back door for me. I carefully slide onto the back seat as he closes the door. Sunglasses gets into the driver's seat. One of my captors rides shotgun, and the other one joins Sunglasses's friend in the truck.

We fall into line behind the truck as it leads the way out of the driveway. My captor starts to say something, but Sunglasses quickly cuts him off. We travel for some time in silence. The tension between the two men in the front seat is almost palpable.

We drive through the mostly deserted countryside with the occasional farm or pasture of sheep or goats. We even pass through two small villages before we turn and follow a road along a small river. The river seems to wind down from the mountain in front of us.

After about thirty minutes, we arrive at a compound of sorts that is comprised of several buildings connecting with what appears to be the main house which is two stories high. There are pastures fenced off with sheep grazing and a couple of horses corralled closer to a barn.

Sunglasses parks in front of the main house. After exiting the car, he opens my door but pauses to wait for my captor to exit the car and join his friend by the truck.

"Where are we?" I ask.

"Don't worry about where you are, just know that this man views you as his property and is willing to fight to keep you." I start to protest, "I am not his property and—"

But Sunglasses stops me with a wave of his hand. "It doesn't matter. It's not for me to decide." He takes a deep breath and continues, "When we get inside, do not speak unless spoken to. This is the best advice I can give you. Do you understand?"

"I understand," I say, but I don't tell him I don't agree. Nausea is beginning to well up in my stomach.

As we make our way to the house, I'm feeling very defeated. How did I wind up being abducted and taken by men who consider me property instead of a person? And in a place where women are seen and not heard? I remind myself that I am far from home in a foreign country and foreign culture. These men don't care about me, nor do they value my life. This thought causes tears to threaten. I hold my side to mask the reason for my tears. I lower my head and pray for mercy. If this is where my life ends, then I pray it will be swift. I'm more afraid of all the possibilities of what could happen if I do live.

I stop as we approach the steps. Sunglasses tells me, "We can go slowly up the steps."

"That's not why I stopped," I tell him. "I know you advised me to remain silent and I will try, but I have a request." I hurry on before he can stop me. "Whatever negotiations we are going into"—I swallow deeply, then continue—"I would like for you to translate it into English for me." Sunglasses begins to shake his head, but I rush on to finish. "I think it is only fair that I at least get to hear the details of the negotiations since I no longer seem to have any control over my own fate."

Sunglasses seems to consider my request and gives the briefest nod of his head.

We are joined by my captors and Sunglasses's friend as we enter the foyer. The house is a buzz with activity. A young girl approaches and tells Sunglasses that someone by the name of Safiya has arrived. She gives our party a disapproving glance before she continues, "And whatever this business is, it couldn't have happened at a worse time."

Sunglasses hands me off to his friend and assures me that I will not be harmed while in this house. I reluctantly let him lead me down the hall while Sunglasses disappears around a corner in the opposite direction.

We enter into an office that has a large walnut desk centered in front of two windows. There are several stacks of papers neatly arranged on the desk. There are bookshelves along the left wall, chairs, and a small table arranged in front of a window to the right. We stop in the center of the room, standing on a plush Persian rug. The room smells faintly of cigarette smoke. I find it odd that my mind is busy taking inventory of this room when I should be more concerned with the fact that my life is hanging in the hands of these monsters. I guess it is the mind's way of distracting me from the truth of my situation.

My captors position themselves to my left and behind me. Sunglasses's friend stands firmly on my right, keeping a watchful eye on the other two men. I get the sense that he doesn't like them any more than I do.

I hear voices approaching before they come into view, and they don't sound happy. A man who appears to be in his fifties enters in front of Sunglasses with a scowl on his face. The man is well dressed in what I would guess is a custom-made suit and very expensive shoes. He glances my way briefly, and what I see is disgust.

Sunglasses looks in my direction, although the sunglasses are now gone, and reverts to speaking in English just as I requested. Custom Suit looks sharply at Sunglasses, at his change of speech and utters what I guess is his displeasure at the conversation changing to

English. Sunglasses continues on in English and explains that I have requested it so that I can fully understand my fate.

There is definitely contempt in his eyes as Custom Suit appraises me from head to toe.

"So this woman is calling the shots, is she?" he intones to Sunglasses who starts to answer but is waved off. "Clearly, she is in no position to make any such request, but if she wishes to hear, so be it."

Custom Suit settles behind his desk and gestures for Sunglasses to begin.

"Amon and I were traveling to Omar's to check on the progress with the north field clearing to ensure it will be ready for the drilling to begin next week. When we arrived, we found Nuru there with this man, and he was dragging this woman by her hair down the drive. It's obvious that she doesn't belong with either of them."

It is clear to me that Custom Suit is of some import as no one speaks until he is called upon. Custom Suit turns to Nuru (now I have a name for my original captor) and asks that he tell his side of the story.

Nuru smiles smugly and states that this woman is his property, and he was transporting her to Qina on the orders of Muhamed al Habib where she will board a ship headed south. There is a sharp intake of breath all around me, for obvious reasons, that make me weak, and I start to sway again. As for Sunglasses and his friend who I think is called Amon, this is not a good sign. I reach for the desk to steady myself and see Custom Suit and Sunglasses locked in a death stare.

Custom Suit narrows his eyes and says something in Arabic to Sunglasses. His tone leaves no doubt that whoever this Muhamed al Habib is, it's not good.

Sunglasses straightens and answers, "Father, I did not know who these men worked for. They were clearly mistreating this woman and attacked and injured Omar when he refused to give them his only vehicle. The things they have done today are not right."

So Custom Suit is Sunglasses's father! Sunglasses then adds a phrase in Arabic, and I shoot him a look of frustration, but he doesn't even glance my way.

Nuru steps forward slightly and grabs me by the arm and pulls me closer to the desk as he addresses Custom Suit again in his native language. He then turns to me and grabs my breast as he states plainly in English, "American whore." I know I'm supposed to stay quiet, but no one said I couldn't defend myself. Since Nuru has positioned himself mostly facing me, I lean into him. His eyes go wide, and he starts to grin as I drive my knee up into his groin. We both cry out in pain, and he lets me go, and I end up on the rug gasping for breath. My well-placed knee hit its mark, but my ribs are paying for it.

My other captor comes to his companion's defense and kicks me squarely in the back. I am blindsided by the pain and can't get a breath in and start to panic.

Chaos breaks out all around me as all the men are yelling and fighting now. I don't know exactly what is going on because my eyes are closed as I try to calm myself and take any kind of breath at all. Even if my eyes were open, I probably wouldn't be able to see much as the tears are flowing freely now.

Custom Suit takes control of the situation again. He starts by saying that there will be no more fighting in this house today. He ends this statement by staring down at me on the rug. Me! I didn't start this, and he is sadly mistaken if he thinks I will just lie down and take whatever they decide to dish out to me. Well, right now I might. I'm spent and hurting like I've never hurt before, but it was worth it to get that scumbag's hands off me.

Custom Suit then advices Nuru and his friend to take a seat at the table while he sorts this out.

Sunglasses bends down and asks, "Are you all right?" I nod my head at him even though I am anything but all right.

He then asks if I would like to sit in a chair. I manage to squeak out that I'm fine where I am for now. So he rises and positions himself between me and my captors.

Custom Suit tells his son that he should not have interfered in Muhamed's business, and he should return Muhamed's property to Nuru and let them leave at once. He finished with, "I'm sure Muhamed would not be pleased to lose his investment." Sunglasses is shaking his head before his father even finishes.

Sunglasses turns to Nuru and asks, "How much?"

Nuru smiles and states, "She is not for sale to you."

"I'm not for sale to anyone," I squeak out, but no one in the room even seems to have heard me or even cares that I've spoken.

Sunglasses speaks again, "How much? Everything is negotiable."

"Not this one. She owes me first before I turn her over to Mr. Habib." Nuru is now leering at me.

Sunglasses turns to his father and leans across the desk. "Father, this is not right what is happening. I know you don't support what Muhamed is doing. Can't you use your influence to stop this? Do it for me."

Custom Suit stares at his son for a brief moment and simply states that he will not interfere in this business.

Sunglasses looks between Nuru and me and then turns back to his father. I watch him as he squares his shoulders. I can tell that he is preparing for a battle. I wait praying that he can talk some sense into one of these men and help get me out of here.

I am ready to argue myself and plead if need be, but Sunglasses's next two statements stun me into silence.

"Then I choose her for my bride. You told me I could marry a woman of my own choosing, and I choose her."

Nuru scoffs and says something in Arabic, but no one responds as all eyes are glued on Sunglasses's father. His father rises from his desk and slams his fist down loudly. I flinch and wince in pain, but I dare not make a sound now.

"You cannot be serious! Is this a joke?"

"No, Father. This is definitely no joke. I choose this woman for my bride, and I will consider it a personal offense if anyone tries to leave this house with my fiancé." He turns to Nuru, "I would hate to have to call in the authorities and lodge a complaint that someone connected to the governorate tried to abduct my fiancé."

Custom Suit's face is so red I'm thinking he might stroke out right here. He speaks quickly and loudly in Arabic to his son, but Sunglasses is having no part of it. "I can and I will! Amon is my witness," he says in response to whatever his father just said to him.

"Amon will swear that these two men accosted my fiancé as she was visiting in the home of our dear friend Omar. I'm sure Omar will gladly speak to this truth, too." Sunglasses is motioning for Amon to help lift me from the floor, but before he moves to help him, he turns back to his father once more.

"Nuru, I'm sure my father would be happy to deliver your gift of the current bride price to Muhamed. I'm sure the governorate will be more than happy to accept this generous gift. And in return, I will let this little disagreement go."

Custom Suit swears, or at least I'm pretty sure he is swearing as he paces behind his desk. He walks around to the front and stands nose to nose with his son. I hear him whisper something about paying, but he will be responsible for the trouble he has brought down on this house today. Sunglasses stands his ground and speaks loudly and clearly. "I take full responsibility for what I've brought into this house today."

His father takes several deep breaths before he speaks again, "You, Gabriel, will handle Safiya and her family on your own, too."

Gabriel only replies, "Yes, Father."

My mind is racing. Sunglasses is Gabriel, only the way they say it his name sounds more like "Gabril." I wonder who Safiya is, but that will have to wait until later because Sunglasses—no, Gabriel—is helping pull me to my feet. I cry out, and sweat beads my brow. I want to stand and walk out of this room on my own, but I can barely keep my feet under me so I'm happy for the support as we slowly make our way out of the room. I'm so relieved that I'm free of my captors, but I know I am not truly free as I've been purchased by Gabriel. Right now, he is definitely the lesser of two evils, so I go along willingly for now. Later when I am stronger, I will find out what this bride price is and repay Gabriel and be on my way home.

We stop at the bottom of a staircase, and I know I will never make it up all those steps. Gabriel must be thinking the same thing as he gestures for me to grab the rail and sends Amon to find someone named Mariam. He then turns to me and says this will probably hurt, but it's the only way.

Before I can ask what, he scoops me into his arms and heads up the stairs. He's right it does, but I'm so tired I just rest my head on his shoulder and let the tears fall anew. I'm shaking violently by the time we reach the top of the stairs, and Gabriel is looking at me with panic on his face.

"Shock," I sputter out. "C-cold," I say.

Gabriel enters a bedroom near the end of the hall and sets me on the bed and wraps a quilt around me. He then goes into the bathroom and starts the water in the tub. I hope he doesn't think he is going to undress me and put me in there. I may be going into shock, but I'm not letting a stranger undress me.

He must read my thoughts because he says, "Mariam will be in soon, and she will help you into the tub, and I will get you a warm cup of tea."

Mariam is an older woman in her late fifties or maybe early sixties. She is dark complexioned with salt-and-pepper hair and very robust. She gives me a quick appraisal and moves to stand next to the bed as she assesses my injuries. "What hurts?" she asks. I point to my ribs and side.

"Well, let's get you cleaned up and see what we can do about that." Mariam helps me slowly rise from the bed. She is surprisingly strong but gentle, too. We maneuver into the bathroom, and I point to the toilet. It's been a long day, and my bladder is suddenly screaming for relief. The button on my capris is a little hard, but I finally manage it. Mariam offers me a little dignity by turning her back to check the running water.

When I am finished, she helps me to remove the rest of my clothing. Modesty is gone now, but I'm happy for her help as I cannot get my T-shirt and bra off alone. I'm tempted to tell her to throw my clothes out, as they are ruined anyway, but they are all I have with me.

I look into the mirror and am shocked at the person staring back at me. The left side of my face is swollen and starting to bruise. My top lip has a small cut and is swollen as well. There are some scratches on my cheek and forearms from being thrown down on the ground.

STRONG AND COURAGEOUS

Mariam interrupts my exploration of injuries and directs me into the tub. The warm water is a welcome relief. I not only want to wash all the dirt and grime away, but the entire day as well. I just sit still letting the warm water envelop me and ease some of the tension. I flinch as Mariam pours warm water over me and begins to wash my hair. I haven't had anyone bathe me since I was a child, and I am uncomfortable but accept her kindness as I would be struggling to do this on my own. My scalp is sore, too, from all the hair pulling, and I'm pretty sure I'm missing a small patch. Add this to the growing list of injuries that I am cataloging. They are all minor in comparison to the pain in my side but no less degrading in their appearance.

"Thank you for the help, Mariam. My name is Sarah." She seems surprised that I know her name, so I tell her that Gabriel told me she was coming to help me.

She nods her understanding.

The bath was wonderful and torturous at the same time. Each movement has added to the pain in my side, which is now growing unbearable as the adrenaline has long since worn off from the trauma of the day. At least I am not trembling as much as before. Mariam helps me out of the tub and dry off. She wraps a soft robe around me and loosely ties it at the waist.

She helps me back into bed as Gabriel enters the room with a cup of tea and a couple of pills. He hands them to me and tells me they are for the pain. I don't even ask what they are, just swallow them with a few sips of tea.

Gabriel asks Mariam to see if she can find something for me to eat. She agrees and leaves the room. Gabriel asks if I need anything else right now, and I tell him just some sleep. He tells me that he has called the doctor to come check on me, but it might me a couple of hours before he arrives. He says he has an appointment to attend, but Mariam will be back shortly with something to eat. "Let her know if you need anything. I will return when I'm finished."

I'm nervous about him leaving me alone in this house. I don't know where Nuru and company have gone. I tell him as much, and he assures me that Amon is on guard downstairs and that he will be on the back terrace for a dinner meeting. "No one will bother you while you rest. You are safe here, Sarah. You are under my protection now."

"Thank you," I reply and relax into my pillow. I feel sleep dragging me deep into its depths. My last thought as I close my eyes is, *Thank You, Lord, for sparing my life today.*

I'm awakened sometime later to someone gently touching my shoulder. I see a tray of food on the table next to the bed and expect Mariam to be standing there, but it is Gabriel. He has showered and changed. It hasn't been long since I fell asleep as the light coming through the window is still bright.

"You need to eat something so that you can take some more medicine soon. Mariam made you soup and fresh bread." Gabriel motions to the tray.

I slowly move into a more upright position and am surprised at how stiff I am now. I try to reach for the glass of water on the tray, but twisting hurts and I give up.

"Here, let me help." Gabriel hands me the glass and waits until I am finished with it. "Would you like some soup?" he asks.

"Yes, I'll try a little. Thank you," I reply.

Gabriel is very patient and doesn't say much while I eat a few bites. I hold the bowl out for him to take, but he says I need to eat more. I tell him I'll eat some bread. That I can do lying down. Sitting up is proving to be painful. He takes the bowl from me and hands me a piece of bread.

Gabriel pulls a chair up next to the bed. "I need to speak with you as you eat."

I nod around a mouthful of bread.

"I don't know your name," he begins.

He must have forgotten because I told him earlier, but it's been a stressful day, so I'll cut him some slack. "Sarah," I say.

"Yes, but your full name," he replies. "Oh, my name is Sarah Grant."

"And I am Gabriel Hafez Ahmad Kattan. But Gabriel will do for now," he says with a smile. "I figured we should start with the basics for now. We can talk more later."

I nod my agreement.

"Where are you from, Sarah?"

I hesitate. I'm not sure I really want to tell a stranger where I live, but he did save me today, so I give a broad answer, "The United States."

"I think we already established that when you said you were an American earlier today."

I'm embarrassed now for my evasiveness and give him the closer answer he wanted, "Texas. I'm from Texas."

My turn to ask a question, "Are you going to return me to my friends in Cairo? I'm sure they are worried sick about me."

Gabriel frowns and is silent longer than I am comfortable with. He finally speaks, "You are badly injured and not in any shape to travel. You will remain here under my protection, as my fiancé until you are healed."

I try to argue. "I can't stay here. I have to get home. My flight is leaving tomorrow."

"I don't think you understand the seriousness of your situation, Sarah. My offering for your hand and threatening to expose Muhamed was no small thing. He is a very respected and powerful man despite what he has done today. He will not appreciate my interfering with his…business." Gabriel all but spits out that last word in disgust for Muhamed's dealings in human trafficking. I'm happy to know he is as repulsed by it as much as I am.

"That is why I exaggerated the truth of how I found you at Omar's today. I needed to plant a seed that maybe his two thugs had inadvertently taken my real fiancé by mistake and not just some random woman. And in doing so, I offer you my protection. I do hope Muhammed will not risk his business dealings with my father over you."

"I hear what you are saying, Gabriel, and I appreciate everything you are doing for me. You saved my life today and I can never repay that, but I will find a way to try. But you can't keep me here. I have a family and friends, and they will be looking for me." My voice is edged with desperation.

"Are you married?" Gabriel asks.

"No, but my brother is expecting me home soon, and he will be worried when I don't show up, if my friends haven't already called him. If they did, he is probably calling out the national guard or worse, on his way here himself."

"Do you have a sister, Gabriel?"

"Yes, two of them." He looks at me quizzically. "Why do you ask?"

"Wouldn't you want to know your sister was safe if she was missing? Can I at least call them to let them know I am all right? Or am I your hostage, too?"

"You are not my hostage, but we will not call them right now. I have some things to work out first." The bread I just swallowed sits heavy in my stomach. I'm not convinced that I am not his hostage either.

"I can see by your expression that you do not trust me, and I don't blame you. But for now, I need you to try." Gabriel offers me more bread, but I shake my head no at him. I'm feeling sick and don't want any more food.

Gabriel rises from his chair and moves it back near the window. Someone knocks on the door, and he moves to answer it. An older man in a white lab coat is standing in the hall with Mariam. Gabriel shakes his hand and thanks him for coming. He then turns back to me and introduces him as Dr. Saliib. What I didn't expect was for Gabriel to introduce me as his fiancé. Dr. Saliib looks surprised but quickly recovers and congratulates Gabriel. Before Dr. Saliib can ask any questions, Gabriel tells him I had a bad fall today and thinks I might have broken some ribs. Dr. Saliib nods and tells him that he will take good care of me.

Gabriel tells me Mariam will stay with me, and we will visit more when he returns after dinner. I don't reply, only watch as he leaves the room and shuts the door.

CHAPTER 5

Gabriel

I walk to the kitchen to get a glass of water and to collect myself before joining our dinner guests on the terrace. I need to be calm and ready to face Safiya and her parents. I steal myself and decide it is better to get this over quickly and with the truth—well, mostly the truth.

I enter the solarium to find everyone having wine before dinner as they wait on me. My father sends me a warning with his eyes. I know he is telling me to tread carefully as Safiya's father is a good friend of his. I notice my older sister has joined them and is visiting with Safiya. I can only hope she holds her tongue and does not make this more difficult.

I greet each person in turn, starting with Safiya's parents, then her, and barely acknowledge my father as I move to hug my sister. I use this moment to whisper in her ear, "I need you to play along." I feel her tense, so I kiss her on the cheek as I release her. She just gives me a questioning look. I move to sit next to Safiya on the sofa and take her hand and remind myself to be quick and to the point. Safiya is the daughter of one of my mother's cousins, and my father believed this match to be beneficial to his business. Her father is in the natural gas business, and we have recently discovered a pocket on some of our property holdings.

"Safiya, it is good to see you again." She is a very pretty girl, and we enjoy each other's company, but I am not in love with her. I am fond of her and had hoped that, in time, that fondness would grow.

That being said, there is a small part of me that is relieved that I will not have to wait and see what grows and what doesn't.

"Thank you all for coming, but I'm afraid I owe you all an apology." Safiya's eyes widen with concern.

I continue on. "I was unaware that you were coming today. Father thought it would be a nice surprise for all of us to have dinner, but I must confess that it was he who got the surprise when I returned home today. I'll just come out with it." Deep breath, "I have kept a secret from my family. I recently met a girl and well...we are engaged to be married. It was very sudden, and I have not even shared it with my family yet." I turn to Safiya, "I didn't mean to hurt you. It was all very sudden, and I wanted you to hear it from me. I'm sorry."

I watch Safiya's face as she subtly removes her hand from mine. I can see the hurt in her eyes, but she has the grace to thank me for my honesty. I hope she never finds out the truth.

Everyone else in the room is silent for a moment until Safiya's mother asks the question, "Is your fiancé here?"

"Yes, she is here, but I'm afraid she was in an accident involving a car on the way. She is upstairs with the doctor now. Maybe you will get to meet her in the future. I hope we can still enjoy dinner together this evening." I turn back to Safiya, "I understand if you are mad at me now, but maybe one day you can forgive me for hurting you." She doesn't reply, only nods her head.

Safiya's father asks, "Is she hurt badly?"

"No," I reply. "Just some bumps and bruises. I probably overreacted, but I wanted to be on the safe side."

Thankfully, my father chose that moment to offer his apologies to Safiya's parents and to scold me for my indiscretion. He tells me that this whole situation could have been avoided if I had been more forthcoming about my "relationship" with my *fiancé*. I realize that he does not know her name, nor have I mentioned it, so I do.

"Yes, Father, Sarah scolded me herself for not telling you sooner, but I wanted to surprise you. I can see now that I was wrong to keep this hidden from you." I will pay dearly for this day later. Of that, I have no doubt, as my father is a hard man. For now, I am just relieved he is playing along.

Father rises from his chair and indicates that we should head out to the terrace for dinner. He and Safiya's father lament the impulsiveness of youth on their way out of the door. I move to escort Safiya, but her mother places herself between us and takes her daughter by the arm.

My sister grabs my arm and lets them file out of the room before she asks, "Are you truly engaged to another woman, Gabriel?"

"Yes, I am. But now is not the time to discuss it. I promise to explain it all later," I answer and move to join the others for dinner.

Dinner drags on for what feels like an eternity, and I can see that my sister feels the same. Her curiosity about my fiancé is eating at her, and she cannot wait to barrage me with all of her questions. As the last course is served, I stand and once again offer my apologies. I thank Safiya for being so gracious this evening and tell them that I need to check in on Sarah.

Sarah

I awaken sometime after dark to a dimly lit room. My side is throbbing, and I need to reposition myself, but it hurts to move. I try to slide a pillow along that side for support, but I end of causing more pain. Suddenly, someone takes the pillow from my hands and says, "Let me." I turn my head to see Gabriel standing next to the bed. I didn't hear him come in, and I wonder how long he has been here.

He helps to tuck the pillow along my right side and offers me a sip of water when my breathing slows. I sip it slowly and hand him back the glass.

"What time is it?" I ask.

"Almost midnight," he answers.

"How long have you been here?"

"A while."

I study the face of the man who is quietly watching me from his chair near the window. He has dark brown, almost black hair that just touches the top of his collar. He has thick dark eyebrows that are currently pulled tightly together either in deep thought or frustration. His eyelashes are long and thick and currently partially hood his dark eyes. In the shadow of the room, he looks much darker than he did in the daylight. I remember his skin being more olive in color. He has slightly full lips that are currently pulled tightly into a frown. The depth and intensity of his dark brown eyes is a little unsettling when coupled with his frown.

I break the silent stare down. "Were you watching me sleep?" He nods yes and I ask, "Why?"

"I was thinking about everything that has happened today and everything you have been through. You are a very brave young woman and…" He doesn't finish his statement.

"And…what?" I prompt. The corner of Gabriel's mouth twitches, and his face relaxes slightly. He rubs his hand across his face, and I see that he is smiling. So I prompt him again.

Gabriel huffs out a breath and smiles fully now. "I was remembering the way you kneed Nuru this afternoon and wondering how gratifying that must have been. After all the pain they had inflicted on you, you somehow found the strength to return a blow of your own. That took courage." His smile is gone as he speaks that last statement and his frown has returned. I wait silently, not knowing exactly what thought brought this serious expression again.

"Why? Why would you do such a stupid thing today? You had no way of knowing that anyone in that room would come to your rescue."

I don't really want to think about what could have happened to me today, but he deserves an answer. He did step up and fight for me. God only knows what would have happened if he hadn't done that.

"You're right. I didn't know for sure if I could trust anyone, but I had already decided that I was not going down without a fight. And when he grabbed me, well, I guess I snapped. I thought if I provoked him enough, maybe he would just end things quickly."

I don't tell him that I knew God put him there, and I was pretty confident he was going to save me. I have that same feeling now that he was sent into my life for a reason.

"That was a foolish move. You were worth more alive than dead, and I can promise you those men would not have done anything quickly. They would have made you suffer greatly and laughed as you begged for death."

I'm silent for several minutes. Gabriel's statement is sobering, and I feel sick thinking about it. Finally, I ask, "What do you think I should have done?"

"I'm not sure there was a right thing to do. I am impressed with your spiritedness. I could see you were barely able to stand when you delivered that blow. I was so shocked that I didn't react in time to stop Jabari from kicking you. So some of these bruises are my fault, too."

"Don't blame yourself. I lay full blame on those two pigs who took me from my hotel."

Gabriel asks what I was doing here in Egypt, and I explain to him that I am on vacation with friends. He then asks how I came to be abducted by Nuru and Jabari. I tell him that I broke the cardinal rule of not going anywhere alone when I stepped outside the hotel for some fresh air. He nods as he listens to my story. My ribs are throbbing, and it takes me a few minutes to get it all out. I'm having to take small, shallow breaths.

We are quiet again for some time before I ask, "So you know and associate with these men." It is more of a statement than a question.

Gabriel bristles at my questions and sits up straighter in his chair. "No. I do not associate with those men in the way that you are implying. I know them through Muhamed and some legitimate business dealings my father has had with him."

He looks angry now, so I say, "Thank you for helping me. And don't blame yourself for any injuries I might have sustained. I'm sure they would have been a lot worse if you hadn't stepped in and helped me." I pause but then ask, "Why did you do that?"

"It was the right thing to do." There is no hesitation in his response.

I decide it's now or never. "Gabriel, I really need to call my family and friends. Please help me to let them know I'm all right."

I hear him sigh and hope that he is caving in. I'm sure my friends have called the police, and I pray my brother is not halfway to Egypt by now. My stomach is in knots waiting for a reply, and the pain is coming back full force. I hope he says yes before I need another pain pill and drift back to sleep.

Finally, he answers, "I'm not sure it is a good idea, but I will help you call them after we get a few things straight first."

I think maybe he is worried that he will be blamed in all of this, so I rush in to assure him that is not the case. "I will make sure that you do not get blamed for this. I will make sure and tell my friends that you saved me. Then you will not have to worry about me anymore."

"Blame me? You think I am worried about being blamed? I know that I did nothing wrong. It is you who doesn't understand." Gabriel raises his voice now, "Do you understand the risk I took bringing you here to my home? In saving you, I put my family, my sisters, in danger!"

"I'm sorry. You are right. I didn't think about that. But don't you see? That's all the more reason to let me make that call and get me out of here as soon as possible. If you let me leave, then I won't be a danger to anyone anymore."

"Except yourself," he states.

"Excuse me? What do you mean by that?" I counter.

"Do you really think they will just let you walk out of here, board your plane, and return home? They are probably already watching your friends and the hotel waiting to see if you return. You have seen them, Sarah. You know their names, and more importantly, who they work for."

"Gabriel, please you have to let me call. I have to warn my friends. What if they are in danger?"

"If your friends reported you missing, then they are probably safe for now. I doubt Muhamed wants to draw any more attention to himself than necessary. For now, you are safer here with me."

"But your father paid them, didn't he?" I ask.

"Of course, he paid them. I didn't leave him any choice. I took their merchandise and then threatened their boss, who happens to be a high-ranking government official. One with whom my father has frequent business dealings. Do you not see what a precarious situation this is? One that I hope Muhamed is content to let go with the sum my father paid him. He could destroy my family's business if he wanted to." He leans forward with his elbows on his knees. "The only way this works is if he truly believes he has inadvertently taken my fiancé. The bride price was nothing more than a promise to not interfere in his business again, an agreement to remain silent. These men don't operate the same way other people do."

"I have some money saved up at home. I could pay your father back, and you could let me go."

"And then when I don't marry an American bride, what do you think happens to my family? You will stay here for now. I will figure something out. Leaving too soon could be bad for all of us." Gabriel pins me with his dark eyes.

"Couldn't we report him to the authorities?"

"Did you not hear me say 'government official'?"

I can tell he is losing patience with me, so I try to change the topic for now. "You don't like me much, do you?"

"What? I'm not the one so desperate to get away from here. I think maybe it is you who doesn't like me."

It's my turn to raise my voice now, "I DON'T KNOW YOU!"

"What do you want to know?" he calmly asks.

"When I can make that phone call." I hold his gaze and vow to myself not to look away first.

"You are singularly focused," he replies, but I still don't say anything. "You may call your family, but you will let them know that you are injured and will remain here for several days while you heal. In the meantime, we will try to figure out our options."

"I agree to stay here for a few days, but my friends will want to come see me for themselves. A phone call will not be enough to satisfy them after everything that has happened. As far as I know, my brother might already be on his way here. And as far as our options go, engagement is not one. I have not agreed to marry you nor will I. This is not how things are done where I come from."

"You forget, you are in my country now, and marriage contracts are harder to break." Gabriel pulls a cell phone out of his pocket but does not offer it to me immediately. "You may call your friends and let them know that you are okay. Give them my name and number and tell them they may call anytime to check on you. Let them know that the doctor has already seen you and advised rest for a few days. Tell them he said travel is out because he is worried about your ribs puncturing a lung. You may also call your parents if you like."

"My parents are dead," I say. I don't know why I said it. It just slipped right out of my mouth.

"I'm sorry for your loss. I understand your loss as my mother died thirteen years ago after my youngest sister was born."

I don't acknowledge his statement about his mother. I'm too angry to be sympathetic right now. "My brother will not be okay with me staying with strangers in a foreign county while recovering from being abducted and beaten. How would you feel if it were one of your sisters?" I ask.

"I would hope that I would be grateful that someone saved you, but I know I would want her home as soon as possible. I will concede that his reaction will be valid, but for all of our safety, I need you to stay here for a few days. That means you need to convince him not to come get you."

"I can't make you any promises."

Gabriel smiles. "Besides, a good marriage arrangement would be considered a blessing, and I happen to be a good catch."

I know he is just trying to get me to lighten up, but I'm still on the defense.

"Again, we are not engaged. You bought my freedom with a lie and your father's money, so in essence, I was purchased by your family. I did not agree to be your fiancé. Would you be fine with your sister being purchased by a stranger and living in a strange place far from home? What if that stranger was mistreating her, too?"

Gabriel patiently considers his reply. "Arranged marriages happen here all the time. Women often leave their homes to live with their husband's family. If it were my sister and her husband was abusing her, I would step in and help her. If I did it for a complete stranger, don't you think I would do it for her? And by the way, no one is mistreating you here."

Still, I press on. "So you would force her to marry someone she doesn't want to marry just for the sake of a good arrangement? Would you force me?"

Gabriel leans back in his chair and looks me in the eye. "If we were to marry, I would take care of you and provide for all of your needs. You would have a good life with me, and I would not mistreat you."

"You didn't answer the question. Would you force me to marry you?"

"I would not force you to marry me, but I would marry you if you agreed."

"You would marry me even if I didn't love you?" I ask.

"If it was for the best, yes, I would. Sarah, you are old enough to realize that we don't always get what we want, and life is not always fair."

Ouch, that was a low blow. "In my country, we don't force people to marry, and generally, we marry for love."

"And what is the success rate of marriages in your country?"

Gabriel is an educated man, and I think that he already knows the answer to this question, so I don't reply.

"Gabriel, you don't know me. Why would you push for a marriage to a total stranger when there have to be other options?"

"You are right, Sarah, we do not know each other, but I made a contract of sorts in order to protect you and for the sake of my family, I am willing to honor that contract. What little I've seen of you so far, I admire. Your willingness to fight for yourself tells me you are brave and determined. You are an intelligent woman who is not easily bullied, and I wouldn't want a pushover for a wife. I offer you my friendship and as a husband, my faithfulness. Is that not a good start to a relationship?"

I think about what Gabriel has just said to me. The conviction with which he just delivered that speech tells me either he really means it or he has had a lot of practice saying that. I know he is honorable by the way he has treated me so far, but it's too soon to say for sure. OMG! What am I thinking? Too soon to say? I'm not staying here long enough to find out! He might be a great catch, but he is definitely someone else's catch. It's not that he is not attractive, because he is, very, but he lives halfway around the world in a totally different culture. And I don't know this man. I have to get out of here and soon!

Gabriel sits quietly watching my mental dialogue. I replay parts of today trying to find something that will convince him that I need to leave. A comment niggles the back of my brain, and I remember what it is. What was all that talk between Gabriel and his father about taking care of Safiya and her father? I venture the topic. "Gabriel, who is Safiya?"

"Nobody you need to worry about." Obviously, he doesn't want to discuss her, but she was important enough to be mentioned in the midst of all of my drama. And she was in this house earlier, so I point this out to him.

Gabriel sighs but answers me this time. "She is the daughter of one of my father's business partners who my father had hoped to make a match with me."

"And I ruined your chances with her, didn't I?"

"You didn't ruin anything."

"It kind of seems like I did."

"Well, you didn't. It was more my father's wish than mine." Gabriel folds his hands in his lap.

"So you didn't have feelings for her?" I ask.

Gabriel obviously is through with this conversation. "I'm not going to discuss my feelings with you."

Just about the time I think Gabriel is going to leave, he holds out his phone to me. "Are you ready to make your calls? It's late, and you are tired as am I. The quicker we get this done, the sooner we get some sleep."

I nod my agreement, but he pauses before he releases the phone to me. "Please, I ask that you respect my wishes for tonight. Tomorrow, we can talk again."

I nod, but he wants a verbal agreement, so I cave. "I agree for tonight."

Gabriel releases the phone and leans back in his chair.

I decide to dial Tyler first and am surprised when he answers on the second ring. I half expected it to go to voicemail. "Tyler, it's me," my voice waivers, but I take a deep breath and bite down on my tongue for a moment to gain control.

Tyler sounds frantic when he asks, "Sarah, is that really you? Are you okay? Where are you? Lauren called—"

I interrupt him to tell him what happened to me. He tries to interrupt several times, but I ask him to let me tell him everything and then I will answer questions. I let him know that I am fine, just a little banged up but going to be okay. I start to explain that a really nice family intervened and took me in and that I will be staying with them for a few days as I heal.

Tyler goes ballistic! "What do you mean staying with them for a few days? I thought you said you had some scrapes and bruises. Why on earth would you need to stay with strangers for a few days? Unless there is something you are not telling me."

"Ty, my ribs are broken, and it would be very painful to travel right now, plus the doctor recommended rest to make sure they don't puncture a lung."

Ty speaks again but is much calmer now. "Are they holding you against your will?"

I laugh and immediately regret it as pain shoots through my side. If he only knew. My sharp intake of breath alarms Tyler. "Are they hurting you right now? Please, Sarah, tell me where you are so we can get help to you."

I blow out the breath I was holding and tell Tyler, "No one is hurting me, Ty. It just hurts to laugh. Everyone here has been very nice and has taken very good care of me. As to where I am… I'm not exactly sure, but my new friend Gabriel might be able to answer that question. Hold on."

I hand the phone to Gabriel who places it against his ear and identifies himself to Tyler. I can only hear one side of the conversation. Why didn't I put it on speaker phone when I had the chance?

"Yes, your sister is safe now. The men who attacked her are gone and will not harm her again. On that, you have my word." A pause and then he answers again, "Trust me, the authorities are aware of what has happened. I made sure of that. You do not need to call them." Another pause, "No, she is not able to travel." Pause, "Of course, I got her medical care. I would hope someone would have done the same for my sister." Pause, "Yes, I have two sisters and a brother. We live with our father on our family farm." Pause, "You may call this number anytime day or night to check on Sarah. She is a strong and brave young woman." Pause, "She is a fighter and will be fine in a few days. She is just tired and her injuries are fresh."

Gabriel concludes by telling my brother the name of the village we are in and how to find us if need be. He hands the phone back to me. I talk to Tyler for about five more minutes and tell him I need to go and call the girls to let them know I'm fine. I'm also hurting pretty badly from all the conversation and need some sleep. We hang up and I ask for a pain pill before I dial Lauren's number. That should give me about twenty minutes to go through this all again before the medicine fully kicks in.

I contacted the girls and after a lot of tears, I gave them the abbreviated version of the story and let them know that I had already contacted Tyler. They wanted to drive out here immediately, but I asked them to wait until tomorrow so that I can get some rest. They tell me they have postponed their flights so that we can all fly back together. I hope that tomorrow, my friends will be able to come for me and that we can leave without a fight.

I hand the phone back to Gabriel and move to get out of bed. He asks where I am going, and I indicate the bathroom. He helps me to stand and waits in the bedroom until I am finished to make sure I am settled in bed again. The pills are definitely taking effect, and I'm already drifting off as he moves to the door.

"I will leave the door open and will be across the hall if you need anything. Good night, Sarah."

"Good night, Gabriel." I want to close and lock the door, but I'm too tired to get up again, so I don't.

CHAPTER 6

September 20

There is a knock at the door, and Mariam enters carrying another tray of food for me. This one contains fresh juice and some sort of broth, flat bread, and butter. She sets the tray down next to me and asks, "How are you feeling this morning?"

"Like I've been hit by a bus," I reply.

Mariam surprises me by saying, "You look like you've been hit by a bus." She is smiling as she finishes her statement.

"Well, thank you for your honesty. I know who to ask if I want the truth," I tell her.

She offers me the juice and helps me to the restroom. Once I am settled back in bed and eating some breakfast, she offers me two more pain pills. My ribs say yes please, but my head says that I will try to take just one this morning. I don't want to be groggy when Gabriel and I speak again. I sip on the broth and find it is very hearty and flavorful. After a few more bites of bread, I'm feeling sleepy again. Mariam instructs me to rest, and she will be back later to check on me.

I must have dozed off because I'm startled awake when someone knocks loudly on the bedroom door. Thinking it is probably Gabriel, I say, "Come in." I am not prepared for Gabriel's angry-looking father, Ahmad, who comes striding into the room. I try to sit up so that he is not towering so menacingly over me.

There is no preamble of good morning, how are you feeling, he just jumps in with, "You will marry my son in two weeks' time. That should give you ample time to heal. It is not up for discussion as my son would have you believe. You are not what I would have chosen for him, but he has left me no choice in the matter."

I brave a response, "On that statement, we agree." I am quickly reprimanded before he continues and told I will not interrupt again until he is finished. My blood is boiling, and I remember Gabriel's advice not to speak until spoken to yesterday. I don't like it, but I know that my presence has caused much upheaval in this household, so I remain silent for now. I am eager to hear the rest of his dictatorial speech or tirade, whatever you want to call this.

He takes my silence as consent and continues where he left off. "As I was saying, you are not my choice for my son, but since he has foolishly chosen you, I have to minimize the damage and trouble he has brought upon this house. The price has been paid for your protection, and my son has chosen to sacrifice himself for, for…" I'm hoping he chooses his words carefully or this is going to get ugly quickly. "YOU!" He throws out his hands, gesturing to me like I am the most undesirable thing in the world. I try to contain my composure and my tongue, but I'm done being insulted.

"If I am so terrible, then send me away from here. Let me go home. Forbid him to marry me. I will reimburse the money you paid." I am so thankful that my little white pill has kicked in or maybe it is the adrenaline, because it has made me bold.

He leans toward the bed. "You have already brought enough shame on this family, and you will not insult my son by running away from his offer of marriage. Not only that, if Muhamed gets wind of this farce and thinks that Gabriel let you go, he will come after my family. You have no idea how much damage he can inflict upon this family. You Americans think you can march into any country you want and disrespect our customs and traditions. You entice our men and have no morals. Then you think you can buy your way out of trouble."

I've had enough of this overbearing, egotistical jerk, and I'm really tired of people questioning my morals! I throw my legs over the side of the bed, wince in pain, and stand as I defend myself.

"How dare you come in here and insult me and accuse me of things that you know nothing about! I didn't waltz in here and disrespect your family. If you have forgotten, I was dragged here by my hair and against my will. I was minding my own business at the hotel, not parading around in public naked and 'enticing men'. I won't sit here and be insulted and bullied by the likes of you. Your son did an honorable thing in saving my life, and if you have a problem with that, then go scream at him!"

"You dare raise your voice to me in my house? I will have you thrown out of here today!"

"Great. Go ahead. The quicker you do, the sooner I get to go home."

Ahmad turns quickly on his heel to leave the room, and that's when I notice Gabriel standing just inside the door watching me. He steps out of his father's way as Ahmad storms from the room. Once Ahmad is gone, Gabriel softly closes the door. I'm gearing up for round 2 as I'm sure he is going to scold me for being so disrespectful to his father.

"Well," he says calmly. "That is a first."

"What?" I ask. "Do you mean that is the first time someone dared to stand up to your father?"

"No," he replies. "It's the first time I've seen someone get the last word during an argument with him." A smile spreads across his face, and he leans in to whisper, "This is going to be interesting." He turns and stares at the door that his father just stormed through and shakes his head.

Gabriel informs me that his phone has been blowing up all morning with calls and texts from Tyler and Lauren. Gabriel says he came in earlier, but I had fallen back asleep. He assured them I would call them back when I awakened. He holds the phone out to me, and I thank him. Before he leaves the room, he tells me Mariam is heading into town for a few things and asks if I need anything. I point to the robe I am still wearing and say that I could use something different to wear. I offer to pay, but he waves me off and says he will take care of it.

Mariam and a girl about my age arrive before I can return any calls. Mariam introduces me to Gabriel's sister, Rana. She studies me openly, curious about the bruised and battered girl his brother has brought into their home. I wonder how much she knows about my situation. She holds out a folded garment which turns out to be a soft cotton dress for me to wear. "I can't stay long," she says. "Papa will be mad if he knows I am in here, but I heard you needed something to wear."

I study her, too, as I take the dress from her hands. She is about my height and looks to be around eighteen or nineteen years old. She has long dark hair tied back in a braid that goes halfway down her back. She is pretty with large brown eyes like her brother. "Thank you. I will return it to you as soon as I can." She smiles at me and quickly leaves the room.

Gabriel tells me he will leave so that I can get dressed. I ask Mariam to help me remove the bandage that Dr. Saliib wrapped around my chest so that I can soak in the tub again before I get dressed. I go into the bathroom and carefully sink into the warm water as I call Tyler and let him know that I am feeling a little better today. I'm not sure it is the truth as the pain is still pretty intense, but I don't want him worrying. I tell him I want to soak in the tub for a while and will call him back this afternoon.

Next, I call Lauren. She is frantic and wants to know why that Gabriel person would not give me the phone this morning. I assure her that Gabriel was only letting me rest since we were up so late last night. She, Nicole, and Stasia insist on coming to get me today. Lauren tells me Tyler told her where I am, and she looked it up. She says she can be here in a couple of hours. I tell her that I am not sure I can ride in a car that far yet and ask her to come in a couple of days. She argues that they are all worried and want to see me with their own eyes. She says she is coming today to see me for herself.

I am worn out from the events of the morning and don't know if I can manage a car ride today without a lot of pain. I ask her to wait until the morning and give me one more day to rest. She is not happy about waiting another day but agrees to call back around lunchtime to see if I am any better.

I am relieved that she is as stubborn as me. I hope that maybe her appearance will change Gabriel's mind, and he will let me go with them. I just hope that no one brings up this engagement business in front of my friends. Maybe they will be ready to be rid of the burden of me and come up with another solution.

I sit in the tub until the water starts to cool and decide it's time to get out. I am getting tired and want to lie down for a little while. It takes a few tries, but I finally get the dress over my head as it hurts to raise my right arm too high. I see Gabriel standing outside the bedroom door with his back to the wall as I exit the bathroom.

"Have you been standing out there the whole time?" I ask. He ventures a peek and decides it safe for him to enter now.

"Not the whole time. You were in there a while, and I wanted to make sure you were all right. Do you feel better now?"

"A little," I tell him as I sit on the edge of the bed. I think I might have to get Mariam to help me rewrap my ribs again as movement is painful.

I tell him I called and let everyone know that I am okay. I also inform him that Lauren and the girls are insisting on coming to see me for themselves. I tell him they might be here later today or in the morning.

Gabriel sits on the edge of the bed with me and sighs heavily. "Sarah, I cannot let you leave with them tomorrow. There are still too many unknowns, and Father has gotten word that Muhamed was furious last night."

"What did he hear?"

"A man my father knows called this morning to ask what my father had done to anger Muhamed. He said they were having dinner yesterday evening when Muhamed got a phone call. They said he returned to the table livid as he made his excuses. He also said he heard him mumble Father's name as he left the table. That is why Father was in here earlier. He is worried."

"Wouldn't it be better if I just left then?"

"Not yet," Gabriel answers. "Not until we know what he intends to do. For now, you are safer here where I can protect you."

"I will be safer in the US."

"I will not argue with you about this all day. First, we need to keep your friends safely in Cairo. Will you please try to convince them to wait a few more days?"

I can concede that I am not really up for visitors today, so I call Lauren back. I convince her that even my short stint out of bed for a bath has left me totally wiped, and I ask her to wait until the morning when I am sure I will be ready to travel then. Gabriel frowns at my comment about leaving but doesn't say anything. I hand him back his phone and lie down to take another nap. As tired as I am, sleep doesn't come for a while as I worry about the potential danger my friends are in. I try to figure out a way to keep them safe while getting me out of here.

Later in the afternoon, I awaken stiff and needing some air. I venture down the hall and pause at the top of the stairs. Gabriel rounds the corner and sees me standing there.

"What are you doing up and where are you going?" he asks, as he ascends the stairs.

"I am tired of lying down and need some fresh air. I thought I would take a walk outside. Do you know where my shoes are?"

Gabriel tells me to wait here, and he will get them from the closet in my room. He returns with them in hand. I slowly make my way down the stairs, and he leads me into the kitchen to sit down so that he can help me with my shoes. I'm grateful for the help and a little uncomfortable that this man is putting my shoes on for me as I can't bend that far yet. It's a little unnerving.

We walk in the yard behind the house and stop to rest in chairs under the shade of a large tree. I lean back and close my eyes. I ask God for wisdom about what to do tomorrow and for safety for all of us. Gabriel must mistake my eyes closed for exhaustion. "Catch your breath, and I will help you back to your room so you can rest."

I don't open my eyes as I answer him, "I'm not resting, I'm praying."

"You are a religious person?" he asks.

"Yes," I reply. "I'm praying for safety for all of us—my friends, your family, you, me. I could also use some wisdom in dealing with this mess I call my life right now."

He is quiet for a few moments, but eventually, he says, "Thank you."

"For what?" I ask. "For thinking of my family's safety, too."

We sit silently under the tree for a little longer before we head back to the house. We are almost back to the terrace when Ahmad comes bursting through the back door. His eyes are wild, and he is gripping the phone tightly in his hand so tightly that I think he might crush it. He barrels toward me with murder in his eyes.

Gabriel steps in front of me to stop his father, but Ahmad doesn't want to stop and tries to force his way around Gabriel. Gabriel grabs him and pushes him sideways to throw him slightly off balance and is yelling at him to stop and tell him what is going on. A younger man comes running from the house and helps Gabriel restrain his father. I wonder if this is Gabriel's brother.

Ahmad is held tenuously in his sons' grips as he spits his words in my direction. "You! I will hold you personally responsible if anything happens to her." I take a step back worried he will break free from their grip.

"Who, Father? What are you talking about?" Gabriel turns his father to face him.

"Rana. They took Rana because of her." Dread fills my whole being and think I am going to be sick. They took Rana because of me. Ahmad is right. I have brought more danger than I could ever imagine into this house.

Gabriel fists his hand in his father's shirt. "Who took her? When?"

"Muhamed's men took her. He knows this engagement is a farce and doesn't like being threatened by you. He intends to see you punished for what you have done. He intends to see you married to her. He said Rana will be unharmed as long as you go through with this farce of a wedding. He will return her at the ceremony." Ahmad has lost some of his steam and is watching Gabriel's reaction. Gabriel lets go of his father's shirt and looks stunned.

My knees turn to Jell-O, and I sink down onto the grass. My stomach is threatening to spill its contents, which leaves me gasping for breath.

Someone helped me up and into the house. My head was still spinning, and I couldn't believe that people could be so evil. It turns out that Muhamed's men snatched Rana when she was at the market with Mariam. Mariam was so distraught that Amon had to go pick her up and drive her home.

Muhamed let Ahmad speak to Rana to ensure that she was fine, just a little frightened. He said he would be keeping her at his mother's house until the day of the ceremony. He also said he did not like anyone messing with his business and since Gabriel messed with his, he would return the favor. Rana would be returned unharmed as long as no one deviates from his instructions.

Mariam returns with Amon and is sobbing and beside herself with worry. She is apologizing and blaming herself for not being able to stop them. Gabriel reassures her that there was nothing she could have done. We are joined by Gabriel's youngest sister as his father explains the situation and issues security precautions for everyone in the house. He has purposefully avoided mentioning me in his precautions, and I don't blame him. Guilt is consuming me by the second.

I can't sit here anymore. I rush from the room with tears pouring down my face. I race for the shelter of the tree we sat under only an hour ago. The pain in my ribs pales in comparison to the pain in my heart right now. That man is sick and twisted and now holds the fate of a young girl in his hands. And that fate rests in my hands, too.

I don't know how long I sit out here, but eventually, Gabriel comes to find me. One look at his face tells me he is just as worried as I am. I can't stop the flood of tears that start again. I shake my head, and all I can say is I'm sorry over and over again. Gabriel kneels down in front of me and hugs me into his chest never saying a word. He holds me until my sobs subside, then quietly leads me back into the house.

I lie awake staring at the ceiling for hours. I don't know how late it is, but the house has been quiet for a while now. I've run through a thousand different scenarios, trying to figure out a way out of this. Someone will have to be sacrificed one way or another. I don't think any of us will be able to walk away from this unscathed, but maybe we can all walk away with our lives. The only conclusion I've come up with is that there is no way out, but maybe a way through this nightmare.

I make my way across the hall to Gabriel's room and tap lightly on the door. I'm starting to think he is not in there when I finally hear the knob turn. He looks tired and pale. His hair is a mess, probably from running his hands through it repeatedly. I ask if I can come in and talk. He hesitates only a moment, then opens the door wide to grant me entrance. I am feeling awkward and nervous about what I came in here to talk to him about. I walk around his room not really seeing anything in particular, just working up the nerve to tell him what I have decided.

I move back to where Gabriel is standing and look him in the eye. He is watching me warily.

"I will do it," I say. He looks stunned. I clarify so that there is no misunderstanding. "I will marry you to save your sister." I expect to see shock, but there is only relief on his face.

His thank goodness is barely audible as he moves to sit on the foot of his bed. I cross over to the chair at his desk and turn it to face him. I tell him I want to discuss some conditions before I fully agree to do this. He cocks his head to the side and says, "I'm listening."

"I've given this some thought, and I know it's the right thing to do. Your sister's life is worth far more than what you and I want or don't want. I'm willing to marry you in name only and stay long enough to convince Muhamed that we are well and truly married. Then we can get a quiet divorce, and I can return to the States. A few months should do the trick."

Gabriel counters, "Muhamed might not take this so lightly. You will have to stay for a while. We can only hope that he loses interest in us after it is done. If you leave too quickly, he will know that we played him only to get Rana back."

"I understand. We need to do this as quickly as possible to get your sister home. I can't imagine how terrified she is right now." I bite my lip to keep it from trembling, then ask, "Do you think he will keep his word and not hurt her?" I regret my question as I see the pained look on Gabriel's face.

He looks toward the window as he answers, "I hope for everyone's sake that he does." He doesn't elaborate, and I can only imagine what Tyler would do if the tables were turned.

I tell Gabriel, "The only thing that has me truly worried is convincing my brother that I really want to stay here and marry you. He will not take this revelation well at all. He will think that I have lost my mind or have been coerced against my will. He will come here and drag me home if he has to, not to mention my friends who are arriving early in the morning."

Gabriel and I spend some time discussing the big hurdles we have to cross in the morning before we can think about moving forward with this wedding. Convincing my friends and family that I am staying is the first and hardest. We can't predict their exact reactions, but we do know that we will have to give the performance of a lifetime to pull this off without them getting the authorities involved.

We agree not to mention the engagement or wedding, only that I have decided to extend my vacation to get to know Gabriel better. We will say that there is a mutual attraction, and we would like to see where it leads. I will call them and tell them about the wedding after it is done. Gabriel will talk to his family in the morning and let them in on the plan. He will also make sure his father is nowhere around when the girls arrive.

Sleep evades me this night even with the addition of pain pills. I can't stop thinking about why this has all happened to me and what God's plan in all of this is. I could really use some answers right now. I remember the pastor's wife telling me to trust the plan and that God can work all things for our good. I say it to myself, but I'm having a hard time believing it right now.

CHAPTER 7

September 21

Gabriel and I rise early and he assembles his family and household staff to apprise them of what we have decided and what we need to do today. He assures them that our main goal is to get Rana home safely. He does not mention our plan to divorce later. The less people who know, the better. Everyone agrees to help except Ahmad who sat quietly with his arms crossed over his chest. I can't say I blame him for being so angry with me. Well, I want to blame him, but I won't. I'm tired of his judgment of me, so I won't judge him.

In the end, everyone agrees that Ahmad should leave the house for a while since he can't or won't play the part. He grudgingly agrees but only for Rana's sake, not ours. Whatever it takes to get him out is fine with me. I will have enough drama to handle without him adding to it.

We all eat breakfast together, minus Ahmad. He will not sit at the same table with me, so he leaves. I need to learn some basics about everyone in the house to help pull this off, especially everyone's names. I'm so nervous I can't eat, but I sip on coffee as we trade information.

I am formally introduced to Gabriel's brother, Aahron, and younger sister, Jasmina. She is quiet and politely shakes my hand across the table. Gabriel's brother is another story. He obviously shares his father's opinion of me and only nods in my direction. Mariam runs the house and has been with the family since Gabriel was small. She has also taken on the role of mother to the girls since their mother's death. I tell them a little about my life back in Texas as a nurse and about my brother and his family. I tell them how I came to be here in Egypt with friends but stop at the part where I was abducted. Now is not the time to go through all of that, but I'm sure they already have heard some version of that anyway.

Mariam is clearing away dishes when we hear a knock on the door. Gabriel and I walk to the foyer to welcome in what feels like the firing squad. He gives my hand a quick squeeze before opening the door.

Lauren, Nicole, and Stasia stare at Gabriel and then notice me standing off to the side. They look shocked at my appearance, whether it's the bruises, or the fact that I really am okay and here, I'm not sure. Lauren rushes past Gabriel and hugs me before I can stop her. I cry out, and she quickly releases me, apologizing for hurting me. She is babbling and moving her hands like she wants to touch me again but is afraid to hurt me. Gabriel steps back and motions for the other two girls to come in and welcomes them to his home. They nod in his direction but make a beeline for me.

I've managed to take some shallow breaths and wiped away the few tears that slipped out. Tears of joy and pain, but now is not the time for tears, or I might lose my nerve. I reach out and squeeze their hands to assure them I am fine. Gabriel invites us into the solarium where they can continue their barrage of questions about my injuries. I walk a little more slowly than necessary to make sure they understand why I needed a few days to rest.

As we all take our seats in the solarium, Gabriel says he will go see if Mariam can help him with some refreshments and leaves us alone to talk.

I can hardly answer one question before they move onto another. Stasia pulls out her phone and is snapping pictures of me and us. I tell her I'm really not up for pictures right now with all the bruises on my face. She tells me they are for Tyler. He wants proof that I am all right, and she promised. I consent, and we all huddle together and smile. I angle my bruises away from the camera as much as I can.

The girls want every detail from the past two days and want to know all about this family that has taken me in. They are suspicious, and I assure them that they are really nice and have taken excellent care of me. Nicole wants to know about Mr. Hottie who answered the door. I decide now is the perfect time to segue into that portion of the story. I decide to build up Gabriel from his rescue and how he saved my life to helping play nursemaid the past two days. I don't mention Muhamed's continued reign of terror, just that he bargained for my release. I'm about to tell them I have developed feelings for him when Gabriel and Mariam enter carrying a tray filled with cups of tea, sugar, and honey.

"Ahh, here are my nursemaids now," I say cheerfully. Mariam smiles and says I have been a model patient.

I introduce her to everyone, and they thank her and Gabriel for taking such good care of me. Gabriel moved to sit in a chair directly across from me after handing everyone their cups of tea.

The girls pepper him with questions, and l learn more about Gabriel in ten minutes than I have learned in two days. He tells them he has a degree in business and accounting and keeps the books for his father's land holdings and other various endeavors. He explains that they have various farms and grow sorghum and maize and raise various livestock. He even offers them a tour of the property after lunch. He explains about a new venture he is involved in, which led him to me two days ago. Gabriel informs us that they will begin drilling for natural gas soon on the property that Omar manages. That is what he was doing out there that day, checking on progress.

I can't believe I haven't asked these questions myself, but I was so preoccupied with getting out of here and then trying to figure out how to convince everyone that I want to stay, that it didn't even cross my mind. I will have time to ask questions once we get through today. For now, I am soaking up information about this man I have agreed to marry. I find that I suddenly want to know as much as I can about him. I might be marrying a stranger, but that doesn't mean we have to be unfamiliar with each other.

Lauren asks Gabriel what he thinks about my attempted abduction. Gabriel leans back in his chair and begins to answer her. I am watching Lauren to gauge her reaction.

Gabriel begins by saying, "I am very impressed with how brave Sarah is and what a remarkable woman she is. She is resourceful, strong-willed, and caring. She faced two monsters and never lost hope." The way he said all of this has me blushing, and I look at Gabriel for the first time since he began speaking and realize he was already looking intently at me. I look away and clear my throat.

Stasia looks from me to Gabriel and bless her, quickly changes the subject. "Where is the rest of your family?"

Gabriel explains that his father and brother left on business this morning, and his younger sister is in the kitchen with Mariam trying to give us some privacy. He tells him his older sister is away visiting family but will be back soon. Gabriel invites us all on a tour of the grounds and moves to help me up from the sofa. He offers me his arm for support. "Let me know if you get tired, and we will stop and rest."

I assure him I will try not to overdo it and let him know when I need a rest. We stop in the kitchen to say hello to Jasmina and then proceed to the terrace. He points out the surrounding structures that house various farming equipment and workers. He explains that Amon lives next door with his family who also work the land. The sun is high when we return to the cool interior of the house. We eat lunch with Jasmina and Mariam in the kitchen.

Lauren thanks Mariam and Gabriel for the wonderful meal and hospitality and tells me it is time we get on the road. She says it is a two-hour drive back to Cairo but will probably take longer depending on how well I tolerate the drive. She suggests I take a pain pill and try to sleep most of the way back.

I see Mariam and Gabriel go deathly still as she talks about my departure. I know they have to be wondering if I will stick to the agreement or cave and leave with my friends. I know deep down that if I truly wanted to leave, Gabriel would not stop me. But I also know that his sister's life may very well depend on my next actions. I made a promise, and this is bigger than just me now, so I know what I have to do.

I straighten my backbone and steel myself for the storm that is about to erupt, but I'm ready.

"I'm not going back to Cairo with you." I deliver my message calmly and smoothly. Lauren pierces me with a glare, but it is Nicole who speaks first.

"What do you mean you are not going back to Cairo with us? Do you need another day to rest? I don't understand."

"I do need a few more days to rest, but that's not the reason." I am cut off as Lauren demands to know what reason could possibly make me stay. I'm pretty sure she already knows as she is now glaring at Gabriel.

"Lauren," I say, trying to get her to stop glaring at Gabriel and focus on me. "I like it here and want to stay and get to know everybody a little better. That's all."

They are all speaking at once now. Demanding to know what is wrong with me. They ask various questions from "Do you have a concussion?" to "Are they making you say this?" to "What medications are they drugging me with?" Stasia even demands to see the bottle of medicine I am taking.

I hold out my hands for them to calm down so that I can answer their questions and explain myself.

"I know this sounds crazy, but I really want to stay. No one is forcing me to stay. It's my choice, my decision. I need you to respect my wishes." I take a steadying breath so that I can continue. This is much harder than I expected. "I know its sudden, but Gabriel and I have formed this connection and have discovered that we really like each other. We want to see where it goes, and we can't do that on two different continents."

It's Stasia who argues against me. "Sarah, you're not thinking clearly. You've been through a terrible trauma, and I think it is normal to develop some sort of feelings for Gabriel as he is the one who saved you. It's probably just infatuation and will pass when you get home." She turns to Gabriel and adds, "I mean no disrespect. You are probably a really great person, but you do see that this is not normal, right? We can't just leave Sarah here with total strangers in a foreign country. It's…it's crazy!" Her voice is taking on a higher pitch now, and I'm afraid she is about to freak out.

My friends all agree with her, but I just shake my head no.

Lauren pleads with me. "Come home. Text, email, video chat, or write letters for heaven's sake. Get to know each other that way and then if you are still interested in each other, meet up again. Plan a visit or have him visit you, at home."

"Lauren, I know I will not convince you that this is normal, I know it isn't. But I've never met anyone like Gabriel. It's not Stockholm syndrome or anything. I just want to stay for a few more days, maybe a couple weeks. See where this goes. And if it isn't meant to be, I'll come home. I promise."

"You know Tyler will not stand for this. You do understand he will fly here and drag you home," she states.

My next statements have to cut the cord and let them know that I am not changing my mind. "I am not a child, and I don't understand why none of you can just respect my feelings. I know this is totally out of character for me. I know the old Sarah would never do anything so impetuous or rash. But this whole situation has made me look at things a little differently. Life is short, and I don't want to do the safe and prudent thing all the time anymore. And I'm tired of being sheltered and told what to do with my life all the time. I can make my own decisions!" I cross my arms over my chest and wince from the pain, but I don't budge.

Lauren walks over to Gabriel and pokes him in the chest. "I don't know what you did to her or threatened her with, but she is leaving with us right now!"

Gabriel stands and steps away from Lauren but holds her stare. "I didn't do anything to convince Sarah to stay. She came to that conclusion on her own. She is welcome to stay as long as she wants. It seems to me that you are the one who is not listening to Sarah's wishes at the moment. I understand your concerns and apprehension. Even my own father has his concerns, but he has enough respect to let me make my own decisions for good or bad. Sarah is asking that you give her that same consideration."

"She is well aware that her brother will have a hard time with this decision. She told me as much last night. She also said she had hoped that her friends would try to see her side and support her."

Lauren is quick with her response. "Then you will not stop her if she decides to leave with us right now?"

"No. I will not stop her. She is free to leave at any time. She is not a prisoner here."

My heart is about to pound right out of my chest. I have made my decision, but this is really difficult. I don't want to ruin my relationship with Lauren. She has always been like a sister to me.

Lauren turns to me. "Sarah, I want to speak to you outside on the porch, without Gabriel." I nod my consent and follow her outside.

We walk out near where their rental car is parked to speak. Lauren demands the truth.

"Tell me the truth. Why are you really doing this? And don't tell me it's because you like him. I know you, and you don't make any rash decisions about any man. Most men have to ask you out several times before you will even agree to have dinner with them. And then when you do go out, it's rarely on a second or third date. You have always said it was because you were waiting for the right man and that when you meet him, you would know. So what gives?"

Everything she has said is true, and she does know me better than anyone. That makes it all the harder to keep lying to her, but I know I must.

"I know what I say when it comes to dating, and yes, I do pray for God to send me the right man. What makes you think that Gabriel might not be that man? Who's to say God didn't send him to save me and that he isn't the one?"

Lauren hits below the belt with her next question. "Is he a believer?" She knows I have always wanted a husband who shares my values and beliefs. She knows that point is nonnegotiable, or it was until yesterday. I can't even find the words to argue right now, so she prompts me to answer. "So is he? Answer me, Sarah."

I go with the truth. "I don't know."

"So you are willing to sacrifice your beliefs for this man you just met? Is that what you are saying? I'll give you he seems nice, and yes, he did save your life, and he might even be handsome, but is that reason enough to sacrifice everything you've ever wanted?" I don't say anything, so she continues.

"You set some pretty high standards a long time ago, and I respect that. I just don't want to see you throw all of that away because you thought you were going to die. Come home, Sarah. Let the dust settle. Process what you have been through and then if you still want to pursue this, then do. But do it with your head straight, because right now, I don't think it is."

I realize she is crying as she finishes her last statement. I want to tell her she is right and that I'm sorry for causing so much trouble, but I think of Rana and don't speak for a moment. I pray for the right words to carry this through and keep my friendship intact.

I decide to hug her and tell her that she is the best friend I have ever had. She hugs me back and whispers, "Thank God." I pull away from her knowing she thinks she has won me over. For Rana, I tell myself one more time. I know what I have to say.

"Maybe God brought me here to minister to this family, to Gabriel. Maybe I was meant to go through this, this hell, to share my faith with them." I silently pray this will be the end of the discussion because I am shaking and ready to drop.

"Maybe he did place you here for that very reason. So come with me to the hotel at least and pray about this, and if you feel you need to stay, then I won't fight you anymore." Lauren looks as tired as I feel.

"I have prayed about this, and I am staying. I don't want you to hate me, but I've made my decision. I'm not leaving with you today. I need you to respect my decision, but more importantly, I need your friendship."

Lauren hugs me again and says, "I support you only because I love, but I don't agree with you. And I am definitely not telling your brother." We both giggle through our tears at her last statement even though we both know there will not be anything funny about that call.

Together, we enter the house and break the news to the girls. I ask Gabriel to give us some privacy while we talk. Lauren backs me up this time, and I make the same case I made to her. No one is particularly happy, but in the end, they agree to let me make my own choices. I promise to stay in touch and check in regularly. I walk them to their car, and it is a very solemn goodbye this time. I watch their car until I can't see it anymore. I turn around to see Gabriel watching me from the doorway. He doesn't speak until I am back on the porch.

"Are you okay?" he asks.

"Not even close, but I have one more person to tell before I can put this day behind me."

I decide to sit on the terrace and call Tyler. I don't know what time it is, and I don't feel like doing the math. All I know is that I need to get this over with now. Gabriel offers to stay for support, but I send him inside. I have to do this on my own, and it's easier to say what I have to say without him sitting next to me listening.

This time, I start with the part that swayed Lauren. I talk to Tyler about how everything happens for a reason and tell him that I have decided to stay and see where this goes. I try to get him to think about it like I am on a mission trip. He doesn't buy it and reacts exactly as expected. He threatened to come drag me home and even said he was calling the girls to insist they come back for me. He even demands to speak to Gabriel at one point. I set the phone down and go get him.

Gabriel endured quite a bit of yelling before he finally spoke. He tried to assure my brother that his intentions toward me were nothing but honorable and that he would ensure my safety as long as I was here. He told Tyler he was welcome to call anytime. Tyler said he doesn't trust him and called him several choice names before I took the phone back.

"Tyler, I know I will not convince you to change your mind, so I won't try. You can either trust my decision or not, but I will not sit here and be yelled at anymore. I'm tired, and I'm hanging up now. Tell Lisa and the kids I love and miss them and will see you all soon." I hang up and hand Gabriel his phone back.

"You might want to turn that off for the night," I suggest. He agrees and powers his phone off.

I'm spent and just want to go to bed. Gabriel touches my arm and asks if I want to talk.

"No," is all I can get out. I stand and slowly make my way up to my bedroom. I stop halfway up to catch my breath. Gabriel stops one step below me and waits patiently until I am ready to climb the remaining stairs. I enter the bedroom without a word and shut the door. Gabriel lightly taps on the door. When I don't answer, he just says, "I'll be across the hall if you need anything."

I want to cry, but the tears won't come. I think I must be in shock, and I know there is no going back now.

CHAPTER 8

September 22

Gabriel is waiting for me in the kitchen when I come down for breakfast. He starts to say something but changes his mind. Mariam brings me some hot tea and offers me something to eat.

Gabriel finally speaks, "How are your ribs today?" I'm grateful he doesn't want to talk about yesterday, smart man.

"Sore but a little better." I sip my tea.

"I left your medicine on the cabinet and told Mariam to call if you need anything today."

I look up and meet his eyes. "Are you going somewhere?"

"Yes, I have some work to catch up on, and Father suggested that I take care of it today. Tomorrow, we are going into the city if you are up for it. We need to make some wedding arrangements."

I look deeply into my cup as I nod in understanding. I have never felt so alone in all my life. I swallow several times to get my emotions in check, because my absent tears from last night have decided to show up now. I hear Gabriel's chair scrap the floor as he stands to leave. I expect him to speak, but he leaves without a word. Only when he is gone do I let my tears fall silently into my lap.

I spend the remainder of the day in my room resting. But mostly, I just don't feel like being around anyone. I don't feel like putting on a happy face today, and I'm mentally and physically exhausted.

CHAPTER 9

September 23

I awake early, bathe, and dress in one of the dresses Mariam got for me. I apply a lot of makeup trying to hide all of my bruises, but it's too much, so I end up wiping it off and starting over. The bruises are still fresh and will show no matter what I do, so I just go with my normal light application.

I send up a quick prayer that Rana is safe before I head out of my room. I'm dreading the car ride today, not because of my ribs, but because Gabriel barely spoke to me yesterday. He checked in on me briefly, but I haven't seen or heard from him since.

We eat breakfast in relative silence, and I am wondering if this will be my life for the next few months. After breakfast, we head out to Gabriel's car, and I am surprised to see Amon standing next to it. Mariam also joins us, and Amon helps Mariam into the car before getting in himself. Gabriel holds my door for me, and I thank him.

Once he gets into the car, he tells me that Jasmina is at school today, and Amon's mother will stay with her until we return. Gabriel surprises me by taking my hand in his. "I am not angry with you, Sarah. I just didn't know what to say to you and decided to give you some time to process everything. I realize that probably wasn't the best way to handle it, and I'm sorry."

Some of the tension in me releases, and I smile at him wondering…oh what the heck, "Mariam set you straight, didn't she?"

That earned us a snicker from Amon followed by an elbow from Mariam and stops mid-chuckle. Gabriel chooses to remain silent which answers my question. He squeezes my hand and releases it, and I see the corner of Gabriel's mouth twitch, and I know he is not mad at me for asking.

Amon and Gabriel talk business most of the way into the city. They are interrupted by Mariam who wants to give us our schedule for the day. She rattles off a list that includes a dress shop, florist, bakery, and a tailor appointment for Gabriel later in the day. Even though I am nervous about what all of this signifies, I am happy to be out of the house for the day.

We stop at a dress shop that has some beautiful, modern gowns in the front window. I'm nervous because I have no idea what is appropriate for our ceremony, let alone what kind of ceremony we will have. I've been in several dress shops with the girls over the past week, but I was always looking at bridesmaid dresses for me, not wedding gowns. Stasia was always the center of attention on those visits, and I am suddenly very self-conscious about my appearance wondering what the salesclerk will think.

I must have reached up and touched my face because Gabriel lowers my hand and tells me that I look beautiful today and not to worry about a few small bruises. I didn't realize he was standing so close to me and watching my reaction. Mariam ushers us into the store and reminds us that we have a tight schedule to keep today.

The salesclerk approaches our group but addresses Gabriel. He promptly introduces me as his fiancé and tells her we are here to select a wedding gown. Mariam tells her we will need a dress within two weeks. The clerk assures her that they have a great selection of dresses in stock.

She smiles politely at me and asks if I have something particular in mind, and I suddenly realize that I don't have any money with me. We are supposed to pick up my backpack and luggage at the hotel while we are in town. I turn to Gabriel and tell him we forgot to pick up my purse from the hotel, and I don't have my wallet with me. Gabriel tells me not to worry that he has everything covered today.

I am even more uncomfortable now spending his money. I will have to reimburse him later. When we turn back to the clerk, Gabriel tells her to help me pick out any dress I want. Her smile widens, and she asks again if I know what I like. She walks us over to a rack of gowns and starts showing me various styles. I notice her glance at my injuries, and Gabriel protectively places his arm around me. He then proceeds to tell the clerk that I am lucky to have as few injuries as I do, seeing how bad the accident was. It has the desired effect, and she asks if the car was a total loss, and he nods that it was.

I'm having a hard time deciding what I like. I always pictured myself picking out a wedding gown with my best friend and sister-in-law. I wish they were here to help me. But then I remind myself that this is not a real marriage. Maybe one day I will have a real marriage and share it with my family and friends.

Gabriel and Mariam point out several gowns and ask my opinion. I like any ivory one that Mariam selected and ask if it comes in white. The clerk pulls several white lace gowns that are similar and leads me to a dressing room to try them on. I hear Mariam dismiss Gabriel and tell him that he can wait outside with Amon. I find I am both relieved that he will not be watching but also a little disappointed as I find I really want his opinion.

I try on five different dresses in all but keep going back to the second one I tried on. I like it the best, and Mariam agrees that it complements my figure. The dress is an off-the-shoulder, white satin gown with a sweetheart neckline covered in sheer lace across the shoulders and flows down the dress. The back plunges into a deep V, low but not too low. There are also pearl buttons extending down the back of the dress. The sleeves are lace and stop three-quarters of the way down my arms. The dress tapers at the waist and then flows out into a full ball gown. It's modest, and Lauren would probably say demure.

My face falls at the thought of doing this without my best friend. I tell myself that this is not my real wedding. Hopefully, one day, I will be marrying for love and not because I'm trying to save someone's life. I look down and rub my hands over the beautiful lace trying to hide my sudden change of mood, but Mariam doesn't miss a thing.

"So you do not like this dress?" she asks. "We can keep looking. We have all afternoon." I know better than that. I know the tight schedule we are on today.

"No, I love the dress. It's perfect," I say. I think fast to cover my sudden change of mood. "I was just wondering what my mother would have thought of this dress. I wonder if she would love it as much as I do." Then I realize Mariam doesn't know my mother is dead. The clerk is watching both of us. I step down from the pedestal and grab Mariam's hands. "Thank you for being here with me today. I imagine she is smiling down from heaven and thankful that I have your help." Her eyes cloud, but she smiles and squeezes my hands.

It's a productive first stop. The seamstress took a few measurements and pinned the hem to fit with my shoes. We select some accessories and a veil before Mariam calls Gabriel back to take care of the bill. Everything is packed up that we are taking today. Mariam arranges for Amon to return in a week to pick up the finished gown.

I walk over and pretend to look at earrings as Gabriel pays the bill. I don't want to know right now. I will ask him later so that I can pay him back.

Next, we head over to the florist where I choose light pink peonies for my bouquet and leave the rest to Mariam to decide. It's lunchtime, and Gabriel suggests that we go find a place to eat. He instructs Amon to stay with Mariam, and we will meet up at the bakery after lunch.

Gabriel finds a little restaurant with an outside seating area. We settle at a small round table, and Gabriel hands me a menu. He asks me what I want. I look at the menu and don't recognize most of the items on it, so I tell him to order for me. He orders a dish full of vegetables and chicken served with rice. I'm pleasantly surprised that it is both sweet and spicy. I eat most of what he serves up for me. It's the most I've eaten in the last few days. My appetite seems to be returning.

Before we leave the restaurant, I ask Gabriel if we can talk for a minute. He nods and waits for me to begin.

"I know our arrangement is not conventional or anything, but I need you to make me a promise. Okay?"

I see his eyebrows go up. "That depends on what your request is. Tell me what you are asking, and I will give it some consideration before I agree."

"I have spent the last few days telling half-truths, no lies, to protect the people I love the most. It's been exhausting and keeps me awake at night. It's eating me alive knowing it will take a lot of hard work to repair the damage I've caused. I pray every night that they will all forgive me when I get home. As much as I want to make my own decisions, I still need their support."

I pause and take a deep breath. I didn't realize how hard this conversation was going to be. It is bringing up so many emotions, but I need his promise if I am going to get through the next few months with my sanity intact. The not knowing and what ifs are chipping away at my conscience.

Gabriel patiently waits for me to gather my thoughts. It's simple really, and I don't know why I'm making such a big deal about this, but it's important to me.

"I want us to promise to be honest with each other. No matter what it is, I need you to be honest with me. I don't think I can take any more lies right now, and I need to feel like I can trust you."

Gabriel leans forward on the table and holds his hand out to me. I hesitate for a second but place my hand in his, and he firmly closes his fingers around mine before he speaks.

"I know this has been very difficult for you, and I'm sorry you are in this situation with your friends and family. I don't want to make this harder on either of us, so trust me when I tell you I will do my best to tell you the truth. I hope you know that you can trust me, Sarah. I would never intentionally hurt you."

"I do trust you, Gabriel. But with all the lies that have been spoken, I wanted you to know that this is not who I am and that it does not sit well with me. I need us to be honest with each other."

Gabriel nods his agreement and then speaks, "I promise to be honest with you."

"Thank you." I relax and gently pull my hand from his. I fidget with the napkin in my lap and tell myself I don't know why him holding my hand affects me so much, (Yes, I do. I just don't want to admit to it.) but it does, and I don't need another complication in my life right now.

When we finish, Gabriel suggests we walk around for a while if I am not too tired. I agree, and we walk around the area stopping every now and then to let me rest a little. We are both more relaxed now and talk a little about our careers. He asks me several questions about my nursing job and asks what I love most about it. I tell him my favorite parts and ask him what he likes most about his job. He tells me he likes being outside when he has to oversee a new project; otherwise, he spends most of his job behind a desk.

I ask him what he does in his spare time, and he tells me he likes to fish. I tell him I like to do that, too, but most of time I spend on the water is in a kayak. Gabriel tells me there is a river running through one of his land holdings and that he will take me there one day to fish. He says he has a small boat but no kayak. He tells me I can row him anywhere I want. I laugh and tell him that sounds like a job for him.

We've walked several blocks when Gabriel reaches down and lifts my hand. I think maybe he is going to hold my hand, but he lifts it up to eye level. That's when I notice how terrible my nails look as several got broken during the attack. I will have to do something about that when we get back to the house. I don't really want to think about how they got broken right now, so I try to pull my hand out of his, but he holds tight. I look at him quizzically and ask what he is doing.

"I almost forgot," he says.

"Forgot what?" I ask.

He rubs my ring finger and simply says, "Rings."

I hadn't thought of that either, and I start to argue that we don't need them, but he says that they are necessary for the ceremony. My stomach tightens again thinking about how much he is spending on this fake wedding that will end in divorce in a few short months.

"Nothing expensive," I say, but he only responds with a sound like "hmmm."

We walk another block and come to a jewelry store and step in out of the heat. Gabriel stops at the engagement rings, but I move onto just the basic wedding bands. He joins me and says he doesn't mind buying me an engagement ring, too, but I tell him that I mind very much. He doesn't argue, just asks, "Do you see anything you like?"

I point to a tray of plain silver bands and ask to see those. Gabriel instructs the salesman to pull out another that has more elaborate bands, some with diamonds.

I try on several of the plain bands, but Gabriel hands me one with diamonds and sapphires encircling the gold band. I shake my head, but he pulls my hand over the counter and slides it on. It is beautiful, but it's too much. I tell him as much, and he holds his hand out. I place the ring in it, and he hands it back to the salesman. I am relieved that he listened to me and move back to the plain bands when I hear him say, "We'll take this one."

I try to argue, but he says it's done and says now we must find him a band. He decides on a band of interwoven silver and gold with a filigree design around the edges. He seems genuinely pleased when we leave the store.

I, on the other hand, am brooding like a wet hen. Steering us toward the bakery, Gabriel asks, "Why are you upset?"

No point in trying to pretend that I am not, so I answer, "Because you are spending so much money on this wedding. Let me help you pay for something, my dress, the rings, something. I should have offered sooner." Although my bank account is quickly shrinking with everything I have to pay back to his family.

"No," is all he says.

I reach for his arm to stop him and make him look at me. I wince in pain as tugging on him pulled on my ribs. How can I keep forgetting about my ribs? Maybe I do have a brain injury after all.

I power through and ask, "Why not? It's my fault we are in the mess, and I want to pay for something."

Gabriel shakes his head at me and says this is not completely your fault. "I'm the one who proposed to you, so I am paying."

I remind him that some sick, twisted men are to blame and that we are in this together and should share some of the cost. I also remind him that he didn't actually propose marriage, and this is more of an arrangement to get his sister back.

He takes my hand and starts walking toward the bakery and says, "No, I didn't propose. But it was my idea, and I want to do this. If you don't stop arguing, you will make us late, and I for one do not want to keep Mariam waiting."

Gabriel walked a little faster than we had been, and I am slightly out of breath. I'm pretty sure he did it on purpose to stop me from talking any more. He hands me a bottle of water and points me to a table to rest while he goes to talk to Mariam. Amon is already seated and he informs me that dress and flower shopping are not to his liking, but cake he likes very much. I smile and have to agree. This part I like, too.

We are brought several plates of samples with various cakes and filling combinations. We taste everything from plain white cake with raspberry filling to spice cake with fruit and nuts. Gabriel's favorite is a spicy cake with salted rum caramel, and I like the white chocolate with raspberry filling. Amon likes them all, so he is no help at all.

Mariam tells us we will need a four-tiered cake as the centerpiece but could use several smaller cakes to share among the guests. The four-layered cake will be my favorite, and the smaller ones will be Gabriel's choice and chocolate torte cake, which I suspect is Mariam's favorite. We are full, but Mariam insists we buy some cookies to take home for Jasmina.

I am tired and full as we pile back into the car, and I am happy to be heading home now. I mention needing a nap and am informed by Mariam that we still have one more stop. Gabriel looks concerned, but I assure him I can survive one more stop.

She directs us to a large department store where we will shop while Gabriel gets fitted for his new suit at the tailor around the corner. Gabriel does not want to leave us alone, but Mariam insists we need some lady things and assures him we will stick together and stay in the store. She links her arm with mine as we exit the car and enter the store. I suspect Gabriel set Amon on task to watch us, but I don't know for sure.

She is a woman on a mission and leads us directly to the ladies' intimates, and I stop in my tracks. She nearly stumbles at my sudden stop. She releases my arm and asks why I stopped. I tell her that this last stop had better be for her. The corners of her mouth twitch as she links arms again and leads on. She insists that I need new undergarments for the wedding gown and lingerie for after. I tell her that my current undergarment situation will be fine once I get my luggage back.

She argues that every bride needs a few nice things to start her marriage with. I remind her that this is not a traditional marriage, but she ignores my protests and is already picking out several items for me. I decide if she is going to make me buy new undergarments, I will be the one doing the choosing. She insists on a few items that are a little skimpier than I would have chosen, but I am quickly learning she is a force of nature and not to be trifled with. She pays for our selections, and I ask for the receipt, but she just smiles and tucks it into her purse.

Gabriel and Amon are waiting outside when we exit the building. They ask how our shopping went and I say, "Wonderful," in the most sarcastic voice I can. He just raises his eyebrows and starts the car. I take some over-the-counter pain meds and fall asleep almost immediately.

I'm awakened as Gabriel touches my shoulder. We are already home, and it's dark. He offers to take my bags from me. I can tell he is curious about my purchases, but I don't want him getting the wrong idea, so I keep them tightly in my hands.

Amon rounds the car with my backpack and suitcase in hand. I don't know when he stopped for them, but I am excited to have my own things back. I realize later that even my passport is back in my possession. I take it as a sign of trust.

CHAPTER 10

The following day, Gabriel is already gone to work when I come downstairs. Mariam tells me he will be back around lunch and asked that I be ready to go somewhere with him. I ask where, but Mariam says she doesn't know.

Gabriel arrives around noon and thanks Mariam for the lunch she has packed and leads me out to the car.

"Where are we going?" I ask, as we head off down the road. "I need to stop by Omar's and check on the drilling preparations and also to check in on him. Are you okay going there today?"

"I'm okay with it. Do you think they are? They may not be happy to see me after everything that happened."

"Omar and Talia are kind people and won't hold you responsible for what happened at their house. They know where the blame lies." Gabriel says we will only be there an hour or so, and then he wants to show me the river he likes to fish. He says we will eat there.

When we pull up to Omar's house, I exit the car and turn and survey the area. I didn't get a very good look the other day and want to replace the bad memories that are threatening to consume me. I wasn't expecting to have such a visceral reaction to this place, but my heart is pounding, and I have a chill in spite of the warm sunny day. Gabriel startles me when he places his hand on my back and asks if I'm all right. I tell him I'm fine and rub my arms to break the spell and make the chills go away.

Talia is a little surprised to find me standing next to Gabriel when she opens the door to us. Gabriel greets her warmly, and she ushers us into her kitchen. Gabriel breaks the awkward silence.

"Talia, I know the two of you did not get an official introduction the last time we were here. Sarah, I would like to introduce you to Talia." I move to shake her hand as he continues. "Talia, meet Sarah Grant, my fiancé."

Talia's hand goes rigid in mine from the shock of his announcement. I'm a little shocked he introduced me this way, too. I smile at her and release her hand. She is speechless for a moment before remembering her manners. "Congratulations, Gabriel. I had no idea."

Gabriel only smiles and asks if Omar is around. She tells him that he is in the north pasture this morning. Gabriel kisses my cheek. "Well, I'll leave you ladies to get acquainted." I am stunned at his display of affection and irritated that he is leaving me to answer the tough questions.

Talia offers me tea and shortbread cookies. I graciously accept and sit at the table and wait for her to join me. She doesn't speak as she sits down, only stares at me. I guess she is waiting for an explanation. I don't really know what Gabriel wants me to say, so I ask about Omar instead. "How is Omar's head wound?"

She tells me he is healing well with an occasional headache but otherwise fine. I tell her I'm sorry that they had to go through that with me. She nods and tells me that I'm looking better than the last time she saw me.

"Yes, soap and water make a world of difference." I try for levity.

"Your injuries are healing well? I was worried the last time you were here. You seemed to be having a difficult time breathing," she adds.

"I have a couple of cracked ribs that are still tender, but each day gets a little better. Thank you for your concern." Silence stretches out between us. I nibble a cookie and sip the tea just to have something to occupy my hands and mouth.

Talia sits watching me as I eat. She does not initiate conversation, but I can tell she is waiting for me to offer some sort of explanation to Gabriel's announcement.

"I guess you are wondering about my engagement to Gabriel," I start. She stuns me with her response.

"Gabriel is an honorable man, and he has offered you his protection. There is no mystery there. But why you accepted instead of returning to your home is the mystery."

I think carefully as to how to respond. I can't tell her about Rana. I contemplate how to spin this tale and finally decide on evasion. "It's as you said, Gabriel is an honorable man, and they are hard to come by. He offered, I accepted."

Talia does not respond, just sips her tea, studying me over the rim of her cup. I finish my cookie and ask how long she has known Gabriel. She replies that she has known him all his life.

We make small talk until the men return. Gabriel thanks Talia for entertaining me while the men attended to business. He helps me from my chair and bids them a good day.

We arrive at Gabriel's favorite fishing spot around two in the afternoon. It is a peaceful slow-moving river that is clear and cool. I take off my shoes and wade into the shallow water. Gabriel watches me from the shade of a tree where he is spreading a blanket and unpacking the lunch Mariam packed for us. I join him on the blanket and accept the sandwich he holds out to me. We eat in companionable silence enjoying the light breeze and birdsong from the trees.

"Do you come here often?" I ask.

"Not as often as I would like. We used to come here more when we were children and had free time, but work keeps me busy, and I only make it out here a few times a year."

"You should make time to come here more often. It's nice." He agrees, and we spend some time just enjoying the day and each other's company.

The next few days pass slowly as I don't really have much to keep me busy. I text Lauren every evening on Gabriel's phone. Our conversations are short and impersonal, but at least we are communicating. We spoke once on the phone, but it was exhausting to sound chipper when I know my lying is hurting the people I love the most.

Tyler hasn't answered my calls the past few days, so I decided to give him time to cool off.

To help pass the time, I offer to help with some of the housework, but I find I am intruding on someone else's job. A young girl comes twice a week to help with housework and laundry. Mariam informs me she came the day after my injuries when I was sleeping and again while we were in town. This explains why I haven't seen her until now.

I settle for watching and helping in the kitchen as much as Mariam will allow. I am curious about all the new dishes, seasonings, and flavor combinations. This also helps to keep me out of the line of fire of Ahmad as he rarely enters the kitchen after breakfast. I'm not sure if this is his normal routine or because he knows I am here.

Aahron rarely makes an appearance and seems to keep to his father's schedule as they share the same opinion of me. Jasmina is more curious and spends a lot of time helping in the kitchen and asking me questions about my life back home. She is bubbly and full of life, and I enjoy her company. She lets me help her feed the chickens and collect eggs. Sometimes, we help with the sheep and goats, but mostly Amon's family takes care of the livestock.

I seem to have befriended a donkey who likes to be scratched behind his ears. I walk out to the fence each day to visit with him. He is very good at keeping secrets, so I pour my heart out to him frequently. He listens to me complain about my situation, and I reward him with a treat each day. I am happy for his companionship.

My ribs are healing, and I take longer walks outside staying within view of the house. I especially enjoy watching the goats play. They are entertaining with their quirky, playful personalities. I am thankful their antics help me smile while passing a little time each day. I'm trying to stay positive and find some joy in this strange situation I find myself in. I still worry a lot about Rana.

Gabriel is working long days in an attempt to get as much done as he can before the wedding. He has informed me he will be taking some time off to spend with me after the ceremony. Even though he is working long days, we usually take a walk in the evening and spend time watching the sun set in our chairs under the big shade tree. We are slowly getting to know each other, and I find I miss his company during the day when he is gone. He is kind and attentive to my needs. I feel safer with him here.

Gabriel took me around a few times to introduce me to various friends and relatives, showing me his family land. I even learn that Omar is his mother's brother. Omar lives on family land that Gabriel manages. I ask him what the exchange of money was for on the day of my abduction, and he tells me he was paying for Omar's medical care. Somehow, Gabriel had Omar's truck returned to him, and I'm sure that cost him as well.

It is obvious that Gabriel is well respected by his workers and friends. He takes a personal interest in their families and always inquires how they are doing. They all greet him warmly when he arrives. My appearance as his fiancé has definitely created a stir, and they flock to greet us wherever we go. I think they want to see if they can catch a glimpse of me.

Gabriel plays his part well. He dotes on me and flirts with me frequently when people are around. I play along, but I confess that I really am enjoying his attentions, even if they are not real.

Rana is allowed to call in the evenings to let her father know she is safe and unharmed. She sounds sad, and it breaks my heart knowing she is separated from her family because of me. Our wedding day cannot get here soon enough for my liking. I want her safely home with her family.

Our wedding is quickly approaching, and Mariam is a flurry of activity as she directs men to set up the back terrace and garden area with chairs, tables, and extra lighting. The house is scrubbed from top to bottom, and new flowers are planted in various areas on the property. I've resigned myself to stop dwelling on the cost of things and tell myself that it is all for Rana. The wedding is a means to an end, because people would question why the Kattan family did not go all out for their oldest son's wedding. It has to look real.

CHAPTER 11

October 5 will be here before I know it or am ready for it. I'm counting down the days until Rana is returned. The sooner she is back, the sooner I can start planning my departure.

I pray that Muhamed will honor his word and release Rana unharmed. I also pray that I will be forgiven for the false vows I am going to speak in a few days. I know marriage is a sacred covenant that should not be entered into lightly and definitely not with the goal of divorce in the future. This has definitely not been a light decision, and I know my actions will help to save a young girl. I only hope that God sees my actions as self-sacrifice and not willful sin.

I have not spoken about religion with Gabriel yet. But as the day gets closer, I find I have many questions about the ceremony. I would like to know what to expect ahead of time. I know that Mariam and Jasmina attend church each week, and she tells me she is of the Coptic faith. I don't really know what that is, and she doesn't elaborate.

After dinner, Gabriel and I take our usual walk, but tonight we walk down the road a short distance. There is a low stone wall that borders a pasture here. I suggest we sit here and talk for a while. As we settle into our places on the wall, I tell Gabriel I have questions about the ceremony. He agrees to answer my questions.

The wind picks up and blows a strand of my honey blonde hair into my face. He reaches up and tucks the strand behind my ear. His fingers run down the length of the strand, letting it slowly slip through his fingers. It is an intimate gesture that causes my breath to hitch in my throat. His eyes linger on mine for a moment before he looks out over the pasture. The countryside is quiet, and the sun is setting in an explosion of pinks and oranges. The sky is on fire as the sun sets behind the trees.

"What is on your mind? Are you having doubts?" Concern lines Gabriel's brow as he turns to look at me once more.

"Not really doubts, but I do have a lot of questions about the vows we will be speaking to each other. I know we will be married in name only and for appearances, but I don't even know what religion you practice or who will be performing the ceremony. I noticed that you did not attend services with Mariam and Jasmina this past week. Do you attend services somewhere?"

"I don't attend services often, but when I do, it is with Mariam and the girls. Religion has always been a contentious subject in our home, and we don't openly discuss it much. My father and mother had very different views on the topic," he offers.

"Isn't that unusual in your culture to have such a division within the same household?" I ask.

"Yes, it is." He explains to me that a lot of families follow the religious customs of the husband, especially in arranged marriages. He explains that his parents were not an arranged marriage, so their relationship was a little unconventional. I save my questions until the end as Gabriel doesn't speak about either of his parents often, and I hope to learn a little about his mother.

He tells me that his mother was an Egyptian-born woman with an Egyptian father and British mother. She was raised in the Coptic faith, and they lived in a village just outside Minya. He explains that his father saw his mother at the wedding of a friend, and he was taken with her. She was fair skinned with dark eyes and sable brown hair. He tells me she was a beautiful woman full of life.

Ahmad went to his father and requested that he inquire into a match between the two. Initially, Malese's (Gabriel's mother) father refused because they were from different religious faiths. Malese was strong in her faith, and her father would not make her sacrifice her religion for marriage. So he turned Ahmad's father down.

Gabriel raises his eyebrows and says, "My father was not easily dissuaded as you can imagine." I make a rude noise and quickly cover my mouth with my hand. Gabriel just smiles and seems to be amused at my response as he continues his story.

He tells me how his father continued to pursue his mother and would arrange meetings with her through mutual friends. "I know you will find this hard to believe, but my father can be charming and kind when he wants to be." Now I raise my eyebrows at him. "He can," he insists.

I shrug and motion for him to continue.

He tells me that, eventually, his mother fell in love with Ahmad and convinced her father that Ahmad would not make her abandon her faith, and so he consented.

"Father loved her very much and did not take it well when she died after Jasmina was born. He is a very different man than he used to be. After her death, he devoted himself to work to escape the pain of her passing. Thankfully, Mariam was already working for us, and she took over raising us and running the house."

He is thoughtful for a moment before he continues, "Mariam attended the same church as my mother and would take us to services with her."

When he stops, I realize he still hasn't fully answered my question. "So where does that leave you?"

He shrugs. "Somewhere in between, I guess. I admit I haven't given it much thought over the years. I attend when I feel like and don't when I don't. I really haven't given it much thought until recently."

"Until the wedding?" I ask.

"That and you," he replies.

"Why me?"

"I've noticed you seem to spend a fair amount of time in prayer. You seem to find comfort in it, and I realized that I rarely pray. It just got me thinking."

He doesn't elaborate, so I ask, "Thinking about what?"

He responds with, "Things." I can tell he doesn't want to talk about it now, so I table this discussion for later.

"So we will have a Coptic ceremony?"

"Yes," he replies. "Mariam would not have it any other way."

We discuss all the aspects of the ceremony, and he answers all my questions but one. I want to know who will walk me down the aisle.

Gabriel says he has talked to Aahron, and he will walk me down the aisle. This does not sit well with me as Aahron barely gives me the time of day. I am trying to figure out how to tell Gabriel that I'm not comfortable with this. He sees I am struggling to find the right words. "Just tell me. You will not hurt my feelings. Do you not want Aahron to walk with you?"

"No, as a matter of fact, I don't. He barely speaks to me and when he does, well…" I'm trying to say it nicely but don't know how, so I just say it. "He treats me like you father does."

Gabriel is not offended and offers his apology. "I'm sorry that he treats you that way. I have noticed he is cold toward you. I hope that in time he will come to see you as I do."

I don't ask how he sees me. I'm not sure I'm ready for that answer. "So could Amon walk with me? He is always kind and never seems to judge me."

"I am sure he will be happy to escort you. I will ask him for you." I thank him.

CHAPTER 12

October 5

I rise early and soak in the tub for a while. I'm hoping the warm water will help to calm my nerves and relieve some of the tension in my shoulders. I am so nervous about this ceremony and wonder if Muhamed will keep his word and show up with Rana. She called last night, and Mariam assured her that a beautiful new dress would be awaiting her. She seemed happy about that.

As my water starts to cool, there is a tap at the door. "Sarah, are you awake in there?" Mariam asks.

"Yes, I'm just getting out. Give me a minute." I step from the tub and towel off before wrapping my robe around me and twisting my hair up in the towel. I find Mariam in my room hanging my dress from the corner of the wardrobe. She has placed a tray with food on my table and encourages me to eat.

"I'm not sure I can eat, for all the butterflies in my stomach," I tell her. "What if it doesn't stay down?"

Mariam unzips the bag and exposes the beautiful satin and lace gown hidden within. "You will find a way to keep it down or you will mess up your beautiful gown," she tells me. "Besides, we can't have you passing out from hunger in the middle of the ceremony."

I obey and nibble on some flat bread that has been spread with fava beans and a cheese wedge.

After breakfast, I dry my hair, and Jasmina helps Mariam to curl and pin it up. She leaves a few strands floating down my back and around my face. She offers to help with my makeup, but I decline and tell her I would prefer to do it myself. I want to keep things light and natural. I feel a little guilty as I turned down an offer a few days ago to have my hands painted with henna. I decided to let Jasmina paint my nails as a compromise, and she chose a deep pink color that complements my fair skin.

Last night after dinner, Gabriel gifted me with a cell phone of my own. I texted my new number to Lauren, Nicole, and Stasia. I sent it to Lisa, too, and asked her to pass it along to Tyler, who still isn't speaking to me. I pull it out now and snap a few pictures of my dress and hair and makeup and wish that I could send them to Lauren. I know this is not the wedding I imagined growing up, but I still wish my best friend could be here to share this with me. Maybe she will be there when I get married for real next time. I probably won't show her the pictures, they are more just for me.

I finish getting ready, and Mariam attaches my veil in place. She hands me my bouquet, and Jasmina snaps a few more pictures before they leave me with strict instructions to meet Amon at the foot of the stairs in ten minutes. I agree, and they leave me alone in my room. Anxiety is eating away at me. My dress feels too tight, I question my choice in putting my hair up, maybe I should have left it down, do I look pretty? A thousand thoughts are threatening to drown me. I decide that it doesn't matter either way. So I close my eyes, say a quick prayer for Rana, and wait it out. It is the longest ten minutes of my life.

I take the stairs slowly so that I don't get tangled up in my dress. Aahron is standing at the bottom with Amon and for a minute, I panic thinking Gabriel forgot to tell him that he is not walking me down the aisle. Amon steps up and takes my hand as I descend the last two steps and places my hand on his arm, making no mistake who is walking me down the aisle.

Aahron surprises me. "You look beautiful, Sarah. My brother is a lucky man." I can't speak, so I just nod my acceptance of his complement, but he is not finished. "Thank you for doing this for my sister."

I'm stunned but quickly find my voice. "Is she here? Did he bring her home?" I will not say that horrible man's name today. It's bad enough he is here, but I don't have to acknowledge him.

"Yes, she is home and safe. I just wanted you to know before you walk down the aisle." With that, Aahron leaves to take his place as the music begins. He is so nice that I almost feel guilty for not wanting him to walk me down the aisle. Maybe he was just worried about his sister before and not really meaning to be rude to me.

"I'm so relieved that tears clog my throat and threaten to pour over my eyelids. I sniff them back, and Amon tells me to take some deep breaths, but is otherwise quiet next to me as I regain composure. I know this day is far from over, and I also know that at some point, I will have to come face to face with the animal who orchestrated my abduction and Rana's. I refuse to be a scared, weak girl in front of him. I think about Nuru doubled over after my knee connected with some very tender parts, and it makes me smile. That is what I will think about today when I have to smile and be cordial to Mr. M.

We exit the house onto the back terrace where musicians are gathered and playing. Their song stops and changes at our appearance. Gabriel stands waiting for me at the front of the aisle. He is so handsome in his black suit. He is freshly shaven and hair newly trimmed and styled. His dark, chocolate eyes meet mine as we descend the steps, and my steps falter. My heart is beating a mile a minute, and I'm short of breath, and it has nothing to do with my ribs. The way he is looking at me sends chills down my spine. Obviously, he approves. I know he doesn't love me, but it is gratifying nonetheless to see that I have this effect on my soon-to-be husband on our wedding day. Every bride wants to feel beautiful, and now I do.

The ceremony seems to last an eternity as the priest goes through the rituals and scripture before he comes to the vows. He instructs us to join right hands and ties a white sash around our entwined hands.

It's symbolic of the entwining of our lives. I realize in that moment that no matter what happens, whether I stay or go, we will always share this connection.

Finally, we exchange vows and rings and with a final blessing, the ceremony concludes. Gabriel lifts my veil and tucks it behind my head. I knew this part would come, even though we did not discuss it. I played out several scenarios in my head and finally decided to just meet him halfway and make it quick. He moves in to kiss me, and I lift my face and gently press my lips into his. He tenses ever so slightly, and I worry that maybe I've done something wrong, but before I can finish that thought, he presses his lips more firmly into mine and cradles my face in his hands. A warm tingle starts low in my belly and is moving throughout my entire body when I am startled by a loud whoop and an eruption of applause. Gabriel and I pull apart, but I can see that kiss affected him as much as it did me.

Amon gives another loud yell and claps Gabriel on the back. I shoot him a look, which only makes him smile bigger. Gabriel takes my hand, and Jasmina hands me my bouquet, and we make our way down the aisle together.

We are congratulated by so many friends and family that it is all a blur. There are too many people for me to even try to remember their names. There are some familiar faces, too, and I am happy to see them. But most of all, we are all relieved to have Rana back. Gabriel leads us to where she is standing next to Ahmad and holds his arms out to her. Rana hugs Gabriel fiercely, and I see the tears streaming down her face.

"Did they harm you?" he asks.

"No," she answers. "I am just happy to be home. Thank you."

Gabriel turns slightly and holds his hand out for me to join them. "There is someone else you need to thank for your safe return," he whispers to Rana. To my surprise, she pulls me into their hug. The three of us stand there for a moment until Gabriel tells Rana that he and I need to mingle with our guests. He assures her that he will make time for her later.

We spend about an hour milling around visiting with guests and accepting well-wishes while we wait for dinner to be served. I hold tightly to Gabriel's arm as we weave in and out of a sea of people. He suddenly stops, and I feel his whole body go rigid. It only takes a moment for it to register who has stepped into our path—Muhamed.

Muhamed is the first to speak. "Good evening, Gabriel, and congratulations on your marriage. You are truly blessed to own such a lovely bride." I can feel the heat of animosity coming off Gabriel in waves now, and I place my free hand on his arm and press lightly to remind him not to give into the baiting of this monster.

It only takes Gabriel a second, but he schools his expression, but I see the narrowing of his eyes as he answers, "I am indeed blessed that this amazing woman freely chooses me for her husband. Now if you will excuse us, we have guests to attend to."

We try to move around him, but he blocks the way and extends his hand to Gabriel. Gabriel hesitates, and Muhamed says, "I look forward to seeing you and your bride again in the future."

Gabriel grasps his hand and follows up with, "It is finished between us now." Whatever game Muhamed is playing, I hope he thinks he has won and moves on.

Thankfully, Muhammed takes his leave immediately after dinner. The tension visibly evaporates upon his departure. Soon after, the dance floor comes alive with dancing and much celebration. Gabriel makes sure to dance with both of his sisters and Mariam during the evening. Everyone seems to be having a wonderful time, even Ahmad is more relaxed and jovial than I have ever seen him. Though he appears to be having a good time, he keeps a watchful eye on his girls.

My feet are sore from all the dancing, and my dress feels tight from all the food we have eaten. There are so many new and wonderful dishes, and Gabriel wanted me to try them all. If I don't eat again for a week, it will be too soon.

The guests linger late into the evening, but the festivities seem to finally be dying down. I see Amon and Gabriel whispering, and it piques my curiosity. "What is all the whispering about?" I ask.

In unison, they say, "Nothing."

I don't buy it for a minute, so I press on. "I don't believe you. You answered too quickly."

"It truly is nothing you need to know about right now," Gabriel insists.

"So it is something I need to know, just not right now?"

I'm determined to get an answer from him, but he replies, "Precisely, so stop asking questions and let me get a good look at you." He spins me around to admire my dress or to distract me. Either way, it works.

"You are stunning in this dress. I meant what I said earlier, I am truly blessed to call you my wife. You are strong and beautiful and brave. You didn't even flinch when Muhamed approached us. I am honored to call you wife and…friend."

He watches me closely, gauging my response and waiting for an answer to his unspoken question. I know what he was asking, so I reply, "Yes, Gabriel. We are definitely friends." He smiles and briefly hugs me before leading me back toward the remaining guests to say good night.

Gabriel walks me to my room, me carrying my shoes and him his jacket and tie. We are both silent as we approach my door. I break the silence by asking, "So how do we do this without raising too many questions?" He knows my meaning and opens the door for me to enter first. Once the door is firmly closed, he turns to face me.

"Father insists that we make sure this marriage looks real. So I guess I should stay in here tonight. It will not look good if we don't share a bedroom, especially on our wedding night." I know he is right, but I'm not comfortable with this. We didn't discuss this arrangement.

My heart starts to pound as he moves closer to me and rubs my arms. I'm afraid and excited that he might try to kiss me again, and I am not quite ready for that. Not ready because I enjoyed the last kiss so much. I look down at the shoes in my hand, but he lifts my face back up.

"I promised to protect you and not hurt you and that includes in here, too." He releases my face and gestures to the room around us. "I know you told me this marriage is in name only, but I won't lie to you. Those vows we just took felt pretty real to me. I am attracted to you, Sarah, and I have feelings for you. There is a part of me that would very much like to be more than just friends."

I take a step back because this was not our deal. He sees the panic on my face and holds his hands up. "Please hear me out. First of all, I would never force you to do anything you didn't want to do, so you don't have to worry about that. I just need you to know what I am feeling right now. You asked for honesty, so here it is. I don't know if it's because emotions are running high tonight because of the vows we spoke and promised ourselves to each other, or if it started that first time I saw you."

Gabriel takes a deep breath and continues, "My head knows this is supposed to be temporary, but I'm only human, and my human side is looking at my beautiful bride and wants more. All I know is that I do feel something for you." He takes another deep breath and sighs, "Hopefully, tomorrow, my head will be clearer. For tonight, I'm sorry that I made you uncomfortable by telling you my human side wants more."

I let his words sink in fully before I speak. "Thank you for your honesty. I'm sorry if I misled you, that was never my intent. I didn't mean to make this more difficult. I like you, Gabriel, really. And I meant what I said. I do consider you a friend, but that's all I can give right now and still walk away. I don't take relationships lightly, and I'm in over my head right now as it is. I promise to be mindful of your 'human side' in the future."

Gabriel rubs a hand across his face and takes a small step backwards. "I don't know how to do this, act like newlyweds without really being newlyweds. I didn't think this would be so difficult."

I suggest, "Maybe we should just try to get some sleep and tomorrow, a solution will present itself."

"Maybe, but I have one more thing to tell you," he says.

I laugh. "Do you think that is wise? I'm not sure we need any more revelations tonight," I say, trying to lighten the mood.

He smiles and says, "Probably not, but there's no going back now." He shakes his head and soldiers on. "I arranged for us to go away for a week. We leave in the morning."

"What? Do you really think that is a good idea after everything you just said to me? I'm not sure we should be alone for a week."

Gabriel tells me he thought it might be awkward to act like newlyweds in a house full of people, so he booked this trip for us to get away and have some time to figure out how to play this.

"That was before this." He gestures between me and him. "I don't know if it's a good idea, but I could really use some time away from here. I'm sure you could, too."

I nod in agreement and he continues, "I booked a suite so that you can have your own room. I can cancel if you don't want to go."

I think about what he said, and he is right. It will be weird spending our supposed honeymoon in a house full of people. Maybe we should go on this trip and figure out how to act around each other. At least, we won't have to pretend while we are gone. And I could use a change of scenery.

I ask, "Where are we going?"

"Amon will drive us to the port in Aswan first thing in the morning where we will board a boat for a three-day river cruise down the Nile. Then we will spend a few days at a resort before we return home."

Gabriel bravely takes my hand. "We will figure something out. I didn't mean to make you uncomfortable. It won't happen again."

I frown, and he reaches up to smooth the frown lines from my forehead with his thumb. I flinch and begin to tremble, so he drops his hand.

"Either you don't trust me or you are still dealing with what happened to you. Maybe both, but you have to trust me, Sarah. I don't want you to flinch every time I try to touch you. People will notice, and I don't like thinking you are afraid of me."

"I'm not afraid of you, Gabriel. My emotions are running high right now, too, and I'm just tired and jumpy." I can't tell him it has nothing to do with nerves.

I suddenly remember him flinching today, too, so I ask, "I am not the only one flinching today. I seem to remember you flinched when we kissed at the altar. Why?"

A smirk pulls at his lips as he remembers what I am talking about. "That kiss was unexpected, and you surprised me."

"Unexpected? Isn't that customary when you get married? We said 'I do', you lifted my veil, and then we kiss. I don't get why you are laughing at me now." He is not actually laughing out loud, but by his expression, he is thoroughly amused by something I've said.

Gabriel is not even trying to hide his amusement as he answers me. "Yes, it is customary, but I think our tradition is a little different than yours."

"Different how?" I ask. I'm confused because a kiss is a kiss. How could it be different?

Gabriel moves a little closer and asks me to trust him for a second. "Hold perfectly still and promise me you will not move. Promise?" I nod my consent.

Gabriel leans toward me, and my heart skips a beat. I know I shouldn't let him kiss me, but I don't want to stop him either. He is watching me as he leans in and kisses me right in the middle of my forehead! I now turn five shades of red as understanding dawns, and I realize what I did today. No wonder Amon and the guests were "whooping." I want to crawl under the bed right now. Gabriel is not helping matters either as he is grinning like the cat who just ate the mouse.

"Now, is everything clear?" he asks.

"Crystal," is all I manage to croak out.

Even though I am thoroughly embarrassed right now, at least the tension in the room is gone, and I'm thankful for that. Gabriel nudges me in the direction of the bathroom and tells me to go get ready for bed. I happily comply, eager to hide my embarrassment.

I spend several long minutes trying to undo all those blasted small, beautiful pearl buttons. No matter how much I bend and twist and try to contort my body, I can't reach them all. I focus instead on washing my face and taking my hair down before I give it one more try, but it's no use. There are just a few that I cannot reach. I consider ripping them off but can't bring myself to damage this beautiful dress. I can't stall anymore, so I straighten my back and walk back into the bedroom.

Gabriel is placing blankets and pillows on the rug next to the bed when I enter the room. He is taken back as I exit the bathroom still wearing my wedding dress. "Are you planning on sleeping in that? It's beautiful, but I can't imagine it's that comfortable." He jokes.

I'm embarrassed and don't want him to see, so I turn my back to him and indicate my dilemma. "I can't reach them all."

"Ahh…" He closes the distance between us and carefully unbuttons the remaining buttons for me. I hold the bodice tightly to my chest as he works. He has made quick work of what I was struggling to do myself. He tells me he is done, and I thank him and return to the bathroom once more.

When I'm done, I tell Gabriel he can have the bathroom now, and I climb into bed. He comes back into the room a few minutes later and turns out the light. I hear him settle onto his palate on the floor.

"Good night, Gabriel."
"Good night, Sarah."

CHAPTER 13

October 6

I did not sleep well. I dreamed about Muhamed coming back here to try to take me. I've had similar nightmares the first week after the abduction, but none since. I guess seeing Muhamed in person yesterday brought it to the surface again. I hope this trip will help to clear my head and chase the demons away.

We leave early the next morning. Gabriel grabs us coffee and fruit while I pack my suitcase. The family is still sleeping after the late night we had. Amon meets us in the foyer and is all smiles. I shoot him a flinty stare, but this only makes him chuckle. He tells us he will take the luggage out to the car. Gabriel locks up the house, and we follow after Amon. I climb into the back seat and assume he will ride in the front with Amon, but he slides in from the other side and sits with me instead.

It takes a couple of hours to reach the port, and I am enjoying seeing more of the beautiful country. I expected all sand when I came to Egypt, and there is plenty of that, but there is also greenery, especially near the rivers and streams.

We reach the port and thank Amon for the ride. We board the boat and get settled into our suite, which consists of a sitting area with a sofa and two chairs that face a balcony overlooking the water and a small bedroom. Gabriel insists I take the bedroom, and I argue that I am smaller and should take the sofa, but he won't hear it. Maybe I can convince him to at least trade off each night. We will discuss it later. For now, we decide to walk around and explore the boat.

As our boat gets underway, we pass landscape that is lush and green, with miles of desert in the background. It is peaceful, and there is a nice breeze. We spend the remainder of the day on deck talking and watching the world float by.

After dinner, we stroll to an upper deck where we hear music playing. When we crest the top of the stairs, we see that there are also several people dancing. Gabriel holds his hand out to me, and we fall in with the others swaying to the music. His hands are strong and warm as he leads me around the dance floor. He asks if I am having a good time, and I tell him that I am.

"You were right," I say. "This is much better than being surrounded by your family. It's the first time I have relaxed in weeks. Who knew I needed a vacation from my vacation?" I joke.

Gabriel takes on a serious mood. "Do you not like my family?" he asks.

I didn't mean to offend him, so I quickly respond, "I do like your family, everyone—most everyone has been very nice to me. Mariam and the girls have been great and very welcoming. It's just odd being in a house full of strangers so far from home and not really knowing my place."

"Aahron and Father will come around in time. You are my wife and officially part of the family now. As for finding your place, that will just take time." He quickly amends his last statement, "If you choose to give it time."

I'm not really sure what he meant by that, but I don't give it much thought right now. I just want to relax and enjoy the evening.

Gabriel asks me to tell him about my family, so I tell him how my parents died in a car accident when I was thirteen and how Tyler is pretty much all I have left. I tell him how much Tyler sacrificed to take care of me. I tell him about Lisa and Danny and Lizzie. By the time I finish, I'm really missing them and wishing Tyler would talk to me. Gabriel tells me he will come around in time. He also says that it hurts to let go of the ones we love, and sometimes, it takes a little space and time to heal.

Gabriel senses my change of mood and quickly spins me around the dance floor until I'm laughing and out of breath. I lean my head on his chest and thank him for the dance.

The boat makes several scheduled stops along the way to allow passengers to tour the surrounding areas. We join the tours but always stray from the group as I get a history lesson from my own personal tour guide, Gabriel. We tour some of the same sites that the girls and I toured, but I find I am enjoying them so much more this time. I try not to go there, but the more time I spend with Gabriel, the more I like him. He is comfortable to be around.

Gabriel passes on the camels this time and says we will walk. I try to talk him into it, but he says I will not change his mind. "You cannot pay me to ride one of those creatures," he states.

"Are you afraid of them?" I tease.

He explains that it is more of a matter of trust than fear. He proceeds to tell me of the one and only time he rode one. He describes the "beast" (his word) as a temperamental, spitting, biting, demon-possessed creature with red eyes and long fangs. I tell him he is exaggerating, and he lifts his shirt to show me a scar on his side as proof. I double over in laughter trying to imagine Gabriel in that scene. He doesn't think it is as funny as I do.

October 9

Today, we disembarked from the boat and made our way to the resort for the remainder of our trip. We decide to just lounge by the pool all day and go out for dinner. Gabriel has made reservations for dinner at a restaurant he loves.

We get settled into our suite, change into our swimsuits, and head down to the pool to soak up some sun. I take off my wrap and notice that Gabriel keeps his gaze straight ahead as he sprawls out on the chaise next to me. At least I think he does. It's hard to tell with his dark sunglasses firmly in place. I smile remembering calling him that, "Sunglasses," until I learned his name. I don't want to think about the rest of that day, so I busy myself applying sunscreen.

I cover all the areas I can reach and walk over to Gabriel and offer him my bottle. "Do you mind getting my back?" I ask.

He sits up and drops his legs on either side of the chair so that I can sit in front of him. His warm hands massage the cool lotion onto my back and shoulders. Butterflies unleash themselves in my belly. Today, I am "human," and this has more of an effect on me than I like. I stand quickly, mumble thanks, and retrieve my bottle.

I fiddle with my towel before lying on my stomach, trying to get my hormones under control. I close my eyes and focus on slow, even breaths. It's not working, so I shift my head from side to side, trying to find a comfortable position. Suddenly, something cold splashes across my back, and I yelp in surprise as I roll into a sitting position just in time to see Gabriel take a long drink from his water bottle. He holds it out to me and asks if I need a sip. I hesitantly take it from him.

"You looked like you needed to cool off." He smiles. "So I decided to help."

He knows! And he is so enjoying this! I go to throw some cold water at him, but he sprints away to the edge of the pool and dives in. I walk over to the edge of the pool, squat down, and wait for him to emerge. No point in trying to avoid my embarrassment. As he breaches the water, I open my mouth to speak, but he is quick and pulls me into the pool with him. When I come up from my involuntary dip, he says, "It's nice to see that you are human, too." With that, he kisses me on the forehead and swims across the pool.

I watch him make several laps and try to get my emotions under control. I'm finding it more and more difficult to deny my growing feelings for Gabriel. I decide not to think about it right now and follow his lead, making several laps across the pool before returning to my chair.

We alternately bake in the sun for a while and then cool off in the pool. The tension is under lock and key for now, and we "humans" keep it light and enjoy each other's company for the remainder of the day.

I've just finished my shower and am drying off when Gabriel knocks on the door. I tell him I will be out soon. He speaks through the door and says Lauren is on the phone. I throw on a robe and crack the door to take his phone from him. He tells me she called his when she couldn't reach me on my phone.

"Hey, Lauren. How are you?" I say, really excited to hear from her.

"You sound chipper," she says. "What has you in such a good mood, or should I say who?"

I avoid her question and tell her, "I just got out of the shower. I needed to wash off the chlorine and sunscreen before we go to dinner."

"I didn't realize Gabriel had a pool at his house." It is definitely not a friendly question by her tone, and I don't like where it is going.

"He doesn't. We are in Cairo spending a few days at a resort. It's been a busy couple of weeks, and we decided to take a few days to sightsee and relax."

She replies with, "Um hum."

I'm not really in the mood for twenty questions, so I ask, "What does that mean?"

"Well, I would like to know what is really going on with you and when you are coming home?"

"I'm not exactly sure when I will be home. Hopefully soon." I hope this will appease her, but it doesn't.

"Really? Because I got a call from one of your coworkers who said you have taken an extended leave of absence. So are you going to tell me what is really going on with you? I'm worried about you."

"Lauren, I'm fine really. As a matter of fact, I am having a great time. I don't know when I will be home, but when I decide, you will be the first one to know." I try to change the subject. "Have you heard from Tyler?"

"Tyler is upset and worried about you. He texts me every evening to see if I've heard anything new. You should call him and work this out."

"I have tried to call him. He is not taking my calls. I texted him my new number and asked Lisa to make sure he gets it. If he wants to talk to me, then he can call me." I know I sound childish, but he's the one who won't talk to me. So, now, the ball is in his court.

There is a long pause, and I'm wondering if the call dropped when Lauren finally speaks, "So are you going to answer my question about what is going on with you and Gabriel?"

"We are having a great ti—" I start to answer her, but she cuts me off.

"Yeah, you already said that. Care to elaborate? You just told me you are at a resort with him, and clearly, you two are sharing a room since he just handed you the phone while you were showering."

I can't believe she is questioning me this way. How dare she?

"Lauren, I'm a grown woman, and I don't owe you an explanation, but since you are my best friend, I will give you one this time." I want her to know that I will tolerate her intrusiveness this once.

"First of all, I was not in the shower. I had just gotten out. Yes, we are staying in a suite together, but he sleeps in one room, and I sleep in the other. And even if we weren't sleeping in separate rooms, I don't see how that is your business."

There is another long pause before she responds. "I don't want to fight with you. But think about it, what would you think if the tables were turned?"

I don't answer because nothing about this situation has made sense from the beginning, and my feelings are hurt right now, and I'm mad for having to lie to her at all.

"I'm just saying that this is totally out of character for you, and I want you to be careful," she adds.

I realize that even though I'm upset with her, I'm more upset at myself for feeling things I wasn't prepared for. If I can't explain it to myself, how am I going to explain it to my best friend? My frustration gets the better of me, and I answer her sarcastically.

"Is a wall between us careful enough for you?" Venom drips with each word, but I am so frustrated with being questioned by her, and with myself, that it just pours right on out. I want to scream at her that I am a grown, *married* woman. I can't seem to stop, so I don't.

"What if I didn't want the wall between us? What would you say about that? I'm enjoying myself and doing what I want to do for once in my life. I'm happy here. Why can't you just respect my decisions?"

"Respect your decisions? Do you even hear yourself? Nothing you are doing makes sense. I can't imagine how horrible your attack was. And a brush with death is enough to make anyone reevaluate their life, but this is insane! You are in a foreign country with a total stranger, living with his family, and traipsing all over the country with him. This isn't you! Just come home and give yourself time to heal and to get your head straight."

"I won't keep arguing about this. You're not listening, and I don't want us to hate each other. Just be my friend. I don't need a judge and jury. Please don't call me if all you are going to do is scold me and tell me my choices are insane. You don't know anything about it. Tell Tyler, tell him whatever. I have to go."

I end the call and drop down on the foot of the bed. I should have told her the truth. I should have confided in her, but I don't want my family or friends to come here and make trouble for Gabriel or his family. I just need to stay long enough to ensure they are safe. Then hopefully I can make this right with everyone else.

Gabriel enters the room. I know he heard every word, and I'm just too tired to care if he thinks less of me right now. He sits down next to me and wraps me in a hug. At first, I resist because I don't want his sympathy, but he doesn't let go, and I stop my protest and bury my head in his chest and wrap my arms around him. Not only do I need this, I find I want this. I am having a good time here, and I do enjoy being with Gabriel. He is smart and funny and caring and…my husband. I'm so confused, and my emotions are all over the place. I let go and just let the tears fall.

When I finally lift my head, his shirt is soaked, and I'm pretty sure my eyes are puffy. I try to smooth the wrinkles, but it's useless at this point. He pulls my hands into his before he speaks.

"I hate seeing you in so much pain. These lies are tearing you in two. Maybe it's time to tell her what is really going on. Maybe we should tell them we are married now. You shouldn't have to defend yourself all the time. I'm well aware that you can take up for yourself, but it's my responsibility now, too."

He pauses, waiting for me to answer. When I don't, he continues, "Talk to me. Tell me what you are thinking." I shake my head, and he reaches up and stops me. I try to pull away, but he won't let me.

"Don't. You have finally started to drop your walls and let me in. Don't put them back up now. I'm not your enemy. I'm your husband and your friend. Tell me what I can do to make this better." Gabriel's pleading tears at my walls that are fighting to resurrect themselves. The tears start again.

The words are leaving my mouth before I can change my mind. "I want them to respect my judgment and stop telling me I don't know what I am doing. I thought they knew me better than this. I understand that everything doesn't make sense, but why can't they trust me. Why is it so hard to believe that maybe I really do want to be here with you, and I don't need any other reason than that? It hurts to think that they doubt my resolve and morals. I've always done the right thing, said the right thing, without compromise. How can she question my morals? How? Twenty-four years, and she thinks I just tossed that out the window without a good reason? I thought she knew me better than that!"

It feels good to give voice to my frustrations and now that the floodgates are open, I can't seem to stop. "Ever since I set foot in this country, people have made all kinds of assumptions about me, and they are all wrong. I'm really tired of being referred to as a woman with loose morals! They are far from loose, you know that better than anyone, they have been locked down good and tight."

Gabriel flinches with my last statement. It takes me a second to realize maybe I said too much. "I'm sorry. You asked what was bothering me, and I told you way more than you needed to hear. I'm done with the pity party. I'll go get dressed so we can go to dinner. You must be hungry." I know I'm rambling, but I can't seem to stop, so I try to get up. Gabriel doesn't release me though.

It's his turn now. "I know that things have not gone the way you planned since you arrived here, and I'm sorry for that. So many of your choices have been taken from you. I can't even begin to think why people would question your decisions or resolve, because I've been extremely impressed with both."

"I'm sorry my father referred to you in such a derogatory manner and that I stood by and watched you defend yourself, twice actually. You shouldn't have to do that. And yes, I do know how virtuous you are, and I respect you all the more for it. I'm not saying that it is easy or that I like it," he says with a smile, "but I respect it. I know I keep telling you, but I think you are amazing. I love you just the way you are. You don't have to prove anything to me."

I'm stunned by his revelation, and I'm not completely sure he even realizes what he just said. I can only blink my eyes. My brain is trying to figure out if he meant it in a friendly way or a romantic way. I'm speechless.

Gabriel holds out his hand. "Now, hand me my phone." I give it to him, and he turns it completely off. "You go get dressed, something pretty, but comfortable shoes, because I'm taking you out for dinner, and I'm going to spin you around a dance floor somewhere until you forget all this and are smiling again." He stands and pulls me to my feet. "And for the record, I'm glad you want to be here with me." He kisses my forehead and leaves the room. I smile, rub my forehead, and thank God that he brought Gabriel into my life despite the circumstances.

Gabriel finds a place with great food and live entertainment, belly dancing. After dinner, he keeps his promise and takes me dancing. We stay until closing at two in the morning, then catch a cab back to the resort. We are still laughing and dancing as we ride in the elevator. He spins me through the doorway, and I stumble into the suite. He catches me and holds me tight. He slows the rhythm, and we just sway for a while. I know I told Gabriel that it was too painful to get too close, but I'm starting to think that not close enough is painful, too. I try not to overthink it right now and just enjoy his arms around me, rubbing slow circles on my back.

Eventually, he releases me and takes a small step backward. I offer for him to shower first while I grab a cold bottle of water from the fridge. I toss him one, and he heads off to the shower. I sink down onto the sofa and close my eyes. Exhaustion kicks in, and I drift off to sleep. I awaken when I feel warm lips on my forehead and smell the clean scent of soap. I smile and open my eyes and gaze up at my husband.

"Come on, Sleeping Beauty, time for bed and you are in mine." I stand to my feet and hug him before I change my mind. "Thank you for this evening and today, well and the three days before that. I've had a wonderful time with you." This time, when he moves to kiss my forehead, I step up on my tiptoes and meet his lips. He stills and but then deepens the kiss. It's wonderful, and I feel it all the way to the tips of my toes. He lingers for only a short time before breaking the spell and holds me at arm's length.

"Go take your bath. You've had a very emotional day, and I don't want you to regret anything." I start to protest, but he places a finger over my mouth. "Go, before I change my mind. I want you to be completely sure. I'm going to remove my finger now, and I need you to turn around and walk away because 'I'm human,' remember?"

I walk into my room enjoying the lingering tingle on my lips. I'm in bigger trouble than I ever imagined.

October 10

I wake and dress quickly eager to see Gabriel this morning. I tossed and turned a long time thinking about that kiss. I wanted to go out to the living room several times and talk to him but decided to let things cool off until the morning.

Gabriel is already up and drinking coffee when I enter the living area. He produces a coffee for me and a pastry bag. "Where did you get that?" I ask.

"I took an early morning walk and thought you might enjoy some coffee and pastries."

I peek into the bag. "Yum," I say, as I reach in and grab a sugary confection. I hand the bag back to him to share.

After I wash down a bite with some coffee, I ask, "Trouble sleeping last night?" I'm hoping we can talk about last night because I don't want any awkwardness to return. He doesn't answer, just narrows his eyes and lifts one brow as he takes another sip of coffee.

"I take it you don't want to talk about last night." I really want him to talk to me.

"No." It's all he gives me before he takes a bite of his pastry.

"Gabriel, don't you think we should talk about it?"

"No, I don't," he says around a mouthful of pasty.

"Why not?" Now I'm just being pushy, I know, but I want to get this discussion out there and over with.

"Because there is nothing to talk about. I think we each said plenty yesterday, and it's abundantly clear that we are attracted to each other. I don't think there is anything else to discuss. I think the ball is in your court, and you need to make a decision." He stops and pins me with his eyes.

I brave the question. "A decision about what?"

"About what you want. No compromises or sacrifices. Just what does Sarah want. When you decide, you let me know. No pressure either way. Totally your decision."

I stuff some pastry into my mouth and think about what he just said. I wanted to talk about where *we* thought this relationship is headed, but I wasn't expecting him to dump it all at *my* feet. I guess I do need to think about what *I* want. He's right, and I know that leaving will be even harder if I choose this. I do still want to leave, don't I? I'm so confused right now. I do miss home, but I can't deny that I do have feelings for Gabriel. Can I picture my life without him? Do I even want to anymore?

There are so many questions running through my mind. My heart is telling me one thing, and my head is doing a great job of arguing both sides of staying and leaving. Not to even mention the fact that Gabriel said he loves me. The pastry feels like a lump of clay as I struggle to swallow. My throat is tight, and my anxiety level is growing by the second. I don't really know what I thought this conversation would be like, but I didn't expect this. I grab my coffee and sip it slowly knowing that either way, this is going to be the hardest decision I will ever make.

We spend the day at museums and shopping. Gabriel acts like nothing ever happened. He holds my hand and keeps things light, and I appreciate it. I walk through the exhibit halls and art exhibits, but my mind is distracted trying to process exactly what I want. I need to be completely sure that I make the right decision. Every time I think about leaving him, my chest tightens. But staying scares me, too. I never expected to feel this way about him.

I ask Gabriel if there is a church nearby. He isn't sure, so we hop into a cab and let the driver take us in the right direction. I know that I could pray anywhere, but it's been weeks since I entered a church to worship, and it just feels like I need to do this.

The cab lets us out in front of a beautiful, old stone cathedral. We make our way up the steps and enter the cool interior. Gabriel is watching me closely as we enter the church, and I take in all the beautiful stonework, statues, and stained glass. The craftsmanship is beautiful. After making a circuit to take it all in, I slide into a pew and bow my head. Gabriel sits silently next to me and allows me this time.

I realized today that after I made my decision and agreed to marry Gabriel, I haven't prayed very much about anything else. Just that my family and friends will forgive me. I haven't stopped to ask what the plan is in all of this chaos. I know God has a purpose for all things. I just haven't asked Him where to go from here. I need direction.

I pour everything out to God and ask him to help reveal to me what all this means. I don't understand why I had to go through all of this. I feel like I've been abandoned to figure this all out on my own. I am struggling to make sense of everything and sort through my feelings.

A phrase pops into my mind, "Trust the plan." I acknowledge that me being here was all part of His plan, but I ask, if this is the plan, why do I feel so alone and confused?

I work through the abduction and being saved by Gabriel. I think about the threat to Rana and the choice I made to save her. As I'm working through that day, I remember what it was I prayed for. It's clear as a bell. I prayed for escape and for someone to protect me. God heard me then, and I know he hears me now.

Tears roll silently down my cheeks as some reflection helps me to see that God answered my prayers and has been with me every step of the way. And I know that Gabriel is a big part of that answer.

I pray and talk to God some more about why I'm having to sacrifice my relationship with friends and family to help Gabriel's family. Couldn't there have been another way? But then I'm reminded of two different verses.

The first one is John 15:13. "Greater love has no one than this, that someone lay down his life for his friends." I know that my sacrifice in marrying Gabriel was done out of concern for Rana's welfare. I couldn't chance not going through with it and waiting to see what might happen. I couldn't have lived with myself if something bad had happened to her. Then the thought hits me again, *Was it really a sacrifice to marry Gabriel? Has it been so bad living in the house with him and his family? Did I sacrifice my life or did I enrich it?*

The second verse that is niggling at the back of my mind is Psalm 68:6. "God sets the lonely in families, He leads out the prisoners with singing, but the rebellious live in a sun-scorched desert." Was I lonely? I had Tyler, Lisa, and the kids. I had my friends and coworkers, but was I lonely? I know I was surrounded by lots of people that I love and who love me, but was I lonely? Am I lonely now?

I think about how to weigh and measure that question and ask myself, "Am I lonely?" The answer is no. Not when I'm with Gabriel. I hadn't thought about that. I've been so wrapped up in missing my friends and family that I didn't realize that I am lonesome for them, but not lonely.

Would I be lonely if I returned to my life back home? Life without Gabriel.

Lonely seems to have taken on a whole new meaning now. My heart aches thinking about leaving Gabriel, his sisters, and Mariam. They have become family to me. I know that I would miss them if I decided to leave.

God has been orchestrating this all along. He has been listening and answering all along the way. I'm the one who hasn't been listening. Time to fix that.

"Lord," I whisper out loud. "I have one more question." I silently ask for guidance with my husband. I need some direction in deciding what I really want. I know that Gabriel is not a believer and that the Bible teaches us not to be unequally yoked, but the scriptures teach that "God can work all things for our good." Is this one of those times, Lord? I know it's a little late to be asking this question now.

But I don't want to make any more mistakes. Please, Lord, speak to my heart and mind.

I sit and wait. There comes a whisper of a verse that flows through my heart and mind. A verse in Genesis that talks about a woman's desire being for her husband. Is that what this is? I think about the vows I spoke only a few days ago and consider the depth of the promises I willingly made. No matter what the reason, I did take those vows. The truth is that they are real and binding and not to be taken lightly. They are meant to be honored.

As I process all of these thoughts and feelings, a final verse comes to mind. First Peter 3 talks about how to show a nonbelieving husband your love for Christ through your actions and with a humble heart. It states that this is how they will come to understand and believe.

Maybe this really is why I'm here—to share that love with Gabriel, to help him believe. I know I said it to Lauren several weeks ago, but maybe it is true. A warm feeling of peace and certainty begins to soothe and relieve my anxieties.

"Thank You, Lord. Thank You for being so faithful to me and loving me. I praise You in all your ways." This is the mantra that is looping through my head now. I have my answer and my decision. It's not what I have to do or need to do. This decision is completely about what I get to do.

I open my eyes and look at Gabriel. He is looking straight ahead. I wonder what he is thinking right now? I walked into a strange church, sat down, closed my eyes, prayed, cried, and mumbled out loud. But I don't wonder long.

"Better now?" he simply asks. I reach for his hand and tell him yes and that I'm ready to leave.

I feel so much lighter as we walk outside. I'm not ready to get into a cab yet. I just want to walk for a while, so we do. Gabriel doesn't press me. He just walks in silence content to wait for me to talk.

We eat dinner at the resort and then dangle out feet in the pool and watch the sun set. We've both been quiet. He asks if I want to watch a movie upstairs. I tell him it's been a long day, and I'm ready for bed. We dry our feet, slip our shoes back on, and head back to our room.

I shower first while Gabriel surfs through television channels. I let him know when I am done so that he can go next. While he showers, I change into one of the lacey gowns Mariam insisted that I buy, and I wait.

Gabriel comes out carrying his towel and stops in his tracks. I'm standing directly in his path. He takes me in from my head to my lacey gown that ends just above my knees and straight down to my bare feet. He doesn't move, and I'm not sure he is even breathing, so I say the first thing that comes to mind.

"Mariam insisted that I buy it."

He barely reacts but says, "I'm glad she did. Is that what was in the bag that you didn't want me to see?"

"Yes," I answer. "Among a few other things."

I don't know why we are making small talk about my lingerie purchases. Doesn't he know what me standing here dressed like this means? Of course, he does. And he told me it had to be completely my decision, so I guess he is waiting on me.

I walk over to him and take his towel from his hand and drop it on the floor. I step up and place my hands on his chest and look up into his brown eyes. I feel him tremble under my hands, or maybe it's me. I can't tell. "I've made my decision," I say.

"And what did you decide?" he asks. His voice is low and husky.

My voice trembles with anticipation, but I manage to tell him, "I want you." It's all the answer he needs before his arms come crushing around me, and he is kissing me.

CHAPTER 14

I wake with the warm sunlight pouring in through the crack in the curtains. I'm wrapped in warmth and strong, tanned arms. I tilt my head back to watch Gabriel as he sleeps, but my movement causes him to stir. He barely opens his eyes, sees me watching him, and smiles. He pulls me closer and kisses the top of my head. "Good morning," he says.

"Good morning," I say back to him. "Did you sleep well?" I ask.

He shifts both of us so that he can look me in the face. His tone is playful. "When you finally let me go to sleep." I blush and duck my head. I'm not used to this intimate banter.

He lifts my face back to meet his eyes. "You're not having regrets, are you?"

"No," I say forcefully. I don't want him to mistake my modesty for regret.

"Good," he says and smiles. He pulls me back into his side and strokes my arm as we just lie there with each other.

"What are you thinking about this morning, Mr. Kattan?"

"If you must know, Mrs. Kattan, I was wondering what other little things you had in your secret little bag." He laughs as I playfully slap him on the arm. I wonder if Mariam knew what she was doing when she took me shopping. Could she have seen something between us then?

With this unexpected, but not unwelcome, turn in our relationship, we decide to stay another night at the resort. I wish we could stay longer, but I know his father will be upset that he is missing another day of work for me. I content myself to just enjoy this extra alone time with Gabriel.

October 12

We've delayed our return home as long as we can. We waited until late in the afternoon before we left Cairo and pointed the car south toward home. The air is cool, and we drive with the windows down for a while.

"You are very quiet over there. Want to tell me what's going on in that pretty head of yours?" Gabriel asks.

With a sigh, I say, "I've made another decision."

"Oh," he replies with a questioning tone.

"Yes. It's time to tell my family that we are married. I dread it, but I can't handle the lies and half-truths anymore. You're right, they are tearing me apart."

"You don't have to do this alone you know. I'm here for you. We can tell them together."

"I know you are. You've been my rock. That's part of what I am dreading. They are going to attack you and say you coerced me and forced me into this when I tell them everything. I just have to figure out a way to convince them that no matter how this started, I'm here now because I want to be."

"So when do you want to call?"

"Tomorrow. It's Sunday and everyone should be home. We will call then." I sigh deeply. "I just hope that Tyler can forgive me for this."

We are greeted by Gabriel's family, minus Ahmad when we arrive home. Even Aahron comes to help with our bags. Jasmina nearly knocks Gabriel off his feet when she launches herself at him. She then hugs me like she hasn't seen me in weeks. Rana is a little less enthusiastic, but she hugs us both. I don't know her well enough to know if she is being aloof on purpose or if she is just reserved. I'm sure she is still dealing with all that has happened to her in the past three weeks. *I know I still wake in a cold sweat from time to time. The nightmare always ends with a hand clamped tightly over my mouth and nose, threatening to suffocate me.*

It's a nice welcome home. Mariam has saved some dinner for us, and we all move to the kitchen while she sets plates of food in front of us. All of his siblings want to hear about our trip. Gabriel stands behind my chair until I am settled, then moves off toward Mariam. He drapes an arm across her shoulders and kisses her on the cheek and says "thank you" before joining us at the table.

"What was that for?" Mariam asks.

There is mischief in his eyes as he answers her. "Because you always think of everything."

Very smooth reply, I think. I know he is referring to the lingerie purchase, but everyone else thinks it's about the food she has prepared. Everyone except Mariam. The knowing smile she sends me says she knows exactly what the thank-you kiss was for. I try to cover my blush by lifting my water glass to my lips and take several long drinks praying my color will return to normal.

October 13

It's a good thing I am not superstitious or I would have to choose another day to break the news to my family and friends. I've decided to tell Lauren the entire story first before I call Tyler. I'm praying for him to have an understanding heart and that he can forgive me. I'm also praying for him to have an open mind where Gabriel is concerned.

I spend the day unpacking and moving my things into Gabriel's room. His is larger than the one I have been staying in and has more closet space. There is also a tall chest of drawers. He told me to rearrange anything I want. His room is decorated in darker blues and tans with a beautiful Persian rug in blues and greens on a cream background. It's all very masculine, but I like it. It smells of his soap and cologne. The work helps keep my mind off the phone calls I will make tonight.

Gabriel leaves to check on things at Omar's and comes home around three and asks if I am ready. "No, but I need to do this," I reply. He hugs me and reminds me we will do this together.

I decide to call Lauren first. I promised to tell her first, and I owe her honesty. I dial her number and put her on speaker phone. I want no secrets today, and I need Gabriel's support. Lauren answers after a few rings with a simple hello. I know she is just being cautious after our last conversation.

"Lauren, it's me. Can you talk for a minute?"

"Are you coming home?" she asks instead of answering me.

"No, not now, but I really want to talk and help you understand where I am coming from. Will you at least hear me out?"

"I don't know, Sarah. I'm not sure I want to hear your excuses anymore. Come home, and we can talk face to face."

I'm hurt and frustrated. I take a deep breath trying to not get angry, because if I do, this conversation will be over. "I'm not coming home for a while. I had hoped to explain everything from the beginning. There are things that you don't know and that I couldn't tell you, but I can now."

"So you lied to me?" her voice is high pitched now.

"Not so much lied as maybe omission of the whole truth," I say quickly. She makes a rude sound, so I amend my answer, "Yes, I did lie, but I had my reasons. Reasons I'm ready to tell you now."

"How could you lie to me? I've been your best friend forever. There is nothing that you couldn't have told me before I left. Why now? Why tell me at all. Nothing you can say will fix the damage you've done. It will be a long time before I trust you again." She is so angry with me. I don't remember us every fighting like this.

Gabriel is sitting next to me quietly watching me try to steel myself for my next statement. I had wanted to start from the beginning, but I think maybe I just need to start with the now. If she doesn't hang up on me, maybe I can explain how all of this happened.

"Lauren, I'm going to tell you something, and I know you don't owe me anything, but I need your word first that you won't tell Tyler until after I have a chance to speak to him." I hold my breath waiting for her answer. After an extremely long pause, she agrees but has a stipulation. She will give me thirty minutes after we hang up and then she is calling him herself. "You don't know the hell you have put him through these past three weeks, and I won't keep any secrets, not even for you."

"I understand," I say. Then I drop my bombshell and tell her, "I'm married."

She doesn't say anything at first, then she laughs, and it is not a happy sound. She doesn't speak to me, so I launch into the whole story, not the edited version I've been telling them. I tell her every single thing that led up to the wedding and my voluntary participation. It takes her a few minutes as she is processing everything I have just said.

She is calmer when she asks, "So this is a marriage in name only, an arrangement to help Gabriel's family?"

"It started that way, but things have changed."

"Changed how?" she quickly asks.

"I am Gabriel's wife in every way that matters, not just name." This is a little awkward with her on speaker and Gabriel next to me. I really don't want to spell this out for her.

"Did he force himself on you?" Her words are angry and direct.

"No," I quickly say. "And, Lauren, I have you on speakerphone. Gabriel is sitting next to me."

Her next statement is directed to Gabriel this time. "Did you make her put this call on speaker so that you could hear and control the conversation?"

He answers that he is only here to support me and answer any questions that he can. I assured her that he is not controlling me, nor did he force himself on me.

She is not convinced and tells him how much his word means. "Why would I believe you? You may have saved Sarah from those other two men, but you are guilty of keeping her there against her will and forcing her to marry you. You've been spinning your web all along and now you have her convinced that she wants this. You took advantage of her. You are a pathological…psychopath! I'm calling Tyler, and I'm calling the authorities."

"Lauren, listen to me. Don't call yet. I know I can't stop you, but please hear me out." Gabriel interrupts me and tells her, "I am guilty of forcing her to stay in the beginning, and yes, the marriage was my idea. Sarah and I discussed the arrangement and decided we would divorce after a few months and my family was safe. I may have taken advantage of the situation but not Sarah. Not the way you have implied. I would never hurt her. She means too much to me."

"That's really touching, Gabriel. This is classic Stockholm syndrome. Sarah has agreed to whatever it takes to stay alive, including convincing herself that she wants this. She is too close to see this sick and twisted marriage for what it really is. She may be confused, but I definitely am not and know that I will fight you with everything I have to get my friend home safe and sound."

Gabriel tries to convince her that however this started, that his feelings for me are real and that he is not my captor, and I am free to go at any time. She is not convinced.

I'm crying now. This just keeps getting worse and worse. I have to convince her that I'm not crazy and that Gabriel is not some psychopath or kidnapper.

"Lauren, do you know how many times I had this same conversation with myself? Do you know how many times I prayed to be rescued? To find a way home? I have been painfully aware of every manipulation and my lack of control from the beginning. No one deceived me. We have discussed it openly from the beginning. I had every intention of running off when I regained my strength. That changed when Muhamed took Rana. It wasn't just about me anymore. It was about an innocent girl. Was I supposed to run away and hope nothing bad happened to her?"

"Yes! You should have run and let someone else handle this. You were an innocent girl, too." Lauren retorts.

"Yes, I was. The day they took me from that hotel, all of my choices were taken from me, and I found myself at the mercy of strangers. Strangers who could have walked away and let someone else handle it. It would not have gone well, I know that. But these strangers, Gabriel and Amon didn't walk away. They did save me. I have no illusions about how slim my chances were without them. I am grateful for that, but my gratefulness did not blind me into a marriage with Gabriel. I chose that of my own free will. I did it for Rana."

"I can understand wanting to help Rana, but how does having a real marriage help her?"

"I took those vows last week to—"

Lauren explodes again. "Last week? Last week? So you were on your honeymoon when I last talked to you, and you lied again telling me you were sleeping in separate rooms. Do you even know the truth anymore, Sarah?"

Gabriel starts to defend me, but I stop him. "Yes, I was on my honeymoon, and no, I didn't lie to you. We had been sleeping in separate rooms. But it wasn't enough. And before you can protest, it wasn't enough for me. I decided I want this. Gabriel didn't force me into anything."

"You've thrown away everything you said you always wanted. You compromised your moral standards. What happened to waiting for a godly man? A man who adores you and that you love? He isn't even of the same faith as you and that has always been a deal breaker for you. Why, Sarah?"

"I did have those dreams and standards and thought that was what I wanted. Things changed, and I was given a curve ball. I wouldn't want to go through any of it again, but the good that has come out of it is that I am married to a good man, who does adore me and who I want to spend my life with. It's crazy! All of it! But it's what I want. Can you just think about it before you start calling out the national guard or white lab coats or whoever else you think can come take me home?"

Lauren doesn't say anything for a while and then responds, "I have one question and depending on how you answer it, depends on what I do. Do you love him?"

My pulse just skipped a beat. "Do I love Gabriel?" I've asked myself that question several times over the past few days, and the only answer I can give her is the truths I've discovered myself. I know I have to answer her honestly, but I don't want to hurt or disappoint Gabriel either. We have not really openly declared our feelings for each other yet. Well, he did, but I haven't.

"That is not an easy question to answer because it is complex. I am committed to Gabriel because I want to be. I've spent some time in prayer about this and am at peace with my decisions. Gabriel has become a great friend, and I enjoy his companionship. I respect him and love the way he values me. I am obviously physically attracted to him, and he makes me happy. I do have deep feelings for him and know that God has a purpose for our marriage. But I don't want to throw the 'love' word out there because it is too important to randomly toss around. And if and when I come to the conclusion that I do love him, he will be the first person I tell, not you."

I don't know, nor do I really care how she reacts, well I do care. But more importantly, I care about Gabriel's reaction than Lauren's. He is watching me intently with a look of tenderness and pride. He pulls me to him and kisses the side of my head and nods what I'm hoping is his approval.

Lauren sighs. "Well, that sounds like the first honest answer you have given me. Thank you for not lying about your feelings."

"You're welcome. Are you going to send in the troops now?" I say, trying for levity.

"No. I'm still not convinced this is for the best, but I can't force you to leave, even though I really want to. Give me some time to think about this. I'll try to respect your wishes for now, but just say the word, and I'll meet you at the airport."

"I know you don't owe me your forgiveness, but I'm really sorry for not being honest with you from the beginning. I know I should have been. I just didn't see any other way." I really need her forgiveness, but I know it may take some time to heal these wounds.

I am completely exhausted when we hang up. I turn to Gabriel and say, "That was the easy one. Now, let's call Tyler." The look he gives me makes me chuckle. He looks like a scared deer about to bolt, but I know better, he'll stay.

The call to Tyler goes about like I expected. I was right, Lauren was the easier call. Tyler is angry, no irate is a better description. He yells at me and calls me delusional and has several choice words for Gabriel, especially knowing he is listening to the conversation. Gabriel endures my brother's vehemence and, to his credit, holds his tongue. He does however defend me repeatedly to Tyler. At one point, he tells him that if he disrespects his wife again, this conversation will be over until he can discuss this calmly.

We basically rehash everything that we did with Lauren but with more testosterone this time. Tyler is angry and disappointed with me and hits below the belt by telling me how disappointed our parents would be in all my decisions. He tells me he doesn't know who I am anymore. It has the desired effect and hits low, just like he wanted it to.

I decide to end the call, but I feel like I need to try to diffuse things if that's possible. "You are probably right. Mom and Dad would not have approved of my decision. They probably would have been hurt by it. They might have even yelled at me, too. But in spite of all that, I know one thing for sure. They would have still loved me." I pause to let that sink in, then continue. "They aren't here now, so you and I are having to have this conversation. You are not my parent, but you are my brother, and I love you and need you in my life. You, Lisa, and the kids have been the only family I've had for a long time. But I have new family now, too. I'm not trading my old one for a new one, just expanding the one that I have. I hope that one day you can forgive me and give us a chance."

I wait for him to reply, and all he can say is that he can't promise anything, and he will need some time.

We hang up, and I force myself not to cry. I'm so tired of crying. I force my tears into numbness for now. I did it. I told them the truth. I'll have to give them time to come to terms with everything. In the meantime, I cling to the family right in front of me who hasn't judged me for my choices whether good or bad. He just accepts me.

October 14

Last night was very exhausting, and I just wanted to crawl under the covers and wallow in my misery, but Gabriel was having none of it. He insisted that I go wash my face and have dinner with the family and try to find a way to move forward. He even insists we play several games of cards with his sisters before we go to bed. He also turned off my phone as Nicole and Stasia were relentless in calling and texting. Not tonight, he says. Wait a day or two, he suggested. I readily agreed. I couldn't handle anymore last night.

This morning, I promise to stay busy today and not hide out in our room or answer my phone. Gabriel promises to call the house if he needs me.

Early in the afternoon, I am in the kitchen learning to make bread with Mariam when there is a knock at the door. Jasmina jumps up from her homework and goes to answer the door. She returns with a beautiful and completely obnoxious display of fresh flowers. They are beautiful. Jasmina removes the card and says they have my name on them. I smile thinking what a thoughtful husband I have. He must have sent them after the really bad night I had last night.

I wipe my hands and take the card from Jasmina. I open the envelope and pull the card out. Written in flowing script are the words, "Welcome back from your honeymoon." The card is signed with a large "M" and nothing else.

I begin to shake and drop the card as the realization of who they are from hits me. They aren't from Gabriel. They are from Muhamed. I guess he has decided to keep the game going a little longer.

The trembling is getting worse. I think I might throw up. Mariam sees the distress on my face and asks, "What? What is it?" I can't breathe let alone answer her, so I just shake my head over and over.

"Sarah…" She bends to retrieve the card and sucks in a quick breath. She turns to Jasmina and tells her to take her homework into the living room. She hesitates, and Mariam yells now.

Mariam sets the card on the table and grabs me by the arms and shakes me to get my attention. "It doesn't mean anything. He is a cruel man and wants to taunt you any way he can. I will throw them out so that you don't have to look at them."

I turn and grab them before Mariam can and storm out the back door and run across the backyard toward the barn. I fling them with a primal scream toward the side of the barn where the vase explodes and flowers scatter to the ground. I scream again just because I need to, and it feels good. I'm raging and proceed to stomp each and every flower into the ground until they are unrecognizable. It takes me several minutes to regain control. But eventually, there is nothing left to throw or stomp into the dirt. Mariam watches from across the yard but doesn't approach me. She heads back into the house as I stalk off toward the pasture to clear my head.

I am just returning to the house when I hear raised voices. I realize it is Gabriel and his father, and I stop in the kitchen. They are in Ahmad's office and arguing about me and the safety of everyone here. Ahmad blames me and tells his son he has brought this evil into his house and that I am to blame for all this trouble. Gabriel defends me and raises his voice to his father. I don't want to listen, because part of me thinks maybe he is right. I turn and go back outside needing to be far away from Ahmad's anger at the moment.

I think about my own reaction today and say, *They were just flowers.* I say it in my head, but I know in my heart it means the game plays on.

Gabriel finds me out at the barn sifting through the dirt, picking up all the shards of glass from the broken vase. He squats down and reaches for me, but I pull away. I don't want his kindness right now. I'm angry and frustrated and hurt, and a small part of me feels guilty that my presence here keeps leading to more and more stress in this household.

"Leave it," he tells me. "I will have someone else come finish this. This is not your fault."

"Stop it! Stop being so nice to me. It is my fault. I'm the one who got angry and smashed the vase. I'll clean up the mess. I don't want anyone else cleaning up my messes around here. I don't need to…" I can't make myself form the words.

"Don't need to what? Finish your statement," Gabriel prompts and waits for my reply.

"I don't need anyone else around here to hate me because they have to clean up my messes, too."

"You mean like my father. You heard us?"

"Yes."

"I'm sorry you heard that. My father is angry and just worried for all of us. We had hoped that Muhamed would move on and leave us alone, but we were wrong. We will figure out a way through this, together. I will talk to Ahmad. He cannot keep saying hurtful things about you. You're my wife, and I love you, Sarah." My head snaps up to meet Gabriel's eyes. He continues on before I can say a word. "You make me happy, and my father will have to accept that if he wants me to stay here. I won't have you upset and feeling guilty for things that are out of your control."

He reaches over and wipes the lone tear that has escaped down my cheek with his thumb. I lean into his touch, and he cups my cheek in his warm palm. "Now, let's finish cleaning up this mess together."

As we lie in bed that night, I really want to talk about Gabriel's declaration. I feel so guilty that he has told me twice now that he loves me, and I haven't said it back to him. I want to, but I'm afraid. "Gabriel, I'm hesitant when I say his name.

"Umm," he responds, half asleep.

"Did you mean what you said today?" I feel him still beneath my hand. He is fully awake now as his chest rises fully before he responds.

"Yes," he answers simply.

"I don't deserve your love you know…and I—"

Gabriel moves to kiss my lips before I can finish, effectively stopping the words I am struggling to speak.

He leans back and tucks me back into his side. "You may not feel like you deserve my love, but you have it nonetheless," he teases. "And as for the rest of whatever it was you were going to say…you can finish it when you are ready. Now go to sleep."

I'm not finished, but I let it go for now. My other question will have to keep until another time. I lie there wondering if he would really leave this house for me.

Life settles down over the next few weeks, and Gabriel and I spend every spare moment together when he is not at work. We even begin to attend Sunday services with Mariam and the girls. Gabriel seems to be enjoying the music and scriptures more each week.

I still help Mariam in the kitchen but have also convinced Gabriel to let me help with some of the livestock. The young man in charge of the animals here took a lot more coaxing to let me help.

He was not used to having a woman in his space, but eventually, he agreed to let me help with some things.

I enjoy being outside and having something else to occupy my time. So I help feed and water the animals in the field closest to the house and barn every morning and collect the eggs from the chickens. Jasmina has happily given the egg collecting over to me as she confesses she does not like the smelly barnyard anyway. I even get to put my nursing skills to use when an animal is injured or sick. I learn what ointments to apply and how to wrap the wound and watch for infection.

It's nearly December when the next assault from Muhamed arrives. It is a letter addressed to me, and Mariam leaves it on the table thinking maybe it's from my family or friends. I pick it up when I come in for lunch and sit down at the table with a glass of water to open it. It's a thick envelope, and I'm eager to see what it contains.

I tear the flap up and pull pictures from inside. Pictures of me, Mariam, Rana, and Jasmina together at the market from last week. How odd that someone would send me pictures of that until I flip one over and look at the signature on the back. Not a complete signature, just the capital letter M.

The water I just swallowed threatens to come back up at the realization of what this means. It means that Muhamed is following me, us. He had someone close enough to take our pictures; close enough to take one of us.

"Mariam," I thrust the pictures at her as I reach for the phone to call Gabriel. I need to know that both of his sisters are safe.

Gabriel sends Amon to check on Jasmina at school. He will wait for her and bring her home when school is out. Mariam calls Rana at work. She works for a seamstress several days a week and is at work today. Everyone is safe and sound, but we know that we will have to make changes again.

Gabriel, Amon, Aahron, and Ahmad come up with a plan that evening. Amon will take Jasmina to and from school each day and then return to the house to watch over me and Mariam. Rana will continue to go to work but agrees to ride with a cousin who works for a market nearby. She will have to leave earlier but concedes so that she can keep her job (Ahmad's condition).

I'm not thrilled that Amon will be babysitting me/us, but I admit I feel safer knowing he is around. He has the grace to not follow me like a puppy, like I think Gabriel wishes. I know that he is not always in sight but is within earshot. I appreciate him trying to give me some space though.

After a few days of our new routine, I ask Gabriel to walk with me after dinner. I guide us toward the field that donkey likes and wait patiently at the fence for him to come greet us. I usually bring him a treat like today, so he wastes no time coming to me. I offer up my carrot and rub his rough mane. We are far enough from the house that I can talk freely here.

"Gabriel, that day, when I broke the vase…you mentioned that you would be willing to leave here if necessary." I word it carefully, trying not to evoke too many emotions from that day. "How far would you be willing to go?"

"How far are you thinking?" he asks.

"With everything that is going on here and the fact that Muhamed continues to taunt us, I was thinking that maybe we should leave, just you and me."

"How far, Sarah?" His tone is serious as I suspect he knows where I am going with this.

"I was thinking that anywhere we go here, in Egypt, will not be far enough out of his reach. Maybe we should consider moving to the States. I've thought about it, and I think he is out to terrorize me. I'm the one that slipped through his grasp, and I think he doesn't like to lose or not be in control. It might be enough to make him leave your family alone with me gone."

Gabriel doesn't answer, just stares straight ahead considering what I've just suggested. After some time, he turns to me and answers, "I don't want to leave my family, my job. This is my home, where I grew up. My work is here, and someday, all this land will be ours. I'm happy here, and I thought you were, too."

"I am happy with you, Gabriel, and the where doesn't matter, but I'm concerned for everyone else's safety. I'm worried how far Muhamed will go to hurt me."

"Are you missing home?" his tone has softened as he asks this question.

"Of course, I miss home a little, but that's not the only reason why I am asking. I can go for a visit when I need to, but this is different. Muhamed is not rational, and you can't keep eyes on everyone twenty-four seven. Eventually, someone will be alone."

"There is no guarantee he will stop if we do leave," he counters. I know he is right. I just feel like we need to do something. "I will consider what you've said, but I'm not making any promises. This is our home, and I don't want some madman driving us away. Maybe we can plan a visit to the States in the spring. Get away for a little while. I would very much like to see where you grew up."

I'm a little disappointed with his answer. I know that he didn't come out and say no to my idea, but I heard it just the same. It hurts a little to think about the fact that I moved my life to Egypt for him, but he is not willing to do the same for me.

Over the next several weeks, there is an occasional card or note and another envelope with a picture of me and Gabriel walking out of church together, all signed with an M. It's clear that he is still having us followed. It makes us all a little paranoid, and I'm thankful that Amon is around all the time now, but I don't feel truly safe until Gabriel is home every evening.

CHAPTER 15

February 5

I awake this morning thinking I have been married for four months today and roll over to tell Gabriel happy anniversary. I must have moved too quickly because the motion makes my head swim and my stomach queasy. I decide to head for the bathroom instead. I break out in a cold sweat and my stomach heaves a few times, but nothing comes up. I felt a little sick after dinner last night and attributed it to all the rich food we ate for Aahron's birthday meal.

I am rinsing my face at the sink when Gabriel comes into the bathroom. He sees the cool cloth on my face and asks if I am all right. I just tell him that last night's meal is not sitting well with me. He looks concerned, but I dry my face and assure him I will be fine. I wish him a happy anniversary and head back to the bed. My stomach is still churning, and I need to lie down. Gabriel offers to bring me some tea and crackers, and I accept, hoping it will help me feel better.

I nibble on the crackers before I fall back to sleep and find that I feel much better when I awake a couple of hours later. Gabriel calls to check on me around lunch, and I assure him that whatever it was has passed and that I'm going to live.

The next two mornings are a repeat performance of nausea and feeling bad. I manage not to wake Gabriel these two times and crawl back into bed before he stirs. I feign sleep and stay where I am until he leaves for the day. I have a pretty good idea that my sickness has nothing to do with my diet.

After he is gone, I pull up the calendar on my phone. I nibble on the crackers I left on my bedside table as I count back. I haven't been really good about tracking my periods, but I think I remember the week I last had one. I count back six weeks. I'm never late. As the understanding of what this means hits me, so does the need to empty my stomach. I race to the bathroom and cling to the cool porcelain as the phrase takes shape in my brain, "I'm pregnant!"

This time, I do feel better after I've emptied my stomach. I rinse my mouth and face and get dressed for the day. I need to stick to my normal routine. I'm excited and nervous about having a baby with Gabriel. I don't want to tell him right now. I want to make it special, so I will have to give it some thought today.

I know Gabriel will be a great father. I wonder if it will be a girl or boy and what Gabriel will want. I try to figure out my due date and realize that the baby will be born sometime in the middle of September.

I'm thinking about all the changes I've had in my life over the past few months and what is still ahead. As I am mentally taking stock of everything, a new concern creeps into my thoughts. What will Muhamed do when he learns about this. It's just one more weapon he can use against me. I can't think about that right now, so I push it to the back of my mind.

I spend the day focusing all my thoughts on the new life growing inside me. I want to tell Gabriel, but I'm still trying to figure out how to make it special. I worry about telling him too soon, so I decide to wait a couple of weeks, which will give me time to plan something special.

It's like Muhamed has a direct line to my thoughts and body because about a week later, a package arrives for me. It is a small box, and Mariam and I sit and stare at it for several minutes contemplating what could be inside before we open it together. I open the top to reveal pink baby booties! Oh my gosh. How does he know? I've told no one. Mariam is not as frozen as me and reaches in to take the card out and reads it aloud. "Hopefully, you will put these to good use in the future. I bet you will have beautiful children. I look forward to watching them grow. M."

It's like a dam inside me bursts, and I can't stop the flood of tears and sobs that escape me. He doesn't know, he is just taking this opportunity to ruin the possibility of children for me. He wants me to have no joy or peace in this life. He is just reminding me that he will always be watching. We will never be rid of him.

Mariam wraps me in her arms and holds me until the worst is past. She is trying to soothe me with her words, but I'm inconsolable. I grab the box, card, and booties and the matches by the stove. I run outside and set fire to the whole thing. I envision him in the flames the whole time. I will not let him hurt me or this baby. Now more than ever, I can't tell Gabriel about the baby. Muhamed's taunt has put a damper on me sharing the news of a baby with Gabriel. I will wait until the sting of this latest barb has dulled.

Gabriel is furious and wants to go to Muhamed's house, but between me and his brother and Amon, we convince him otherwise. He sees this new taunt as a personal threat to his future children and says he has had enough. Surprisingly, it is Aahron who reminds him that he has a wife to think about now, and he can't go off threatening Muhamed. He tells him it's best to just ignore this latest attack and not stir up the hornet's nest. I know Aahron is worried about Gabriel's safety, and I am thankful for his calming words. Gabriel storms out of the house, and Amon tells me he will follow him and make sure that he doesn't do anything stupid.

The next few days are tense, and everyone is on edge worried about what Muhamed's next move will be and when.

I find that if I keep a little something on my stomach, the nausea is not so bad, so I just snack frequently. Gabriel and I climb into bed, and I toss and turn for quite some time. I have so much on my mind, and I need to tell Gabriel about our child soon. I want to share my joy with him.

I have decided I will do it soon. This family could use something good to focus on. Maybe tomorrow.

My stomach rumbles, and I decide not to fight it and move to get out of bed. Gabriel raises his head, "Sarah, are you okay?" I knew my tossing was keeping him awake.

"Yes, just can't sleep, so I am going downstairs to fix some chamomile tea." I reach over and kiss his cheek. "Go to sleep. I'll be back soon."

I pull on socks as I know the kitchen tiles will be cold and wrap my robe around me. I quietly descend the stairs and head for the kitchen. As I move to pass Ahmad's office, I realize he is up, and I hear voices—angry voices. I move closer and realize that Ahmad and Aahron are arguing and I stop to listen. Aahron rarely disagrees with his father.

"No! You can't keep asking this of me! This isn't right, and if Gabriel finds out what you are doing, he will never forgive you." Aahron's mention of Gabriel has my full attention now and I dare to move a little closer. What could Ahmad be asking of Aahron that could anger Gabriel that badly?

"Do you think that your brother will not include you in his anger? You would be a fool to tell him and to disobey me." There is a menace to Ahmad's tone that I have not heard before. Whatever it is that is driving him makes him willing to risk hatred from both sons. What on earth could drive him to that extreme?

"Father, please just stop this madness. Give her a chance. She is not a bad person, and Gabriel truly loves her. Don't you see how happy he is with her. Please don't ask me to do this anymore."

Aahron's words are like a punch to my gut as I realize what Ahmad could hate so much to risk the loyalty of his sons…is me. I want to run, and my stomach is threatening to turn inside out. I know I should run from this hallway, but one question has my feet rooting to the spot as I try to get my stomach under control, what is it he is forcing Aahron to do?

"That woman is evil and an embarrassment to this family. She has no respect for our culture or our ways, and I want her out of my house immediately!" He lowers his voice and continues, "You will go into Qina tomorrow and pick up the package as I told you before. You will leave it in the barn on Saturday when Gabriel will be here to witness her finding it."

"Father, what if it forces Gabriel out, too? What if he finds out you are behind the taunts from Muhamed? What then?"

There are no words to describe the shock of that one statement. I feel as though my blood has turned to ice. I can hardly comprehend how cold and callous this man is. Cold enough to terrorize not just me, but every member of this household. No one is immune from his hatred.

I'm startled as Ahmad issues his last order to Aahron, "You will not mention that name in this house again (*Too late*, I think to myself. *I already heard it*.), and you will do as I say or you will regret your defiance."

I flee from the hall and hide in the shadows of the living room as Aahron storms out of his father's office and Ahmad closes the door behind him. I am shaking violently and have broken out in a cold sweat. I want to run to Gabriel and tell him what I've just heard, but I have more than just me to think about now.

I decide to slip outside and walk to the barn to think. I can't stay in this house a minute longer with this deplorable, narcissistic man. I decide he is in the same category as Muhamed, but maybe worse. Muhamed terrorizes and hurts strangers. Ahmad has been doing it to his own family.

How can he sit at the table with these people every day and not feel any remorse for what he has done? And why? Because I stood up to his bullying and refused to be cowed by him. I'm not safe here anymore. No, I place my hands on my abdomen and cradle the innocent life within me and realize we are not safe here. There is no way I will let this man have any influence in my child's life, not even for one more day.

I spend several hours pacing and planning my escape tomorrow. I know that my leaving will hurt Gabriel, but our child's safety is all that I can think about right now. I have to leave and sever all ties to this madman. I can't risk Ahmad knowing I gave life to his grandchild. I don't trust what he might do. I worry that if he hates me so much, how much worse it might be for my child. But then I wonder, what if he doesn't hate my child? What if he takes an interest? How much influence would he have and would he see it as an opportunity to use that child as a weapon against me, too?

I won't stay here and risk having my child used as a pawn. The truth is, I just don't know what he might do, and I've decided to not stick around to find out. At least in the States, I can raise my child without constantly worrying about them being used as a pawn or their safety.

I decide that I am going to turn the tables on this situation and use Ahmad's errand boy as my means for escape. Tonight, I have to write the hardest letter of my life to Gabriel. I have to be ready early in the morning. After my letter is written, I quietly return to bed and lie next to my husband for the last time. Silent tears slide down my cheeks, and I want to shake him awake and tell him everything, but I can't. I know he will believe me, but I'm worried it won't be enough for him to leave with me. I'm also worried that Ahmad might retaliate, and I can't risk it. So, tomorrow, I leave.

I make sure I am up early. It's not hard, I didn't sleep. I dress quickly and go down to breakfast so that I can make sure I catch Aahron before he leaves. I know I won't have to face Ahmad as he makes it a point to only have to endure me once a day, and that's usually dinner. He is usually gone by now and won't return until this afternoon.

Aahron is at the table when I arrive, and by the looks of it, he is almost finished. I make small talk to delay him. Gabriel enters a few minutes behind me and goes straight to the coffee. I tell myself it is now or never.

"Gabriel, I think I will go into Qina today to do some shopping."

"Oh, Amon didn't mention your plans yesterday, but I will arrange it with him," he says and walks over to kiss me good morning. I inhale his unique scent and almost cave.

"Oh," I stammer. "There's no need. I already have a chaperone and ride today. Aahron mentioned last night that he was going into town today on an errand for your father, and I'm sure he won't mind taking me." I smile sweetly in his direction and find satisfaction as the color drains from his face. Now he knows I know.

Gabriel notices his brother's discomfort at my statement and walks over to pat him on the back. "Buck up, brother, it won't be all that bad. How much shopping can one woman do?" Gabriel chuckles as he takes his seat at the table.

"What is it that you are on a mission for today?" he asks me.

I play coy and just shake my head and say, "It's my secret." He takes my comment exactly the way I hoped he would and winks at me. He thinks I am referring to my "secret" purchases that I made with Mariam. It's the result I was looking for. He doesn't question me any further.

Now, my only concern is keeping Aahron quiet until we are safely in the car and away from this house. I grab a piece of fruit and tell them I am going upstairs to get my backpack and will be back soon. I don't want Aahron to suddenly find a backbone and spill everything before I get out of here.

Gabriel walks us to the car, and Aahron is thankfully silent the whole way. I hug Gabriel goodbye and jump into the car before I can think too much about what I am about to do.

Aahron is silent until we are out of sight of the house before he speaks. "You heard us talking last night." The way he says it is more of a statement than a question. He is probably trying to replay every word to figure out how much I know. I just nod my head repeatedly.

"How much did you hear?" There is the question I was waiting for. I grab hold of my anger and use it to fuel my impending ultimatum.

"All of it." I just let it hang there between us for a minute. He turns to look at me and flinches when he sees the fire in my eyes and looks back to the road.

"Now, since you are so good at following directions, I have a few of my own and you will cooperate, or I will tell Gabriel about your part in all of this. And this 'evil woman' might embellish a little, too." I throw his father's term of endearment out there just to make sure he understands everything I heard.

It has the desired effect. He is sweating now and silent.

"First of all, hand me your phone." He does, and I turn it off and place it in my backpack. "You'll get it back after you do a few things for me." He just nods and swallows.

"First, you will drive me to the bank and then the airport." He swerves a little, and I can tell by the widening of his eyes, this is not what he was expecting.

"You are leaving?"

"Yes, isn't that what your goal was? To drive me out of this country and your family?"

"N-n-no, not my goal. My father's." He starts to speak again, but I cut him off.

"I don't want to know your reasons why you allowed your father to manipulate and blackmail you into this. I just want your cooperation. Nothing more. The quicker I can put this place behind me, the better."

"Are you going to tell Gabriel about everything we've done?"

"Not if you follow my directions. I wrote him a letter and told him I just couldn't do this anymore and that I want to go home." Aahron doesn't need to know all the hurtful things I listed that bother me about his father, this culture, and this country. I even throw in the words he used to try to reassure Lauren that I was not a prisoner here. I tell him that if his words were true, then I don't want him to follow me and try to convince me to stay. Writing it down was a little easier, I don't think I could say it aloud if I had to. Because most of it is not true.

"You will wait several hours before you contact Gabriel and tell him I gave you the slip at the store. You will tell him you found a letter when you went back to the car to look for me."

"Why are you doing this? I thought you loved my brother. This is going to kill him, and he will come looking for you."

I scoff at his why. "Why? You know better than anyone 'why' I am leaving. Your father has made it clear that he is willing to destroy his family to get rid of me and you know what? Your family obviously means more to me than him. I'm not willing to sit here and watch him destroy all of you. He refers to me as evil. Well, if your father wants to see true evil, tell him to take a long look in the mirror. He is like a cancer, and I want no part of it. Tell him he wins. I don't want anything to do with any of you anymore." I've raised my voice, but I don't care.

"Sarah, you can't just leave like this. Let me talk to my father. Please, don't do this. Gabriel won't get over this. He loves you, and this will destroy him. You could tell him everything, and maybe he would go with you. I don't want him to leave, but I don't want to watch him suffer either."

"Just so you know, I do love him, and I don't want him to look back someday and hate me because I forced his hand and made him choose between his family and me or his home. He will get over it, but he will need all of you to help him through. That, Aahron, is why I won't tell him."

"Sarah, I don't know that I can sit by and watch him suffer and not say anything."

"Sure you can, Aahron. You've had several months to practice. You should be a pro at it by now." My statement has the desired effect, and he stops his protests.

When we arrive at the bank, I make Aahron park and accompany me inside. I don't trust him alone or not to leave me stranded. I could take a cab, but I've decided that him knowing my every step is part of his punishment.

I transferred all my checking account and some savings when I decided to stay. I will take enough money out of my account now to buy my tickets and get me home. I can transfer the rest later. I set the account up with Gabriel as a joint user, and I don't want him notified before I leave. I don't know what their policy might be, and I can't chance it.

Next, I have him drive me to get something to eat. I have three and half hours before my flight to Cairo. I'm not hungry, but I know I need to eat something to keep the nausea at bay. I can't afford any delays today. So we eat. Well, I eat, and he just pokes at his food.

That only took up about forty-five minutes, so I order him to just drive around until closer to my departure time. As he pulls up to the departure area, I dig his phone, my passport, and Gabriel's letter out of my bag. I hand him his phone first, then the letter, but I don't release it immediately. I have one more demand. "Make him believe it. I don't want him to come after me." With that, I release the letter and get out of the car.

I purchase my ticket and make my way to security. I place my backpack on the conveyor belt and think about how much I am leaving behind. I only grabbed one change of clothes and my passport. I couldn't risk taking more with me. But it's not just stuff that I am leaving behind. It's more than just stuff, it's part of my heart, but I can't think about that now.

The security guard motions me forward as I'm trying to focus instead on all that I am taking back with me, my baby. I stop just a few inches short of the X-ray scanner. He tries again to motion me through, but I shake my head and tell him I can't. He asks me why not, and I say the words out loud for the first time, not to Gabriel, or Lauren, or even Mariam, but to a random airport security guard, "I'm pregnant."

I am led around the scanner, and they use a hand wand and pat me down before releasing me to make my way to my gate. I collapse into a seat, close my eyes, and send up a quick prayer to get me back home safely.

I don't turn my cell phone on until we touch down in Miami. When I do, I am not surprised to see numerous texts and four voice mails from Gabriel. Even Mariam and Rana have reached out to me. I don't bother to read or listen to them now, I can't. I just pull up my contacts and call Lauren as I wait in line for customs.

Lauren answers on the third ring. "Sarah. Are you okay? Gabriel called me looking for you. Where are you and what is going on?" It's been a few weeks since we last talked. Our conversations were strained for a while, but we have managed to maintain contact with each other. But right now, this is my best friend, and I hear the concern in her voice. I know she will help me.

I'm on the verge of breaking down and know that I still have customs to get through, a two-hour layover, and a three-hour flight before I land in Dallas. I can't afford for any cracks to appear in my armor now, so I remember my anger. It focuses me so that I can answer. "I'm in Miami, and I need you to pick me up this evening at DFW."

"Sarah, are you all right? What happened?"

"I'll tell you everything when I get there. I can't talk right now. I'll text you my flight information."

Lauren answers, "Sarah, I don't know what happened, but we'll get through this. I'll be there when you land."

CHAPTER 16

I'm exhausted and nauseated when I make my way to the terminal exit to meet Lauren. My feet are lead, and I feel like my backpack weighs a hundred pounds. There is so much relief when I finally spot her worried face, that I am sobbing before I even reach her. She wraps me in her arms and just lets me cry.

When the worst of it has passed, she guides me outside toward the parking garage and gets me settled in the passenger seat before she asks, "You want to tell me about it?"

I can barely speak, "Not yet. I just need to sleep for a minute."

She can't stop the questions anyway, and I guess I don't blame her, so I answer her as briefly as possible.

"Did he hurt you?"

"No," I reply.

"Did someone else hurt you?" she continues on with her barrage of questions.

"Not the way you think. Not physically."

She keeps digging, and I'm just too tired to keep this up. Exhaustion is dragging me down as I haven't slept in two days, and I'm emotionally drained. I tell her the one thing that I'm sure will shut her up. "I'm pregnant."

I am right, and she just looks at me, eyes wide, and nods her head. I lean back in my seat and slip into blessed sleep.

My rest is not nearly long enough as it only takes about forty minutes to get to Lauren's apartment, my old apartment. I know that she has a new roommate now, but I will happily settle for her sofa tonight. I can figure out living arrangements tomorrow.

Lauren gently touches my shoulder, and it takes me a minute to remember where I am. We make our way into the apartment, and she fixes me a Coke and sits across from me at the table. I know she will not let me just go back to sleep, so I drink most of the soda and lean back in my chair. "I'll tell you everything, but I need something to eat first."

I help her fix some peanut butter toast and return to the table to nibble on it as I pour the whole, sickening story of Ahmad's insanity out to her. She doesn't interrupt me at all, just lets me tell it piece by ugly piece. My hands are in my lap cradling my belly as I finish. She considers everything for a minute before she says, "So Gabriel doesn't know about the baby then." I just shake my head.

"Do you love him?" She is watching me closely for an answer.

"Yes."

"Are you going to tell him?" She means the baby, and I realize I kept two secrets from Gabriel—the baby and my feelings. I regret the latter, but maybe it will make it easier for him to accept my leaving thinking that I never did love him.

Lauren is still waiting for my answer. "No. I don't want to risk a custody battle."

She pauses, then says, "We need to call Tyler and Lisa. Gabriel called me. He will eventually call them, too. They need to know you are safe."

"I know. Will you call for me? I'm too tired to go through this whole story again tonight."

"Of course," she answers, as she moves to retrieve her phone.

"And, Lauren, don't tell them about the baby. I will tell them tomorrow in person after I've had some real sleep."

She agrees and paces in the kitchen as she makes the call.

Tyler wants to come over now and hear the story for himself, but Lauren convinces him that I am safe and unharmed and too tired to go through the story again tonight. She tells him she will call as soon as I'm awake in the morning.

I sleep for about ten hours before my bladder and stomach insist that I get up and tend to them both. Lauren insisted that I sleep in her room last night instead of the sofa. She said I would not be disturbed and could sleep longer that way. Lauren's roommate came in late not long after our call to Tyler but had the decency to excuse herself to her room after a quick hello. Lauren must have given her a heads-up that I was coming.

I leave Lauren's room and find her having coffee in the kitchen. She asks if I would like some, and I wave her off and reach for juice in the fridge. I ask if she has any crackers and points me to the cupboard where they are. I nibble the crackers and sip the juice slowly. Thankfully, my morning sickness has not been bad and food seems to be the remedy, so I slowly fill my stomach with crackers but know that I will need something more substantial later.

Lauren decides that I need a real breakfast and insists that I go shower and get dressed so that we can go in search of "real food" as she says it using her hands and making some air quotes to go along with it. She says she will drive us over to Tyler and Lisa's after breakfast. I thank her and am glad we will be going there this morning. I'm looking forward to seeing them all, I've missed them so much, but I dread having to go through the whole story again. A knot forms in my stomach thinking about it.

Lauren has offered for me to stay with her as long as I need to, and I am grateful. I'll need to retrieve some clothes from Tyler's while I am there. Lauren boxed up my things and sent them to him when she realized I wasn't coming back. I hope he didn't throw them away. A new wardrobe will be expensive, and I have a lot of expenses coming up in my future.

We decide on IHOP, and I order pancakes with a side of bacon. Lauren orders an omelet and more coffee. I opt for decaf, but tell myself it's the real thing. She texted Tyler to let him know we would be there in about an hour or so, and we take our time eating our breakfast. Thankfully, she is content not to ask too many questions this morning. I'm not sure if she is just letting me have time to prepare for my conversation with my brother or if she really just doesn't know what to say to me right now. I decide not to over think it and am grateful for the reprieve.

I still haven't checked my phone again, but I know I will have to listen to all the messages soon. I had Lauren text Gabriel last night that I was safe and to stop blowing her phone up that I would contact him when I was ready. Her phone pinged several times while we were driving from the airport and before I went to bed. He must have checked flights and known approximately when I would arrive.

Lisa has sent the kids to her mother's for the day, and I am both disappointed that they are not here and grateful that we don't have to have this conversation with them around. I want to get this over with, with as few interruptions as possible. Like pulling off a Band-Aid in one quick motion.

I start with "I'm pregnant" again and after the shock wears off, I launch into my story so that they will better understand my motives for leaving Gabriel, especially after I fought so hard to convince them that I really wanted to be with him.

Lisa is the first one to speak. She tells me she thinks I made the right decision and asks how I feel about the baby. I tell her I am excited and scared. She gets up and hugs me and tells me that she is happy for me and will help any way she can. Tyler is pretty silent through this exchange. Lisa offers to move the kids into a room together so that I can stay with them for a while, but I decline. I didn't come back here to move in with my brother and his family and let them take care of me. It's not right, and I'm pretty sure it would be awkward being in the same house as Tyler. We have a lot to work through right now.

"Lauren has agreed to let me stay with her for a while. My nursing license is still current, so I will look for a job and a place to stay this week. I tell them that I will probably use the insurance money I have been saving and look for a place by myself. They try to convince me that I don't need to be alone, but I think I need the space to sort through everything and get my head straight before this baby makes its appearance.

Lisa helps me locate the box with my clothes in the garage before Lauren and I leave. I ask if I can return the next day after church to see Danny and Lizzie, and Lisa invites me for lunch. She tries to get me to join them for church, too, but I'm not ready for people and questions yet. I thank her and climb into Lauren's car to leave.

I lock myself in Lauren's room and wade through the numerous texts and voice mails. At first, Gabriel is frantic with concern, but his messages take on more anger that I am avoiding him. He is not threatening or anything, just angry and hurt that I won't talk to him. I knew this would be hard, but I feel like I am dying with each new message. My heart is breaking for what I am doing, but I remind myself it's for the best and that Ahmad is responsible for this mess. I can't talk to him, so I send off a text and tell him that I am fine and reiterate some of what I said in the letter. I ask him not to keep bothering me or my family and encourage him to file for divorce.

Gabriel responds back that he doesn't want a divorce and wants to come see me. He is convinced we can work this out. I hold my ground and sob as I text him, I don't want him here. It's a lie, of course. I want him here more than I can breathe right now, but I know he won't stay, so I tell him not to come. He keeps trying to call, but I ignore each phone call and finally send him a text not to call anymore, that I am turning my phone off. I send it and power my phone down and dissolve into a fit of sobs in the middle of Lauren's bed.

I spend the next few days alternating between trying to find my new normal and tears. By the end of the week, I decide that it's time to try to pull myself together and make an appointment with an obstetrician. I need something to keep me from slipping into the black hole that is tugging me down, so I focus on this baby—my baby.

CHAPTER 17

The next couple of months pass by in a blur. I found a job on a pediatric unit where I will work three twelve-hour shifts a week. That way, I have four days off a week and so that I can be home with the baby as much as possible.

I visit the OB routinely, and everything is progressing well with the baby. He confirms my estimation of gestation and that I should deliver early in September. Lisa and Lauren both insisted on going with me to my appointments and for my first ultrasound. They have decided to take turns attending the rest of my visits and have worked out a schedule. I don't mind and am happy to have their support.

I've also been house hunting and have put a bid on a small two-bedroom, one-bath house about twenty minutes from Tyler and Lisa. It's small but has a fenced-in backyard and is close to work, and the monthly note is manageable.

My first few weeks back in the States, I was having lots of nightmares and anxiety. Lauren suggested that I talk to a therapist. She points out that she knows I am putting on a strong front for everyone but thinks it might help to have an unbiased, professional opinion. I agree and ask around for some recommendations.

I finally settle on a counselor named Lucy Schafer. She is in her fifties with slightly graying hair and is patient and calm during our first session as I lay out the abbreviated story of why I am here. I can see by her expression that I am not her run-of-the-mill patient, but she recovers quickly, and I can see the determination set in as she leans forward on her desk and tells me that it might take a while to sift through all of this, but she is willing to try if I am.

I like that she doesn't make any guarantees and states her willingness to help me try to sort through everything. She seems genuinely interested in helping me, and I think she is the kind of person who enjoys a challenge. She asks what my goals are in coming here today, what I hope to get out of our sessions.

"Peace and no more nightmares. And help with my anxiety." I rattle them off without hesitation. It's what I pray for every day. I also want someone to tell me I'm not crazy, but I don't mention that one today.

We agree to meet again in a week, and she gives me some homework to take notes on what my nightmares entail and what situations give me the most anxiety. She suggests a few exercises to do that might help reduce my anxiety when it starts to creep up on me. I notice that we have gone way over our allotted time, but she assures me this is not a problem. We will work on managing our time better in the future.

The next few weeks are busy as I juggle settling into my new house, work, and all my appointments. The counselor and I have decided to meet once a week. I want to deal with as much of this as I can before the baby gets here in September. It's now May, and I know the summer will pass quickly.

CHAPTER 18

Gabriel
April 17

I wake up confused as to where I am and why everything feels stiff and sore. I feel like I am strapped down to my bed and lift my right arm to find an IV sticking out of my hand. My left arm is strapped across my chest and hurts to move it. It takes me a few tries to pry my eyes open and a few seconds to register that I am in the hospital. How did I get here? Everything is foggy right now.

I try to sit up and a strong hand presses on my shoulder as Amon tells me to lie still and that I am all right. I turn and look at him wondering what happened. I glance to the other side of the room and see Mariam and Rana rising from their chairs to come stand at my bedside. Rana has obviously been crying.

Mariam looks angry, so I look back to Amon and ask, "What happened? I can't remember how I got here." My throat is dry and scratchy, and it takes two tries to get it out.

Rana presses a cup of water into my hands and gets me to take a few sips before Amon answers me.

"You wrapped your car around a tree," he tells me with very little emotion, but I can see the anger simmering just below the surface. I see the way his jaw is set, and I know he is ready to lash out at me but is probably holding his tongue because Mariam and Rana are in the room.

I'm trying to piece everything together as I am remembering bits and pieces of what happened last night. Or is it still night? I don't know how long I have been here. I'm about to ask when Mariam cuts in. "You are lucky to be alive," she says with disdain dripping from her voice. I have rarely heard this tone with her, but I know that a lecture is coming.

She proves me right by asking, "What were you thinking driving your car drunk?"

She doesn't wait for my answer, just continues on. "You could have killed yourself or someone else. It was stupid and careless." She continues to extol the stupidity of my actions, but I am only half listening as I close my eyes and try to stop the pounding in my head.

She takes this for me ignoring her and taps my leg and tells me to wake up and pay attention. She is obviously not finished with her speech. I open my eyes and look at her as she finishes with, she will not stand for any more of my foolishness and tells me her heart can't take it. She also tells me this little stunt of mine has taken at least twenty years off her life.

Her eyes are shimmering with unshed tears as she tells me, "I love you, Gabriel, but I will not stand here and watch you destroy yourself like this. You have to decide to either move on with your life or fight for what you want. But this," she motions to me, the bed, and I know she really means my actions, "this is not the answer. I will not sit quietly anymore and watch you kill yourself." With that, she storms out of the room, and I am grateful for it. I don't need or want any more lectures from anyone. God knows I get enough of them from Amon.

Rana sniffles, and I turn to look at her. She leans over the bed and kisses my cheek and says, "I'm glad you are okay, but Mariam is right. It's not easy to watch you do this to yourself." I start to argue that they have no idea how hard this is, but she spins on her heel and leaves the room in Mariam's wake.

"You sure know how to clear a room," Amon comments.

I fear he will take his turn to scold me now, too, but he doesn't. He just sinks into the nearest chair and stares at the floor.

After several long minutes of silence, I venture a question. "Mind telling me where I am and filling in some gaps while they are gone?"

He sighs but looks directly at me as he says, "You got drunk. You refused to let me drive you home, and you wrapped your car around a tree. We are in the hospital and have been waiting for you to fully wake up for about eight hours." I just nod my thanks for his honesty.

I lift my right arm and point to my splinted left arm in question. "Possibly fractured, they will know for sure when the swelling goes down," Amon replies.

As I lie here trying to make my alcohol-soaked brain put all the pieces together and think about what Mariam said (even though I really don't want to think about her—Sarah, not Mariam, I do anyway). My heart clenches, and my stomach returns to its normal acid-filled state, and I try not to go down that road right now. I instead focus on everything going on here right now and notice for the first time that my father is visibly absent from this room.

I wonder if he even showed up to the hospital to check on me. Not that it really matters, our relationship has been strained lately. He can't seem to understand why I can't just move on with my life. He had the gall to tell me her leaving was a blessing and tried to get me to call Safiya. I start to run through the whole, ugly argument but decide my head hurts enough right now, so I stop that train of thought.

After a while, my curiosity gets the better of me. "Did he even show up to the hospital?" I don't have to tell Amon who he is, he knows I mean my father.

"Yes. He stayed until the doctor told him you were lucky and that you would make a full recovery. Aahron is here, too. He's in the waiting room. He and your father are still not speaking." He pauses for only a second before he asks, "You still do not know what is going on with the two of them?"

I just shake my head slowly as the pain is getting worse. I ask Amon if he can find me a nurse and see if I can have something for my head and arm. He goes in search of one for me. I feel bad. He is such a great friend to me, and I have not treated him or anyone else very well lately.

Amon returns with a nurse carrying a syringe. She checks my vital signs, asks me several questions, gives me the injection, and leaves. Aahron slips in as she leaves. He stands near the doorway almost like he is scared to enter. I motion him all the way into the room. He comes to stand at the foot of the bed but doesn't quite make eye contact.

"Don't look so sad, Aahron. I'm not dead yet," I say, trying to lighten the mood, but no one laughs.

He does look up at me now and says, "No, thankfully you are not. I wouldn't have been able to live with myself if you had…" He can't finish the statement.

"It's not your fault I'm in here. You didn't put those drinks in my hand. I did this, not you. So don't feel guilty."

"But I am guilty, and it is my fault you are in here. I should have told you sooner." Aahron is looking down again. The hair on my neck begins to tingle with anticipation as to why he thinks this is his fault, or maybe it is the medication. Either way, I have a feeling what he is about to say is not going to make me happy.

Amon moves to leave to give us privacy, but we both protest, me because I want a witness to what he is about to say. I want someone to make sure I understand, afraid the drugs will kick in fully any minute.

Aahron tells Amon to stay, saying, "You have been a better brother to him than me, and he will need you when I am finished." Now the anticipation turns to fear as I can only think of one reason I will need Amon around. I know that whatever Aahron is about to say has to do with Sarah.

"What did you do?" I demand. "Tell me what you did to her!" I'm sitting up in the bed now.

"Please, Gabriel, let me get this out. I should have told you months ago, but you know how father is. He threatened me. I knew it was wrong, and we shouldn't have done it, but I didn't know how to tell you without you hating me. I see now that I was wrong. I should have stood up to Father."

I am trembling with anger now and the next words drip acerbically from my lips, "What did you do to Sarah?" Amon places his hand on my chest to keep me in the bed.

He tells how the flowers arrived shortly after the honeymoon and that they really were from Muhamed. He tells me that they were what gave father the idea to taunt Sarah with the notes and pictures. He hated her and wanted her gone. He tells me he tried to reason with Father, but he was beyond reason and that Aahron was frightened of him. He goes on to tell me that the ideas were all Father's and that he only delivered them. As if that makes what he has done any better. He continues on, pleading for my forgiveness until I tell him to stop. I have questions of my own now, and I don't want to hear anymore from him.

"She found out, didn't she?" I say, knowing that this is why she left.

He nods in reply. I am slowly putting the pieces together, but I need him to confirm a few things.

"She made you take her to the airport, didn't she?" It's a statement not a question. Again, he nods. I'm seething with anger now. I thought Sarah's betrayal in leaving was bad, but it pales in comparison to this. I'm so angry I can't see straight right now, and it has nothing to do with the accident or medicine.

"Why tell me now? She is gone." My voice reverberates off the walls. I'm so angry I try to get out of this bed. I don't know where I am going, but I need to move. Amon blocks my way, and I try to push him aside, but I'm weak, and my medicine is making the room spin. He holds his ground and doesn't let me up.

"She loves you, Gabriel. She said she couldn't stay here knowing what we did, and she knew you wouldn't leave. She said she didn't want to be the reason you came to hate your family, so she left. I'm sorry."

"Get out! And don't come back." I fall back onto my pillow. I am so angry and hurt and stupid. I should have gone after her. Why would she think that I would not have gone with her? I don't understand. I thought she knew that I love her. My thoughts are all mixed up as the medicine finally does its job, and I drift off to sleep.

May 25

I never went back to my father's house when I left the hospital. I was too angry. I'm assuming Aahron told Father that I know because he hasn't tried to contact me. I had Amon find us an apartment in Cairo. I stayed in a hotel for a few days as I recovered. I quickly found a job at an accounting firm and started work last week. I don't know that I like it, but it's a job, and it keeps me busy while I try to decide what to do. Amon moved with me and is driving a car part-time for a local hotel. Two days a week, he drives back home to help oversee and check on the drilling on one of my land holdings. Omar was kind enough to let him stay with his family for those two days each week.

Amon hasn't really pressed me about everything Aahron told us. He asked once at the hospital what I plan on doing and has not asked again. I suppose he is giving me time to process this betrayal.

Mariam and the girls were upset that I didn't return home, but she and Rana understand. I told them what Father and Aahron did. We have chosen not to tell Jasmina for now, but she is not stupid and has put some of the pieces together. She knows I am angry with Father and that it has to do with Sarah. For now, that is all she needs to know.

I want to go to Sarah, but I have some things I need to work through first. I've spent the past few months being very angry and feeling betrayed by her. I need to work through some of that before I can talk to her. I am still angry and not sure I have my temper under control yet. I also need to firmly establish my career to ensure I can provide some stability for us if I can convince her to come back home. I have some savings, but I will need it all to buy a house and provide for Sarah the way I want to. I won't rely on anything from my father. I don't need his money or land. I can provide well enough on my own. I will miss my children not being raised where I was raised, but I can start a new tradition with Sarah.

Oh my… I am so stupid. It hits me as I sit here thinking about everything I am willingly giving up for her, for us. I flash back to the conversation Sarah and I had that day, standing at the fence of the pasture. She asked me how far I was willing to go then. She wanted me to leave with her, and I basically told her I wouldn't go, that this was my home. She wanted me to leave with her then, and I told her no.

How could I have been so selfish? She gave up everything to stay with me. I didn't even consider leaving, and I promised her I would. Would she have stayed if I had been more willing to discuss it with her that day? Would she have confided in me and tried to get me to go with her? Guilt is beginning to set in as I realize I did not fully consider how my wife felt. I can't let it derail me now though. I can't change the past, and I've already started to build a new future. Hopefully, it will be enough for her to come back.

CHAPTER 19

Sarah
May 25

I've met with Lucy a few times, and it seems to be helping me not have so many nightmares. Maybe just talking has helped them to be less frequent. I did end up asking her if she thought I was crazy, I needed to know. She turned the question back on me. She words it a little more delicately.

"What makes you think that you might not be thinking rationally?"

I don't really want to answer. I want her opinion, but I know this is why I am here, so I reply, "Because it's what my family and friends have been thinking and saying since the beginning, and now after everything I've put myself through, I'm questioning my sanity."

Lucy counters with, "Yes, you are responsible for the decisions you made, but you are not responsible for the decisions that Muhamed, Ahmad, and Aahron made that negatively affected you. That burden is on them. You just have to find a way to deal with and work through those negative effects." She pauses to let that sink in for a minute then continues, "As to your sanity, you understand the difference between right and wrong, and you made the decision to remove yourself from a potentially dangerous situation. That shows you were thinking rationally and that you are not insane."

"But my decisions resulted in me placing myself in that dangerous situation."

She asks, "What was the first decision that you made?"

"To leave the country and go on vacation," I say.

"And do you think that this couldn't happen here in the States?" Lucy counters.

"No, I know it could have happened anywhere." I sigh deeply.

"Let's agree that several events were out of your control, and let's focus on what you did have control of." Lucy eyes me expectantly, but I just nod. "After you were taken, what was the first decision you made?" She gives me a minute to think through everything.

"To stay and go through with a fake marriage to save Rana."

"Was that really the first decision you made?" she asks.

I'm not sure I understand, and my confusion must show because she clarifies. "Go all the way back to when you were taken outside the hotel. What were you thinking when they took you?"

I sort through all the feelings and emotions trying to remember what I was thinking. I tell her I remember thinking that I was going to die. I thought about all the awful things that might happen to me before they killed me and then I tell her that's when I decided to try find a way out. I tell her about praying for someone to help me. When things weren't looking very hopeful, I decided that if I was going to die, that I would at least go out fighting.

Lucy replies, "So you decided to fight. You fought for escape, fought for hope, and fought for your life. You went into fight or flight, and you decided on fight. That was your first decision. It shows strength, and we will use that strength to work through all of this." She smiles at me. "You are strong, Sarah. You've been through a lot, and if you put in the work, you will get through this."

Her words are like an arrow straight through my heart. Didn't Gabriel tell me something very similar? I can't even think about him right now. It's too painful.

I appreciate her vote of confidence and ask her another question, now that we've established I'm not crazy. "Do you think I am suffering from Stockholm syndrome?"

Again, she asks me if I think that I might be. I explain that maybe that's what started my attachment to Gabriel and his family, and we discuss the specifics of those first few weeks. She points out that I didn't delude myself about why I willingly married Gabriel to save his sister. She also pointed out that I didn't try to convince myself that I needed Gabriel to survive, because when I felt in danger again, I was able to reason for myself what I thought was best. We agree that I was probably suffering from some post-traumatic stress, but not Stockholm syndrome.

She does show me that I did have other options than just marrying Gabriel. There were options that I might not have liked but options just the same. They were decisions that would have removed me from danger and may or may not have put others further in danger, but options nonetheless.

She asks me if I regret my decision to marry Gabriel. I think about it for a while before I answer, "No, I don't regret marrying him. I regret that I hurt my friends and family. I regret lying to them, and I regret the pain I have caused everyone."

"Does that include Gabriel?" Lucy frequently circles back to him.

I know I have to deal with it eventually, but I keep putting her off because it hurts too much to go there now. "Yes," is all I say.

She watches me for a minute before continuing, "What is your biggest fear concerning Gabriel?"

I am not ready to deal with this topic, so I tell her I don't know. She encourages me to give it some thought, and we can revisit this topic at our next visit. I know I will have to think about it sooner or later, but I just want to focus on the positive right now. We wind up our session, and I half-heartedly agree to at least give it some thought.

I decide to stop by the park for a walk to clear my mind before I return home. I need the exercise, and I skipped my walk this morning.

CHAPTER 20

Gabriel
August 15

Things have been going really well at work lately. I am enjoying my new job and settling into life in the city. I still miss home and the countryside, but the city has many distractions that keep me busy. I still think about Sarah often but try to distract myself by staying busy which usually works well, but not today. I'm still struggling to forgive her for leaving so suddenly, even though I understand her reasons. I'm angry that she did not follow her only rule…honesty.

She is heavy on my mind today, and I can't seem to focus on anything but her.

I'm supposed to meet Amon for dinner, so I decide to leave work a little early and go for a walk to try to clear my head or I won't be very good company. I don't really have a goal in mind, I just walk, not really seeing where I'm going. The walk is not helping, and I am about to just call it a day. I stop on the sidewalk and focus on where I am, and I suck in a breath when I realize where I've stopped. I have stopped a few feet from a church—not just any church, but "her" church. The one we visited that day on our honeymoon. The one that changed everything. I haven't been back to church since Sarah left, and I'm not really in the mood now, so I turn to go in the other direction.

I only get a few steps when I get this tugging in my gut to turn back around. I argue with myself, and the farther I walk away, the more I feel like I should turn around. I stop again and ask myself what I am running from. "What do I have to lose?" I say out loud. This place brought Sarah comfort and helped her sort through her feelings, maybe it can do the same for me. I square my shoulders and turn back in the direction of the church.

It is cool and quiet with just a few people scattered around the sanctuary when I enter. I don't really want to be noticed, so I choose a pew near the back. I sit staring ahead for quite some time, not really sure what to do. I pick up the Bible in front of me and randomly open it up. I read a verse in Psalm 52. "Cast your cares on the Lord, and He will sustain you."

I think about this for a minute and decide I would love to cast all my worries away. I'm tired of this burden of guilt and anger and bitterness that I have carried for so many months. I've been angry at so many people and now, as I sit here, I realize just how tired I am. I wish it were that easy to just toss it all away. How? How do I do that?

I think back on that day with Sarah and remember how she bowed her head and silently poured out her heart in prayer. I decide to give it a try. I bow my head and ask for help in not being so angry with Sarah. I ask for help in knowing what I should do next and wait for a response. I wait several minutes and don't get an answer. I absently flip through the Bible in my lap.

This time, I find myself in Ephesians 4 where I read a lot about anger and sin. Verse 26 says not to let the sun go down on your anger. Well, I can't count how many sunsets have passed since I first became angry, it's been a while. I read on hoping for some direction on how to remedy this.

Verse 31 tells me, "Get rid of all bitterness and slander, along with every form of malice. Be kind and compassionate to one another, forgiving each other." That's the problem. I don't really know how to forgive anyone and am not sure I am ready to do that especially with my father. I'm not ready to even go down that road, but what about Sarah? Am I ready to forgive her? Do I even want to?

It doesn't take long to come up with that answer, yes, I am ready. I miss her and don't want to let another sunset pass without speaking to her. I have to try to make things right between us. I have my answer, and I quickly exit the church so that I can try to remedy this tonight. I pull my cell phone out and begin dialing her number before I've even cleared the doors. My heart is pounding, because I haven't talked to her for so long. It's been months since I have even tried. I'm not even sure if she still has the phone I gave her. I never turned off the service as it is my only link to her.

I anxiously wait as the phone connects and goes directly to voice mail. My heart skips a beat. I have no way of knowing if it is just turned off. I hang up. I don't want to leave a voice mail. I want to talk directly to her. I start walking back in the direction of my apartment as I decide what to do. I know I have to find her. I've tried going through her friends and family in the past, but they were very protective of her and would not give me any information. I will have to do this the hard way. I need to go to Texas and talk to her face to face. No matter how it turns out, I need to speak to her in person one last time.

By the time I reach my building, I have a plan in place. I meet up with Amon for dinner and share with him my plan.

"I've decided to go to Texas and talk to Sarah." No point in beating around the bush.

He immediately asks, "What took you so long?"

I just smile and press on. I know his comment was rhetorical anyway. "I'm not really sure where she is living and concerned that it might take me a few days to find her. I don't mind searching, but I have limited time off from work since I just started."

"Couldn't you call her or her family to get an address?" Amon asks.

"I tried calling her number today, but it goes directly to voice mail, and her family wasn't very helpful the last time I contacted them. I think the best course is to just go there. If I travel all that way, she has to at least hear me out. She owes me that much."

"We can do some online searches to help narrow it down before you go," Amon suggests.

"Yes, I thought of that. But I would prefer if someone could physically locate her before I go. That way, I can have more time to try and work things out with her," I say, waiting to see if Amon picks up on what I am suggesting.

Amon nods and replies, "And you want that someone to be me?"

"Yes. I trust you with my life, and you know how important this is to me. I will pay your travel expenses if you think you can manage some time off from work. Once you locate Sarah, I will join you in Texas. You can spend the remainder of your time vacationing and sightseeing."

Amon contemplates my proposal for only a few seconds before agreeing to help me. We spend the remainder of dinner discussing travel plans and searching websites for information to help us find Sarah.

Three days later, we have a travel plan and a destination. We found a listing for a Sarah Grant in Red Tree, Texas. It's a small community outside of Dallas. Amon leaves in a few more days. Hopefully, he will find her quickly. I'm packed and ready.

Sarah
August 20

I am watching the clock counting the minutes until my shift ends. My feet are swollen, and my lower back is killing me. I only have a couple of more weeks before this sweet baby makes an appearance, and I am beyond ready. Sleep has been greatly diminished due to frequent bathroom visits and trying to find a comfortable position. I just want a hot shower and a soft bed. Thankfully, I have the day off tomorrow and can sleep in before I go for my doctor's appointment.

I awake around eight in the morning feeling refreshed and decide to take a walk after breakfast. I decide on a bagel and juice this morning. I have craved carbs this entire pregnancy, so I have been walking three to four days a week to help burn off the extra calories. There is a nice park two blocks from my house.

After I put on my tennis shoes, I pull my hair up into a ball cap. I grab a bottle of water, my phone, and keys and head out into the warm, humid day. I turn onto the sidewalk and head in the direction of the park. I have a few hours to kill before I meet Lisa for lunch. She is going with me to my appointment this afternoon.

The park is fairly busy for a weekday. There are several joggers, dog walkers, moms with toddlers, and babies in strollers enjoying this beautiful day. Having the park so close to my home will be nice when the baby gets here. I've even considered getting a dog but decided having a baby by myself is all the challenge I want to tackle for now. Maybe in a couple of years I will get a puppy. I feel my mood drifting to a place I don't want to go. I made my choice and stand by my decision. I just never imagined I would be a single mom. I pick up my pace and decide to focus on all my blessings today.

CHAPTER 21

Amon
August 23

I arrived at DFW airport late yesterday evening, picked up my rental car, and checked into my hotel. I have an address that we hope is Sarah's that I will check out in the morning. I opt for takeout in my room so that I can be up early. It's has been a long couple of flights, and I am tired. I pull up the map on my phone and calculate the distance based on traffic in the morning. By my calculations, Sarah is only about fifteen minutes away.

I rise around six in the morning and stop at a donut shop for pastries and coffee. I drive to the address and find a small red brick house with a single car garage attached. The yard is fenced with several shade trees. The houses are all well cared for in this quiet neighborhood. I wonder if this is really where Sarah lives and hope that she is home. I want to try to get a feel for her routine so that when Gabriel arrives, he can try to meet with her alone. The less people around, the better.

I continue past the house and survey the street for a good vantage point. I don't want to be so close that I'm noticed. I'm not even sure if she is home because her garage is closed. I will wait a couple of hours to see if she shows up.

Just as I am about to give up my watch for the morning, someone exits from the red brick house. I realize I must have the wrong address as a very pregnant woman emerges. She seems to be going for a morning walk. I'm disappointed and don't want to tell Gabriel that we had the wrong address. I decide to head back to the hotel and will focus on finding Sarah's friends or family. Maybe one of them will lead me to her. I start the car and slowly make my way out of the neighborhood. I pass the pregnant woman on the way, and something seems familiar about her. Her familiarity bothers me as I round the corner. The hair on the back of my neck stands on end as I consider the possibility that that woman could be Sarah—a very pregnant Sarah.

Could it really be her? Would she really have left Gabriel and not told him about the baby? Why would she keep something like that from him? So many thoughts are flooding my mind right now that I can't process them all. I pull over on the side of the road to try to figure out how I am going to tell Gabriel he is going to be a father. Again, I ask myself why she didn't tell him. She should have told him.

I shake myself and decide that I better be certain that really was Sarah. I can't tell Gabriel without verifying that it is really her. I turn the car around and head in the same direction that the woman was walking. I circle around a few blocks and stumble upon a park. I pull into a parking place and scan the park for the woman in the hat. After a few minutes, I spot her on the walking path. I decide to wait where I am and see if she walks past the car.

My heart is beating violently inside my chest as I anticipate the woman turning the final corner and walking in my direction. This turn of events changes everything, and I am worried how Gabriel will handle this news. It's only been in the past few weeks that he has started to act like himself again. I think about the wreck after Sarah left and worry what he might do if she rejects him again.

As I worry about all these things, part of me hopes I am wrong and that the woman walking in my direction is not Sarah at all. The closer she gets, the more my hopes are sinking. The sun illuminates her face under the brim of her cap, and there is no mistaking who she is. It's Sarah!

I silently watch Sarah go by and out of sight. I can't think, can't move. I can't tell Gabriel, I won't, at least not until he gets here. He will have to see this for himself.

I don't follow Sarah back to her house. I need time to figure out what I am going to do next, so I head back to the hotel.

August 25

I wake up extra early this morning, not that I slept much last night. Gabriel texted me the evening I found Sarah wanting to know if I had any luck. I called him to let him know that I located Sarah. He promised to be on the next flight out and should arrive this evening. The sooner he gets here, the better.

I make another pasty and coffee run in preparation for another long morning. Sarah left early yesterday morning and did not return until the evening. I assume she went to work, but I need to know for sure, so I leave earlier than yesterday.

I arrive on Sarah's street just in time to see her pull out of her garage, so I decide to follow her. Twenty minutes later, we arrive at Cedarview Memorial Hospital. I worry that maybe she is here to have her baby but realize this is her place of work when she steps out of her car with scrubs on. I park far enough away to hopefully not be noticed and wait for her to enter the building before I leave. I will return in the afternoon to resume my watch. At least now I can tell Gabriel a little more about Sarah's schedule.

Sarah

Today has been another long day at work, and I am once again experiencing swollen feet and a sore back. Only a few more shifts before I can start my maternity leave. I am definitely counting down the days. When my shift ends, I just want to head home and soak in my tub, but I promised the girls I would meet them for dinner. I talk myself into going since it might be the last girl's night before the baby arrives.

I drive to the restaurant and join the girls already seated at a booth. It was a rough couple of months when I first returned. Everyone was so mad at me and hurt by my actions. It took some time, but we have finally come to a place where we can all hang out together again. It's not the same, and I know that's my fault. I'm just happy to have my friends back in my life when I need them the most. They are all excited about the new baby and getting to be "aunts."

I don't eat much of my dinner. My appetite has been lacking today, and I chalk it up to being tired. Lauren notices and asks if everything is okay.

"I'm just tired from a long day at work. The bigger this baby gets, the more my back hurts. I just need a nice hot bath and bed. I will feel better in the morning."

I stay a little longer before I say my good nights. The girls all walk me out to my car, making me promise to take my vitamins and drink plenty of fluids. I promise to comply and slide into my car. My back is really aching now, and I can't wait to get home.

I soak in the tub for just a short time before I decide to get out and just head for bed. The warm water wasn't helping so much today anyway. I think I just need sleep.

August 26

It has been a long night. I only managed to sleep a few hours. The ache in my back continued to increase and around four in the morning, I got out of bed. I think I might actually be in labor. I drink some water and eat some toast as I make sure everything is in my bag. My contractions are not very close together yet, so I will wait to call Lauren in a couple of hours. I do some laundry and pick up around the house before I get dressed. I called work to let them know that I would not be in today and probably starting my maternity leave a little early. They were excited and made me promise to call and keep them all updated.

Lauren and Lisa are both going to be with me in labor, but Lisa will have to drop the kids off first, so Lauren has agreed to be my ride to the hospital when the time comes. I called Lauren around six thirty and to tell her the news. She screams her excitement and promises to be here soon. I tell her not to rush that I think I am in early labor. I tell her I want to walk a little to see if things speed up, so she agrees to come walk with me. I tell her to drive carefully that I still have plenty of time. My contractions are irregular, so it might be a while.

CHAPTER 22

Gabriel
August 26

I arrived late yesterday evening, and Amon picked me up at the airport. I had a thousand questions and wanted him to take me to Sarah's immediately. Amon argued it was too late to go last night, but I argued it wasn't even nine o'clock yet. Amon said Sarah gets up early for work and might already be in bed. We compromised, and he agreed to at least drive me by her house before we headed to the hotel. We decided to get up early and resume Amon's now daily watch. If Sarah goes to work today, then I will have to wait until the evening to see her. If it is her day off, then I will talk to her this morning. Now that I'm here, I'm not sure how much longer I can wait.

Amon insists we stop for breakfast sandwiches and coffee. He promises we will not miss her. We arrive in Sarah's neighborhood around six o'clock and wait. I sip my coffee but am too nervous or excited to eat.

By six thirty, Amon says, "It must be her day off. She is usually gone by now." I nod my understanding as he continues. "She usually takes a morning walk around eight or nine, so she should be getting up soon. Do you want to give her a little more time to awaken?"

I want to scream no that I've waited long enough, but I know he is right and need to give her a few more minutes. So I answer him, "I've waited five months. As much as I don't want to, a few more minutes won't kill me."

Amon settles into his seat, but I feel like a caged animal. I want to get out and pace but don't want to risk her seeing me before I am ready. Around seven fifteen, I can't wait anymore. I tell Amon that I'm going now, and he wishes me luck. He agreed to stay as long as needed.

I open my door and step out of the car just when a car pulls into Sarah's driveway. My heart sinks and can't believe my luck when Lauren emerges from the car. I stand still and watch her approach the house hoping to get a glimpse of Sarah as she answers the door. But as luck would have it, Lauren uses her own key and enters the house. I feel totally deflated. I need to talk to Sarah but don't know if I want to risk a confrontation with Lauren, too. I had hoped to talk to her alone. I sink back into my seat and wait. Amon squeezes my shoulder but doesn't speak.

I only wait a few minutes before the front door opens, and Lauren steps back out followed by a very pregnant woman… Sarah! I can't breathe, and the coffee I had earlier turns to acid in my stomach. I shake my head trying to make sense of what I am seeing. I hear someone saying breathe, and it takes me a minute to realize that it is Amon. I had forgotten he was next to me.

I glance at him and then quickly back to Sarah, afraid to take my eyes off her and still not believing what I am seeing. As the shock begins to wear off, I find my voice. It takes a few tries, but I manage to croak out, "You knew?"

"Yes," Amon answers. "I didn't know how to tell you and decided you needed to see it with your own eyes. I'm sorry I kept it from you."

I don't even know how to answer him. My shock is slowly turning to anger, but I know that I am really not mad at Amon, so I say nothing. I just watch Sarah and Lauren walk away and turn the corner. I point and tell Amon to follow them, and he insists he has a good idea of where they are going. He tells me about the park and says we will give them a few minutes before we follow.

We watch Sarah and Lauren walk the path at the park, and I notice that Sarah stops occasionally to catch her breath. Lauren keeps handing her a bottle of water and checking her watch. It dawns on me she is timing contractions. Sarah is in labor.

How can this be happening and happening today! Of all the days for me to arrive, I choose the day that Sarah is going into labor. I couldn't have chosen a worse day, and I say so out loud, but Amon counters with, "Maybe this is the best day. Sarah is giving birth to your child today, and somehow fate has brought you here today. Maybe you should go tell her you are here."

With as much urgency as I had to speak to Sarah today, I now can't seem to get my feet to move in her direction. She will not be happy to see me and even as mad as I am at her now, I can't bring myself to confront her when she is obviously in labor.

"Even if I confront her now, there is no guarantee that she will let me be a part of the birth today. She obviously didn't want me here, and she absolutely didn't want me to know about the baby." I look at Amon. "You saw how her friends acted back home, how protective they were of her. Today won't be any different. I need to speak to Sarah now more than ever, but it will have to wait until she can think clearly." Amon nods his agreement.

Lauren and Sarah don't stay long at the park before heading back to Sarah's house. Thirty minutes later, they exit the house with bags in hand and head off to the hospital.

I fluctuate between anger and worry as I think about Sarah in labor today. Part of me wants to be there with her while another part of my brain is telling me to catch the first flight out of here. Fortunately, or not, my heart keeps thinking about that tiny baby she is carrying—my baby—and I can't leave. I wonder is it going to be a girl or a boy, and I pray that it will be healthy. I even find myself praying for Sarah, too, as I think about my mother. I want to call Mariam, but not until I know more details and where things stand with Sarah. I didn't even tell my family that I was coming here.

Amon and I spend a long few hours walking the grounds of the hospital. I've been trying to figure out how to get information without letting anyone know I am here. I know the hospital will not give any information out, even if I am her husband. I make a suggestion to Amon.

"Amon, will you go into the waiting area and see if Sarah's family is in there? Sarah is the only one who will recognize you, and she won't be a problem. See if you can get any updates and text them to me."

Amon agrees.

Amon

I enter the hospital and ask for directions to the maternity waiting area and coffee. The receptionist points me to the elevators and tells me to follow the signs on the second floor. She assures me there will be fresh coffee in the waiting area.

I exit on the second floor and find the waiting area a short distance down the hall to the left. I scan the room for the coffee and am thankful it is pretty full with waiting families. I pour myself a cup and find a seat in the corner near the vending machine. I'm trying to hear conversations, but it is hard and so far, I can't spot Sarah's family.

I am on my second cup when Lauren enters the waiting area and joins a man and two women. She is excited and tells them that this baby is in a hurry and will be here within the next couple of hours. She hugs the man and assures him that Sarah is doing well. I send a quick text to Gabriel and promise to send more information as soon as I can.

Lunchtime is quickly approaching, and I need more than coffee, but I don't want to leave and miss any news. I settle for cookies and chips out of the vending machine. There is a woman sitting in the chair across from me who asks who I am waiting for. I tell her my sister is in labor, and I am waiting for news from her. I lift my phone to indicate how I am getting information so that she doesn't wonder why no one comes in to speak to me. She smiles and tells me she is waiting on her fifth grandbaby. I congratulate her and wish her well.

When I'm done with my vending machine cuisine, I cross the room to the trashcan by the door. I am knocked sideways as Lauren comes rushing in the door. She quickly apologizes without even looking my way. By the looks of her, the baby is here. She confirms my suspicions and announces to the room, "It's a boy!"

A boy! Gabriel is a father, and he has a son. He will be so excited. I stick around long enough to hear that mother and baby are doing well. I decide not to text Gabriel, I want to tell him this in person. I text him and tell him to meet me at the car.

Gabriel is pacing in front of the car as I approach and is questioning me before I even get close. I assure him everything is fine and get straight to the point. He has been suffering out here long enough.

"It's a boy!" I tell him and enjoy the look of pure joy that crosses his face. He crushes me in a hug that lifts me off my feet. We are both smiling and commenting about Gabriel having a son. I can't imagine the roller coaster he has been on today—finding Sarah, discovering she is pregnant, and learning that he has a son.

When the excitement starts to die down, Gabriel sinks onto the hood of the car. I guess all the emotions and revelations of the day have finally drained him of all his energy. He looks like he is going to pass out.

"Gabriel, are you okay?"

"Yes," he replies. "I'm just overwhelmed and tired. This day has not gone the way I had planned or hoped. I just need a minute to let everything sink in."

"You haven't eaten today. Let's go find something to eat and you can decide what to do next." I can tell he is hesitant to leave, but I assure him that they are not going anywhere, so we leave to find something to eat.

CHAPTER 23

Sarah

I can't believe the flood of emotions that I am experiencing right now as I hold my baby skin to skin with me. He is perfect! All seven pounds and three ounces of him. I stroke his velvety soft skin and silky brown hair as I marvel at how perfect he is. Tears of joy stream down my face as I thank God for this tiny blessing. There is a twinge of guilt and sadness mixed with my tears as I think about how much he looks like his father. I hope Gabriel doesn't hate me, and I hope even more that this tiny baby will someday forgive me for keeping him from his father.

Tyler must notice my change of mood. He places his hand on my shoulder and asks if I'm all right. I assure him I am fine. Just tired and needing a nap after the sleepless night I had. He reassures me that he and Lisa are here for me if I need anything. I thank him for being here today. He kisses the top of my head as he heads out to pick the kids up from his in-laws. He congratulates me on my beautiful son, and I smile from ear to ear. I still can't believe it myself. I have a son!

Gabriel

I don't even remember eating my burger and fries but realize my plate is empty as Amon comments he is glad to see I have found my appetite.

"I haven't had much to eat the past few days, and I'm starving all of a sudden," I reply. Amon pushes his onion rings in my directions and moves to get us both refills on our drinks. I eat a few onion rings before pushing his plate back in his direction.

"So what's the plan?" Amon asks, setting my drink in front of me.

"I guess we can go back to the hotel for a while. I have decided I am going to visit Sarah later this evening. I can't put it off any longer, and I want to see my son. Hopefully, most of her family will be gone if I wait long enough."

"Do you think they will let you in?" he asks.

"They will have to. I am still her husband and that baby's father." I know that I will have to keep my head cool when I go there this evening, but I will not be turned away without seeing either of them.

Amon and I return to the hotel. It is a long afternoon and evening. I called the hospital and learned that visiting hours end at eight o'clock, but fathers can come and go as late as they want. I get Sarah's room number and plan to go after visiting hours.

I can't seem to sit still, so I opt for laps in the pool to burn off some energy. Amon convinces me to accompany him to dinner before he drops me off at the hospital.

Sarah

Visiting hours are almost over, and I am still arguing with Lisa and Lauren about staying by myself. I convince Lauren to leave because she has work tomorrow. She promises to come by after work and take a shift tomorrow night. I thank her for all of her help today and tell her that Auntie Lou can come get more snuggles tomorrow.

Lisa is a little harder to get to leave. She insists I need someone to stay the night.

"Lisa, I feel really good and am just going to sleep most of the night tonight. Jackson has been the perfect baby this afternoon. I don't need you here to watch me sleep."

"What if Jackson wakes up to feed?" she counters.

"Then I will feed him," I respond.

"But you will have to get out of bed to get him out of his crib."

"I am capable of lifting my baby in and out of his crib. And besides, the nurse is here if I need any help. I would feel so much better knowing you are at home getting some rest so that you can help me when I get home. I will need you then, I'm sure."

"Are you sure?" she tentatively asks.

"Positive. Now go home and get some rest. You can come back in the morning and bring donuts when you come," I tease, but I know she will arrive with a wide variety of sugary confections to choose from.

She kisses the top of Jackson's head and hugs me before she leaves. I retrieve Jackson from his crib and settle into my bed for a snuggle. It has been a long day, and I appreciate all my family and friends being here to support me, but I am thankful for this quiet time to spend alone with my baby. I unwrap him and study his tiny features, memorizing his long fingers and toes. I still can't get over how much dark hair he has and again find myself thinking about Gabriel. I wonder what he looked like as a baby.

I feed Jackson, but he only nurses a few minutes before he is fast asleep again. I guess it has been a long day for him, too. It's been a long time since I last took any pain meds and could use something now, so I wrap Jackson and place him in his crib. I press my call light and request my pain medication. I lie on my side in the bed watching my baby sleep as I wait for my meds.

There is a knock at the door, and I tell them to come in, expecting my nurse. I think that was really quick, but maybe she was not busy. The door opens and closes, but she is unusually quiet. I turn to see who has entered and am totally shocked to see Gabriel standing there. I blink several times in disbelief before I can even speak. It's almost like my earlier thinking about him has somehow conjured him to my room.

"Gabriel?" I know it's him, but it still comes out sounding like a question. I don't know how he found me and can't believe he is standing in my room right now. My heart begins to pound wildly in my chest wondering why he is here.

"Sarah," is all he says, as he stares at me with dark eyes.

I can't tell if it is anger that has his expression schooled into stone or disdain. I've never seen him look at me this way before, but I guess I deserve his anger right now. I just didn't expect him to ever show up here. No point in delaying the inevitable anymore.

"What are you doing here?" I ask.

"I came to see you," he answers. "Imagine my surprise seeing a pregnant version of my wife. I almost didn't believe it."

"When did you see me?" *Was he following me?* I wonder.

"In front of your house today and at the park with Lauren," he states matter-of-factly.

"Were you following me?"

"Yes. I came to your house to talk to you today and saw you and…well, I had to get my head straight before I could approach you."

"Oh," is all I can say. I can't believe he is standing there so calm. My palms are sweating, and my heart is still drumming a steady beat in my chest. We just stare at each other waiting for someone to say something.

I guess it will be me. "Why did you come here, Gabriel?"

"I told you I wanted to see you and talk to you," he answers.

"I told you several months ago that I didn't want you to come here. I don't know what you want to talk about now after all this time."

Gabriel humphs and shifts his feet. "Don't you? Don't you think we have a few things we need to talk about? Like my son," he says, pointing to Jackson's crib.

I cringe and guilt knocks the wind out of me. He knows, and there will be no going back now. I don't know what I thought, but I know Gabriel is not the kind of man who would walk away from his child, no matter the circumstances.

"You're right. I guess we do have a lot to talk about." I move to get out of bed and motion him over to Jackson's crib. I don't want to fight right now, so I say, "Come see how beautiful he is."

Gabriel steps up to the side of Jackson's crib and reaches his hand down to touch his head. He looks back at me and has the hint of a smile on his lips as he says, "He is beautiful."

Thankfully, some of the animosity that was dripping off him has started to ease. I'll take what I can get at this point. I was expecting him to ream me out. I know I probably deserve it, but I don't think I can take it today.

The nurse breaks the spell as she enters with my medication and stops mid stride and looks directly at Gabriel. "I'm sorry but visiting hours are over. You can come back tomorrow," she informs him. I am a little relieved but know that we will have to resume this conversation in the morning.

Gabriel's reply shocks me into silence. "I'm her husband, and I just arrived from out of the country. I will be staying a while longer."

The nurse looks from Gabriel to me for confirmation of his statement, and all I can do is nod my agreement. She proceeds to hand me my medicine and tells me to call her if I need anything else. I thank her and set my water on the bedside table. Gabriel has resumed his inspection of his son. He looks to me and asks, "Can I hold him?"

"Of course," I answer and move to help him, but he is already sliding his hands under his tiny body. He lifts him to his chest and cradles him like a pro. I motion him to the chair at the side of the bed. I try to make myself comfortable on the edge of the bed but am having trouble finding a comfortable spot. Hopefully, my medication will kick in soon.

Gabriel notices my discomfort and asks how I am feeling.

"I'm a little sore, but not too bad considering." He nods his acknowledgment, and we lapse into awkward silence again.

After a few minutes, he asks, "Does he have a name yet?"

I am a little nervous to share it with him, so I watch his face for a reaction as I tell him. "Jackson Gabriel."

"You gave him my name? I thought you didn't want to have anything to do with me. So why would you give him my name?" He holds my stare waiting for an answer.

"Because he is your son, Gabriel, and I thought it was the right thing to do. He is a part of you, too, and I wanted him to have a part of you."

Gabriel scoffs, "Really? The right thing to do? The right thing to do would have been to tell me you were pregnant, not run away from me and hide my child from me. Don't you think? How would you feel if I had kept something this important from you?" Gabriel's voice raises as he speaks and Jackson squirms in his arms. He soothes him and lowers his voice as he continues.

"I know this is not the best time to talk about all of this, but we will talk about it later. I just need you to answer one question tonight."

"Okay," I answer, knowing I owe him a lot more than one question. I'm just relieved he doesn't want to hash it all out tonight.

"Did you ever love me?"

"What?" I am totally thrown off guard by his question. I didn't expect this one and totally don't know how to answer, so I tell him as much.

"Sure, you do. It's a simple question that deserves an honest answer." He continues on before I can reply. "You asked that I honor one request from you before you agreed to marry me, and I did. Now I am asking for you to do the same."

He doesn't have to remind me of what that request was. I remember it well. Honesty.

He patiently waits for my answer never breaking eye contact. I only thought my heart was beating wildly before. Now it is downright erratic in my chest. "Gabriel, it doesn't matter what I felt for you, I had no choice but to leave."

Gabriel cuts me off. "I know why you left and what my father did, and we will talk about that later. Right now, I asked you a very simple question, and I expect an honest answer. And, Sarah, it does matter to me."

There are so many emotions running through my head right now, so many questions. Tears are threatening to spill over now as my emotions are already on overdrive today. I look down at my folded hands in my lap and take several deep breaths before answering. "Yes." It is a simple answer, and it is the truth. He deserves the truth.

Gabriel rises from his chair and comes to sit next to me on the bed. Our shoulders are touching, and he leans into me and says, "Thank you."

"You deserve honest answers, and I don't want to lie to you anymore."

Gabriel places a hand over mine and tells me we can talk later.

"You look tired and have had a busy day. Why don't you lie down, and I'll just get to know this little guy while you rest." I start to protest, but he assures me he will wake me when needed.

I don't know how long I sleep, but I awaken to a warm hand on my shoulder and grunts from Jackson.

I move to sit up and Gabriel tells me, "I think he is hungry."

"What time is it?" I ask.

"Almost one," Gabriel tells me.

"Have you been holding him all this time?" I ask.

"Yes, and before you scold me, the nurse has already done that. She told me I was going to spoil him, and he would not want to sleep in his bed if I kept this up," he tells me as he smiles down at Jackson. "I told her he would not be spoiled, just well loved."

I smile at him and know that it is true. He will never be lacking in love. I reach for Jackson after I get comfortable sitting up. He hands him to me and sits on the edge of the bed. I don't know why I feel uncomfortable feeding Jackson in front of him, but I hesitate. I don't want Gabriel to know I am uncomfortable, so I quickly tell him, "You can go back to your hotel now. I feel bad that you stayed so late already."

Gabriel tells me, "I don't mind staying and besides, I don't have a ride."

"How did you get here?" I ask.

"Amon dropped me off. I sent him back to the hotel when you didn't kick me out of your room. I texted him when you fell asleep. It's late, and I don't want to wake him, so I will just stay until the morning."

"Amon is here with you? Why didn't you say something? He could have come in and said hello."

"He is looking forward to seeing you and Jackson, but tonight was not the right time." I agree and wonder how true that statement is. Amon can't be all that happy to see me after everything that has happened. I guess we will see when he visits. For now, I need to focus on feeding Jackson as he starts to protest in my arms.

I unbutton my shirt and offer Jackson my breast. He readily latches and settles into nursing. I am so happy he has taken to feeding so well. I watch him as he suckles and am thankful for yet another blessing. I feel Gabriel watching me with Jackson and look up to see him watching his son as he feeds. My subtle movement catches his eye, and he looks up at me with a look of contentment. Gone is the angry man who entered my room just a few hours ago. This is the Gabriel I remember and am happy that he is here with me.

"Beautiful," he says, and I don't know if he is referring to me or Jackson, so I just smile at him.

I don't know exactly where we go from here, so I just focus on this moment. I enjoy the intimacy we share with this child. No one could ever fill that place but him, and I was stupid to ever think otherwise. I can't believe how selfish I've been. Why didn't I trust him more? He never gave me one reason to distrust him, not once. I let my fears overwhelm and blind me to the truth.

Here we are in a hospital room together enjoying our newborn son peacefully, when he should be railing and angry with me, but he is not. At least, not at the moment. He is a good man. Hopefully, we can find a way through all of this. I don't want Jackson to suffer because of my bad decisions.

I can't hold the tears in, so I look down at Jackson feeding, trying to hide my emotions. A few silent tears land on his blanket. Gabriel lifts my face to him and wipes my eyes.

"It's going to be all right, Sarah. We will figure all of this out." I nod at him and try to speak and tell him I'm sorry, but he just shushes me and tells me not tonight. We will talk later. I don't deserve his kindness but am thankful for it.

Jackson feeds for quite some time, and Gabriel and I make small talk. I tell him about my job and house that I bought, and he tells me he has moved to Cairo and taken a job there. I want to ask what prompted the move and have a pretty good idea I already know, but I don't want to bring up that topic just yet. So I keep it light and ask him about his new apartment.

When Jackson finishes, I burp him and hand him off to Gabriel. I get out of bed and retrieve a diaper and wipes and offer them to Gabriel. He tells me he will let me get this one but will watch and learn. Once we get Jackson cleaned and settled, I place him in his crib. I make my way to the bathroom. My bleeding seems a little heavy, but I don't really know what is normal or not since I've never done this before. I will mention it to the nurse when she rounds.

I return to bed and point Gabriel to the pillow and blanket in the closet. He settles into the recliner and immediately closes his eyes. I need to ask him a favor, and I hope he doesn't get offended, but I need to do it now.

"Gabriel."

"Yes," he replies with his eyes closed.

"I know this is going to sound really bad, but would you mind leaving early in the morning before Lisa arrives? I know we will have to tell them you are here soon, but I don't think the hospital is the right setting. And they will have a lot of questions that I won't be able to answer. After you and I have had a chance to visit, then we can tell them." He doesn't answer immediately, so I press on. "You do remember how they all responded when I told them I was staying in Egypt with you, don't you?"

That earned an immediate response, and he agreed it was probably better to tell them after I am discharged.

Gabriel left a little before six after several kisses and cuddles from Jackson. I promised him he could return this evening. I told him I would text him later.

CHAPTER 24

Gabriel
August 27

I walk out of the hospital this morning feeling lighter and heavier at the same time. I am overjoyed about Jackson and how perfect he is. I am excited about being a part of his life but worry just what that means between me and Sarah. I decide I will worry about it later. Right now, I need breakfast and a nap. I didn't sleep much between watching Jackson and watching Sarah.

Sarah

Lisa shows up with donuts as promised. I enjoy a couple while she snuggles and gushes over how handsome Jackson is. She asks how we did last night, and I tell her we did well. Jackson only woke twice during the night. She continues her gushing and cooing to him about what a wonderful baby is he already. I don't mention our late-night visitor, mostly because I don't know what I would even say about Gabriel's arrival.

Lauren came by during her lunch break and offered to come back after work. I told her that Stasia and Nicole are coming by this afternoon, and some of my coworkers are supposed to stop by as well. It will be pretty busy in here today and asked if she will wait and come visit when we get home. She and Lisa worked out a schedule for our first week home. Lisa will come during the day, and Lauren will check in after work and on the weekend. She agrees and tells me she will see me in two days.

It turns out to be a very busy day, and I am a little tired after everyone leaves. I just want a nap, but Gabriel has texted a couple of times asking when he and Amon can come by. I tell them now is good and decide to close my eyes until they arrive.

Thirty minutes later, I am awakened by a knock on my door. It is Gabriel and Amon. I'm still a little worried how he will react but relax as soon as I see him smile in my direction. I greet them both and motion Amon over to where Jackson lies in his crib. Gabriel gently lifts him up and introduces Amon to his son. Amon congratulates us both and is grinning from ear to ear. Gabriel asks him what he thinks of his nephew. I didn't think his smile could get any bigger, but it did. Gabriel proceeds to hand Jackson over to him despite his protests. He moves to sit on the sofa as he inspects his tiny hands and touches his soft hair. Jackson gives a tiny whimper, and Amon quickly hands him back to Gabriel. Gabriel walks around the room patting and rubbing his back until he settles down again.

Amon catches me up on what he and Gabriel have been up to since I left. He tells me that he will be returning home tomorrow as he has to report back to work. He says he is enjoying dividing his time between the country and the city. He says he has the best of both worlds. I agree with him that he does.

Amon stays for about an hour. I have never heard him talk so much and have enjoyed the visit. He stands and tells us it is time for him to go. He asks what time he should pick Gabriel up in the morning, as he moves toward the door. I stammer slightly as I look from him to Gabriel.

"You don't have to stay tonight. We will be fine," I say.

Gabriel looks hurt, and I continue, "I really appreciated your help last night, but I would feel bad if we kept you up all night again." He still looks defeated, so I just keep talking, this time addressing Amon. "Can you pick him up around six thirty again?"

"I'll be here," Amon answers and turns and winks at Gabriel. Somehow, I think I have been played. Amon quickly leaves before I can confront the two scheming rascals.

Gabriel's triumphant look quickly turns to guilt. "I didn't mean to pressure you into letting me stay. I just wanted to spend more time with Jackson. I can call Amon back to get me if you would like."

Now I'm the one who feels guilty. "No, I want you to stay and spend as much time with Jackson as you like. I just don't want to impose on you so that I can get extra rest."

"Jackson is not an imposition, Sarah. He is my son."

"I didn't mean to imply that he is. I meant me." I sigh. "I know that you are still angry with me about keeping him from you all these months. I don't want to fight with you. I know we need to talk about all of this, but I just can't do it today or here."

Gabriel agrees and moves to sit with Jackson for a while. I think it is going to be a long evening.

Surprisingly, Gabriel doesn't seem to be angry with me. He is content to hold Jackson and help attend to his needs.

We slip into a comfortable routine of taking turns with Jackson. As the morning dawns and Gabriel prepares to leave, I assure him this would be the last time he would have to hide from my family. I inform him I am going to tell Tyler and Lisa today that he is here. He asks if he should stay and help explain. I tell him that I would prefer to introduce him once the shock wears off. He says that his offer stands if I should change my mind.

Lisa arrives around ten o'clock and helps me pack up to leave the hospital today. I'm ready to be back at my house, but dread the conversation that I have to have today. Tyler is meeting us at the house later to let the kids meet their new cousin. I will tell them both about Gabriel then.

Our ride home is uneventful, and I debate telling Lisa first, but lose my nerve and decide I only want to have this conversation once. I know that she will be the more reasonable out of the two, so I hope that she and the kids will be a sort of buffer when I break the news. I don't think the past few months have changed Tyler's opinion of Gabriel, and I know he is going to be angry.

We arrive home, and I start to unpack, but Lisa sends me to rest and starts a load of laundry for me. I'm keyed up and end up walking around the house with Jackson. I wonder what Gabriel is doing today, so I send him a text to let him know we are home and waiting on Tyler and the kids to arrive. He offers to come be with me when I tell them, but I decline and tell him I'll call him after it is done.

Tyler, Danny, and Lizzie arrive around one o'clock, and the kids are so excited that Lisa has to remind them to not be loud around the baby. She sits them on the sofa, and they take turns holding him and getting to know their new cousin. Tyler brings in brisket and sides and sets them in the kitchen. After Danny and Lizzie have finished taking turns, Uncle Ty swoops in and takes Jackson from them. He says he will be on baby duty while we fix our plates. He and Jackson settle into the recliner and find sports to watch on the TV. Lizzie is a mother hen and hovers near by in case Jackson needs her help.

After lunch, I feed Jackson and get him settled in his crib in his room. I tell Ty and Lisa that I would like to speak to them alone. Ty turns on cartoons in my room for the kids so that we can talk.

Ty and Lisa sit on the sofa, and I perch on the edge of the recliner facing them. I steel myself and send up a quick prayer that this goes well.

"I wanted to talk to you both about something important, and I need you to promise me you will hear me out before you ask questions." The both agree, and Tyler leans forward and rests his elbows on his knees.

I take the plunge and tell them, "Gabriel is here."

They are both stunned into silence for a moment before Tyler speaks. His face goes from shock to red in just a few seconds. I start to speak, but he cuts me off.

"You called him?" he asks, but it is more of an accusation.

"No, he just showed up."

"When?" he demands. Lisa places her hand on his knee trying to calm him, but it doesn't help. I can see how mad he is. He has always seen Gabriel as the bad guy, and it will probably take a miracle for him to see him any differently.

"Two days ago," I answer.

"The day Jackson was born?" he asks. I nod my answer. "Don't you think his timing is a little suspicious?" he asks, as he rises from the sofa and begins pacing in the room.

I don't get a chance to answer because Lisa launches into her questions.

"Does he know about Jackson?" she asks, and I tell her he does. She follows up with asking if he has seen Jackson, and I indicate that he has, in the hospital.

Tyler stops pacing and faces me when she asked her questions. "Are you crazy, Sarah? How can you let him back in your life and Jackson's after everything that happened to you over there?"

"He is Jackson's father." I try to answer calmly, but my defenses are up. "And I am not crazy. Gabriel isn't the one who hurt me. As a matter of fact, I'm the one who hurt him."

"So he has you believing that you did this?" he counters.

"He doesn't have me believing anything. I'm the one who left him. I panicked and left. I didn't trust him or anybody else at the time," I say.

"But you trust him now? So I guess you are just going to take him back and move halfway across the world again where he can separate you from your family."

"Yes, I do trust him and no, I am not going anywhere. This is my home now and Jackson's. I don't know how Gabriel fits into all of this yet, but I do know that Jackson needs him in his life. You are going to have to trust that I am doing what is best for Jackson and for me."

Tyler shakes his head and scoffs. "That's just it. When it comes to him, I don't trust your decisions. You don't think straight when it comes to that man. And I still think his timing is suspicious. Why now? It's been how many months, five, six, and he just happens to show up the day your son is born. I'm not buying it, Sarah."

I'm angry now, so I stand as I speak. "I didn't tell you about Gabriel for you to stand here and judge me. I just wanted you to know the truth. Gabriel is here, and he is going to be a part of Jackson's life whether you like it or not. I am capable of making my own decisions, and you can either accept them or not."

Tyler starts to speak, but I tell him I'm not finished. "If you are going to keep insulting me, then this conversation is over." I need him to understand that I am serious, so I hold his stare for a minute before I continue.

"Gabriel came to Texas to look for me. He admits his initial goal was to get me back and have me move back with him." I see Tyler start to comment, so I cut him off. "He moved out of his father's house when he found out what he did to all of us. He moved to Cairo and got a new job, too. So, no, he wouldn't have expected me to go back to that house.

"As for the timing, I can't even begin to explain how he showed up when he did. He actually showed up a few days before to talk to me but was blindsided when he saw that I was pregnant. It took him a few days before he could even approach me and unfortunately, I had already gone into labor by then.

"All I can say about the timing is that maybe it was God's timing," I tell them.

Lisa ventures another question before Tyler can say anything else. "How long is Gabriel here for?"

"I'm not really sure. We haven't had a lot of time to talk, and he had a lot to digest with finding out about Jackson. I'm not going to shut him out of his son's life. He is a good man, and he deserves a chance to get to know his son."

"After we talk, I really would like for you to meet him. But I need you to promise, Ty, to be civil and give him a chance. He is not a bad guy, and I think you will like him if you will just give him a chance."

"Do you really think I want to meet the man who forced my sister into marrying him and then let his father torment her?" Tyler all but yells at me.

"I'm not going to go through this with you again. Nobody forced me to do anything. I made my own choices, and you are going to have to respect them if you want to be in my life. I'm done arguing about this. All I'm asking is that you just consider giving Gabriel a chance. Pray about it, Ty."

"I very much want to meet the man who saved your life," Lisa says, as she moves to hug me. "I support you and Jackson. So, for your sake, I will give him a chance." I hug her back and thank her for her support.

"I don't know how you can expect me to accept this man back into your life," Tyler says.

"I'm not asking you to make him your new best friend," I counter. "Just give him a chance."

"I'm not making any promises," Tyler says and then leaves the room to retrieve his children.

"Give it some time, Sarah. He was just caught off guard. I think we all were. He loves you and just wants what is best for you and Jackson. I'll talk to him, but he will need some time to come to terms with all of this."

I release the breath I have been holding and feel totally exhausted. This went about how I imagined.

Lisa offers to help with the kitchen, but I assure her I can handle it today. I thank her again for lunch and tell her I'll talk to her tomorrow. Tyler lets the kids give me a quick goodbye before he rushes them to the car.

I made quick work of the kitchen and settled onto the sofa to take a quick nap, but Jackson decided he was hungry again. After I got him back to sleep, I took a long nap before calling Gabriel.

It's late in the evening when I awaken, and I see that I have a missed call and text from Gabriel. He wants to know how everything went and if I'm all right. I call Gabriel and reassure him I am fine. I just needed to rest for a while. He asks about Jackson, and I tell him he can come over if he wants. I know it's late, but I really want to see him again. Of course, he wants to come, so I sit rocking Jackson as I wait for him to arrive.

Gabriel arrives, and I welcome him into the living room. Gabriel is studying my house taking everything in. I ask him if he would like the grand tour, and he says he would love to see the rest of my house. The tour doesn't take long as my house consists of a living room, kitchen, two bedrooms, and one bathroom. There is a small screened-in porch on the back that I will enjoy more when the weather cools off, and I have some fans installed.

Gabriel compliments my house and asks how I like living alone. "It took some getting used to all the quiet. It's the first time I've ever lived totally alone. But overall, I enjoy the peace and quiet, and it gave me a lot of time to think and work through some things."

I ask about his apartment with Amon. He tells me where it is located and that he too had to get used to not having so many people around. He says he misses Mariam's cooking the most. He says he is not very good at cooking, and Amon works in the evenings, so he eats out a lot.

I ask how Mariam and his sisters are. He tells me they are doing well but miss all of us very much. He tells me that Jasmina took it pretty hard when I left. She took it especially hard after he moved out. He tells me they come visit him from time to time.

I ask him if he told them about Jackson yet. He shakes his head. He says he really wants to but needs to work some things out first. I nod my understanding.

I hand Jackson to Gabriel as we return to the living room. I aim him to the rocker recliner, and I stretch out on the sofa. It's been a long day, and I am tired, but I have so many questions I want to ask. I start asking him what his plans are, but he tells me that can wait for another day.

"I know you are tired, and I would rather have this discussion when you are rested," Gabriel tells me.

"Why aren't you tired?" I ask. "You slept less than me last night."

He smiles and says, "That's true, but I was able to sleep for about four hours when I got back to the hotel. And I didn't just give birth either. Why don't you go get ready for bed, and I will watch this little guy for you."

"Gabriel, I didn't invite you over to watch Jackson all night so I could sleep."

"Why did you invite me over, Sarah?"

I hesitate, but then tell myself "honesty," so I answer truthfully, "Because I missed you." My pulse is racing, and my heart is in my throat as I wait for his reaction.

He continues to rock Jackson but never takes his eyes off me. After several beats, he tells me, "I missed you, too. I'm not going anywhere tonight. Go get ready for bed, and I'll bring Jackson to you to feed when you are ready. That way, you both can sleep a few hours."

I can't swallow past the lump in my throat, so I get up and head for my room.

I decide a nice long, hot shower is needed and take advantage of having Gabriel here. When I'm done, I head to the kitchen for some over-the-counter pain pills and something to drink. Gabriel comes in and asks if he can help. I tell him I am just boiling some water for some chamomile tea and taking something for the soreness. He hands Jackson to me and tells me he'll bring the tea when it's ready. He counts out two pills and pours me a glass of water. I take the pills and head back to my room to get comfortable so that I can feed Jackson.

Gabriel pauses in the doorway holding my tea. I tell him he can come in, but he stays where he is another second. "Gabriel, you can come in," I say again.

"I know, I was just watching you hold and feed our son." He steps into the room now and moves toward the bed. "I don't mean to stare, it's just such a beautiful and amazing sight, and I still can't believe we have a son."

"He is pretty amazing, isn't he? I knew I loved him from the moment I knew about him, but I didn't grasp how intense that love would be until they placed him in my arms. I'm so thankful for this beautiful blessing."

"I know what you mean. I was pretty angry with you when I found out about the pregnancy, but one look at him at the hospital, and, well, I wasn't quite so angry anymore."

"Gabriel, I really am sorry that I hurt you. I—"

"Thank you, Sarah. We can talk tomorrow morning." Gabriel sets my tea down and sits on the end of the bed.

I'm half asleep when I finish feeding Jackson. Gabriel helps me change his diaper and walks around the room with him to settle him back to sleep. I ask him to place him in his bassinet in my room so that I can hear him when he is ready to feed again. He looks hurt that I want him to put him down, but I explain that he needs to learn to sleep in his crib at night. I reassure him that he can hold him as much as he wants when he is awake.

STRONG AND COURAGEOUS

When Jackson is fully asleep, Gabriel reluctantly lays him down in the bassinet. I tell him that there are blankets and a pillow in the hall closet. He tells me to call if I need anything. He turns off my lamp and says good night and makes his way back to the living room.

It was a very long night as Jackson only slept for three hours before he decided to cluster feed for the next three hours or so. Gabriel was convinced something was wrong, but I reassured him that this is normal in the beginning. I told him that I read all about it in the breastfeeding book I bought a couple of months ago. I tried to get him to go back to sleep, but he insisted that as long as I was up, he was up. He assigned himself diaper duty between feedings and would walk Jackson so that I could try to catnap.

I awaken around seven thirty with my stomach cramping and needing the bathroom. I'm not really ready to get up, but my stomach wins the battle. I could use some more over-the-counter pain reliever, too.

Gabriel is asleep on the sofa, so I do my best not to disturb him as I fix coffee and something to eat. I don't want to take my medicine on an empty stomach. As I am pouring myself a cup of coffee, Gabriel's sleep-deprived, raspy good morning startles me, and I jump.

"I didn't mean to startle you," Gabriel says.

"I thought you were still sleeping. I didn't mean to wake you, but I need something to eat and…"—I rattle the pill bottle and pour two out—"and thought coffee might be appropriate after no sleep last night."

Gabriel moves to the fridge to retrieve the creamer, and I hand him a mug. "I can run out and get you something to eat if you'd like. My culinary skills are a little lacking."

"Don't bother," I say, sipping coffee. "I was thinking about making some oatmeal and having a banana. I have eggs, too, if you want me to fix you some."

"You just gave birth. You will not be standing at the stove fixing me breakfast. Coffee is fine for now. Point me in the direction of the oatmeal, and I will muddle through." I point to the pantry and tell him where to find the instant oatmeal, brown sugar, and cinnamon.

I tell him he can just pop it in the microwave once he has everything measured out in the bowl.

Just as the microwave beeps, I hear keys in the front door and remember that Lauren is coming over to help today. I guess she didn't want to bother me in case I was sleeping, so she used her key. I didn't get a chance to warn her last night, so this should be interesting.

I move into the living room to greet her. She smiles when she sees me. "Good, you're up. I brought cinnamon rolls." She is trying to balance a pastry box, her purse, and coffee as she pulls her key free of the door. I move to take the box from her but don't move into the kitchen yet.

"Lauren, I hope you brought more than two cinnamon rolls, I have company this morning." I'm trying to keep it light as I break the news that Gabriel is here.

I see the intrigued look on her face wondering who could be visiting so early in the morning. She verbalizes those thoughts. "I was wondering whose car was in the driveway."

"I will tell you whose car it is, but I need you to not freak out."

"Why would I freak out?" she asks.

"Because Gabriel is here."

She doesn't say anything. I see her blanch, and I think her eyes might bug out of her head. She recovers quickly and asks if I invited him here. "To my house, yes. To Texas, no. He showed up the day Jackson was born and is staying in town for a while."

"Is he staying here with you?" She is now looking at the blanket and pillow on the sofa.

"He stayed last night to help with Jackson, but he has a hotel room, too."

"You could have called me to help you last night." I can't tell if she is hurt or angry.

"I knew you would be here today, and I thought I could handle nighttime by myself. It was late when he got here, and he insisted on taking the night shift so that I could rest. Unfortunately, Jackson had other plans last night and no one slept much."

"Is he okay?"

"Yes, Jackson is fine. He just wanted to feed all night. I plan on waking him soon so that maybe we won't have a repeat tonight."

"Where is Gabriel now?"

She is much calmer than I expected. "In the kitchen having coffee. Let's go join him. These cinnamon rolls smell amazing!"

Gabriel rises from his chair as we enter the kitchen and moves to greet Lauren. "Hello, Lauren. It's nice to see you again."

Lauren shakes his hand but only replies with, "Gabriel." Her reply is bordering on rude, but at least she shakes his hand. I'm sure she is a little in shock from seeing him standing in my kitchen.

I open the box to see there are six cinnamon rolls, so I pull out three plates. Gabriel moves to take the plates and box from me and tells me to sit. He also motions Lauren to a chair as well. He places a cinnamon roll in front of each of us and refills his coffee before he joins us at the table.

Lauren breaks the silence first as I dig into my cinnamon roll. "So, Gabriel, how long are you in town?" I haven't even gotten a chance to ask him, so I am curious about his answer as well.

"I originally planned to stay about six days," my stomach drops. That means he will be leaving in a couple of days. It's not enough time to figure all of this out. "But finding out about Jackson has changed my travel plans."

"So you didn't know about Jackson, and you just happened to show up the day he was born." Lauren's skepticism makes her direct and to the point. She sounds like Tyler right now. I hope she doesn't blow up like he did.

Gabriel is patient as he answers. "Actually, I came a couple days before he was born. I wanted to talk to Sarah, but my plans took an unexpected turn when I saw a very pregnant Sarah. It took me a couple days to collect myself enough to approach her. It just happened to be the same day Jackson was born."

"So what was your plan? Did you come here to try to trick her into going back home with you?" Now she is just being rude, and I've heard enough.

"Lauren, that's enough. Gabriel never tricked me into anything and what I choose to do is my business, not anyone else's." My body language and eyes are trying hard to send her a warning that she is treading on thin ice here.

"Are you really considering going back with him?" Her voice has an edge and raises an octave with her questions or assumption, whatever it is.

"I'm not going anywhere. This is my home. I've already told Tyler as much. And no, he hasn't tried to get me to leave. In fact, we haven't had much time to discuss anything." I take a deep breath to calm myself. "Look, we have a lot to figure out, and right now, we are just trying to survive being new parents who didn't get a lot of sleep last night. Now that you are here, maybe we can both get a good nap. We can talk when we can keep our eyes open."

Lauren is quiet and picks at her cinnamon roll. "I'm sorry I was rude. I just don't want to see you get hurt again."

I start to answer that neither do I, but Gabriel beats me to it. "I don't want that either. I'm not the enemy, Lauren. I care very much for Sarah and Jackson. I regret that she was hurt before, and I will do my best not to cause her any more pain. Truce?"

"Truce, for now. But if you—"

Gabriel doesn't let her finish her statement. "I won't."

We eat our cinnamon rolls and finish our coffee. Lauren cleans up the kitchen, and Gabriel goes to wake up little man so that I can feed him. He definitely has his days and nights mixed up.

I excuse myself and head for the bathroom. My bleeding feels a little heavy, and I need to get cleaned up before I feed Jackson. I'm a little shocked to see that my bleeding is heavier than I've seen it. The nurse said that my bleeding might be heavy for a few days and showed me how to massage my uterus to help it contract, so I do this now. I'm having trouble finding it, and the bleeding seems to be getting heavier. I rub harder, but it's not having any effect. As a nurse, I know that this is not normal and call for Lauren.

She taps on the door before she enters. "You need something?" she asks and then she spots the blood, and fear darts across her face. "Sarah, that's a lot of bleeding. Is that normal?"

"No. That's why I called you. Can you bring me my phone? I want to call my doctor. They showed me how to massage my uterus, but it's not slowing down." She doesn't move, so I prompt her. "It's on my bedside table." With that, she leaves to get my phone. I hear her tell Gabriel that I am bleeding a lot, and he appears in the doorway behind Lauren when she returns with my phone.

He is holding Jackson and worry creases his forehead. "Are you all right?"

"I'm bleeding a little heavy, and I want to call my doctor to see if there is anything I can do. You and Jackson can wait for me in the living room. I'm sure it will be fine." But he doesn't move. He and Lauren stay where they are while I dial the number. As the phone rings, the blood continues to flow.

I get my doctor's nurse and explain the situation, and she suggests that I go to the emergency room to get checked out. She says she will notify my doctor. We hang up, and I relay the conversation to Gabriel and Lauren.

Lauren asks if I need help cleaning up, and I tell her I think I can handle it. She turns to leave, but Gabriel hands Jackson to her. I'll take her to the hospital if you will stay here with Jackson. She starts to argue, but he insists, noting that I am still his wife and that he wants to go. I don't have time to argue with them. I ask Lauren to call Lisa and see if she will pick up some formula for Jackson and bring it here as I'm not sure how long I will be gone. Lauren nods and leaves the bathroom with Jackson.

I do my best to clean up, but it's in vain as the bleeding continues. I'm starting to worry about the volume of blood that is coming out of me. I know that this is serious. I do the best I can and move to stand. I sway slightly, but Gabriel is there to steady me. I wash up and ask him to grab an extra towel. I'm not sure how long this pad will last.

I ask him to retrieve my purse and tell him I will meet him in the living room. I'm a little lightheaded, so I use the walls and furniture to steady myself. Lauren is just hanging up with Lisa and tells me that Lisa will run by the store and come help with Jackson. "Tyler will meet you and Gabriel at the emergency room."

I don't know that I can deal with Tyler's drama right now, so I ask her to call him back and tell him I'll call when I know something.

Gabriel is moving toward me now with my purse in hand. I reach to take it from him and the room spins, and I tilt sideways. My vision is starting to tunnel, and I know I'm about to pass out. The last thing I feel are his arms coming around me before everything goes black.

CHAPTER 25

Gabriel

I park my rental car in the driveway in front of the emergency room. Sarah has been in and out of consciousness on the ten-minute drive here. She is so pale, and her pajama bottoms are soaked in blood. I was worried she would bleed out before I could get her here. But we made it, and she opens her eyes briefly when I talk to her. I run around the car calling for help.

I open the door and lift her out of her seat and am met at the door by a woman with a wheelchair. I'm reluctant to set her down, but logic kicks in, and I place her in the chair. They take her directly back, and a team of doctors and nurses begins examining her. They ask me questions. Some I can answer, some I just don't know, but I tell them she delivered a baby two days ago. They try to send me back to registration, but I refuse to go. I'm not leaving her side until I know she is going to be all right.

The doctor in charge tells the nurse to call the OR and to get Sarah's obstetrician on the phone stat. They have started an IV and are giving Sarah medications, trying to get the bleeding under control. I hear the doctor order two units of blood stat. I stand there holding her hand, too paralyzed by fear to say anything or ask questions.

Eventually, a nurse touches my arm and asks if I am Sarah's husband. I nod yes, and she tells me they need me to sign some papers so that they can take Sarah to surgery. I nod, and she places a clipboard in my hands. The doctor is talking, but I don't comprehend any of what he is saying. I just sign everywhere she points and hand her back the clipboard. I reach for Sarah's hand again, but they are already wheeling her out of the room. I can't force my feet to move. I just stand there and watch as they wheel her down the hall.

Another nurse gently guides me to the elevator and takes me to the surgery waiting area. She tells me they will give me updates as soon as they know anything. She hands me Sarah's purse and reaches into her pocket and pulls out the car keys. "The security guard parked it in visitor parking for you." I had forgotten that I abandoned it in the driveway.

I lower myself into a chair and place my head in my hands. I can't get the image of all that blood out of my head. I've never seen so much blood. How did everything go so badly, so quickly? Sarah was fine minutes before. "Oh, God. Please don't let her die. I'll do anything, just don't take her from me." I don't know if I am praying or pleading, but right now, I would do anything to save her. I just found her again, and I'm afraid that I might lose her.

I vaguely hear someone say her husband is right there in the gray shirt; the man with his head in his hands and realize they are referring to me. I look up to see a man standing there watching me with hatred in his eyes. I realize this must be Tyler.

He comes to stand in front of me, and we just stare at each other for a minute. I can't think clearly enough to say anything at the moment. He studies me for a minute and then speaks. "Any word on how Sarah is?"

I can only shake my head. I realize that I am crying and wipe my eyes with the back of my hand. Tyler sits in the seat next to me and is silent while I try to compose myself. I don't really care that I am crying, I just need to be able to speak and answer him, so I take several deep breaths.

When I'm sure my voice won't crack, I tell him, "She was fine this morning. We all had breakfast, and I went to get Jackson so that she could feed him. Sarah went to the bathroom, and the next thing I know she is calling for Lauren and…" I have to stop again. I keep picturing all the blood. I close my eyes trying to clear the image, but it only makes it worse. "I've never seen so much blood," is all I can tell him. Tyler doesn't say anything, just nods his head and leans back in his seat.

Forty-five minutes later, a nurse comes out to give us a report. She tells us that Sarah lost a lot of blood, but she is stable now. She tells us that the doctor will be out in about thirty minutes and will explain everything then. I thank her and drop back into my seat. I'm relieved, but I won't feel better until I see her for myself.

I place my head in my hands again and don't really realize I've spoken out loud until Tyler asks, "Are you a believer?"

My head snaps up to look at him. "What?" I'm confused by his question.

"I heard you thanking God for sparing Sarah. Are you a believer?"

"I guess I believe in God," I say, not quite sure how to answer this question.

"You guess?" Tyler gives me a sideways glance. "If you are not sure, then why were you praying?"

I sigh and think about it for a minute before I answer. "I once saw Sarah do it when she had an important decision to make, and I observed how much comfort it gave her. She was able to find direction and had peace through it." Tyler nods, so I continue. "Recently, I had some pretty big decisions to make and needed some direction, so I tried it and found that I had some peace afterward. I can't really explain it, but I just sort of knew what I had to do after that."

"And what about today?" Tyler prompts.

"Today… I didn't know what else to do. Everything was out of my control, so I just prayed that God would save her. I need her, and Jackson needs her."

Tyler doesn't answer for a long time, but when he does, he gets right to the heart of things. "You love my sister very much, don't you?"

"Yes." I heave a big sigh and lean back in my chair, too. "I have been miserable without her, and now that I've found her, I don't want to lose her again." I take a deep breath and ask, "Do you think she will be all right?"

"The nurse said she was stable. Hopefully, the worst is past," Tyler replies.

We don't speak anymore. We just sit silently waiting on the doctor. When he arrives, he assures us that Sarah is going to be fine. He informs us that she retained some placental fragments that caused her to hemorrhage. "We cleaned them out and were able to get the bleeding under control. We gave her two units of blood in the OR, and a third is infusing now. I'm going to keep her in the ICU tonight as a precaution. If her lab work looks good in the morning, we'll move her to a private room. With any luck, she should be able to go home in a couple of days."

I thank the doctor, and Tyler and I shake his hand. He tells us Sarah is in recovery and that we can see her when they get her settled in the ICU.

Tyler walks across the room to call Lisa and Lauren and update them on Sarah. I inquire about Jackson when he returns. He tells me he is being sufficiently spoiled by his two favorite aunts. I tell him I need to call a friend and pull my phone out of my pocket. I dial Amon's number. I tell him about Sarah and the surgery and let him know I will be staying at the hospital. I ask him for a clean set of clothes, and he agrees to bring them and some lunch as soon as he can.

I walk across the room and fix myself a coffee and bring one to Tyler as well. I don't know what he takes in his, so I bring sugar and creamer, too. He thanks me as I hand him the cup.

He asks who Amon is as I sip my coffee. I explain that he is my oldest friend and more like a brother to me. I tell him that we work together and that he is very fond of Sarah as well. We exchange a few more pleasantries and then sit quietly sipping our coffee.

It seems that Tyler and I have come to some kind of an understanding for now, and I am thankful.

Tyler and I wait for almost an hour before a nurse comes to escort us to ICU. Sarah's color is a little improved, but she is hooked up to several IVs and monitors. She appears to be sleeping, so I quietly walk up to her bedside and reach for her hand. She squeezes mine and turns to look at me with sleepy eyes.

"How do you feel?" I ask.

"Drugged," she replies. She looks past me and notices Tyler standing just inside the doorway. "I see you two have finally met, and you're both still standing. I must have been worse off than I thought." I flinch at her attempt at humor. I don't know that she knows how close we came to losing her.

Tyler steps up to the bed before answering. "And it would seem you have gone to extreme measures to get us together. You could have just invited me over for coffee. Your coffee has to be better than what they serve here." He jokes.

Sarah smiles and closes her eyes. I pull a chair up closer to her bed so that I can resume holding her hand. I need to feel her warmth and am comforted that she lets me. I know the nurse said fifteen minutes, but I've decided I'm not leaving. Tyler sits on the other side of the bed.

Sarah opens her eyes again and asks how Jackson is. Tyler reassures her that he is fine and in good hands. He encourages her to rest so she can get home quickly. Sarah nods and closes her eyes again.

As promised, the nurse returns in fifteen minutes and tells us that our time is up. I inform her that I am staying. She tells me that Sarah needs her rest, and I counter that I don't plan on bothering her. She starts to protest, but Tyler comes to my defense.

"Gabriel is Sarah's husband, and I'm sure she would rest better with him here." The nurse concedes and moves to check Sarah's vital signs. I nod my thanks to Tyler, and he tells me to call if I need anything. I assure him I will keep him informed if anything changes.

After everyone leaves the room, I finally relax and am overcome with thankfulness that Sarah is all right. I feel sick even thinking about what I would have done if I had lost her. I can't imagine my life without her. I lean forward and press her hand to my lips and squeeze my eyes shut and thank God again for sparing her. I'm thinking about my conversation with Tyler. I guess I do believe. I find comfort in that thought. It gives me hope that everything is going to be all right.

Sarah startles me out of my thoughts. "What are you concentrating so intently on?"

I kiss her hand again and open my eyes. "You. I was thinking how thankful I am for you. And I was thinking about a conversation I had with your brother earlier. About how much you have changed my life for the better and that I don't want to live life without you in it."

Sarah responds, "I'm fine, Gabriel. I'm not going anywhere." I know she is probably referring to her current situation, but a big part of me is hoping she is referring to us. The medications have her drowsy, and she drifts off to sleep again.

"Neither am I," I tell her.

The next two days are fairly uneventful as Sarah has no further episodes of heavy bleeding, so they discharge her home. As we drive back to Sarah's, I tell her my return flight is scheduled for tomorrow morning.

"Do you want to go back to Egypt?" she tentatively asks.

I pull over into a parking lot so that we can talk. "I know we haven't had a chance to really talk yet, but I need to know one thing before I can answer your question. Do you want me in your life, Sarah? Not just for Jackson's sake but for yours, too."

Sarah only hesitates for a moment before answering, "Yes, I want you in my life, Gabriel, but I can't go back to Egypt. Maybe one day for a visit but not to live there."

"Then I will cancel my flight until we can figure this out. And to answer your question, I only want to go back to Egypt if you and Jackson go with me."

Introductions are made as we arrive back at Sarah's. It is my first time meeting Lisa, and she tells me she is glad to finally put a face to the man who saved Sarah's life. She thanks me with a hug and gathers her things to head home. She promises to check in on Sarah in the morning. Lauren follows Lisa out and leaves the three of us alone.

CHAPTER 26

Sarah

It's been a crazy and scary few days, and I am relieved to be home. I know we have a lot to talk about, but I really could use a shower and maybe a nap first. I tell Gabriel I would like to take a quick shower while Jackson is sleeping. He tells me not to rush that he will look in on Jackson while I bathe.

I finish my shower and slip into some clean pajamas. I hear Gabriel talking as I enter the living room. I find him on his cell phone, and he motions that he will only be a minute. I suspect he is talking to Amon, and he confirms this after he hangs up.

"That was Amon. I called him to let him know that I would be staying here a little longer, and I asked him to do a few things for me when he gets home."

Gabriel looks tired. I know he has not gotten much sleep over the past few days. "Why don't you go back to the hotel tonight and get some rest. Jackson and I will be fine."

"I'll worry about you if I go back to the hotel. I can sleep on your sofa again if that's all right with you. That way if you need anything, I'm just one room away."

"Then I want you to sleep tonight, and I will get up with Jackson," I tell him. He only nods, and I don't believe he will comply.

I get up and head to the kitchen to get a snack and something to drink. Gabriel asks where I am going and I reply, "The kitchen." He moves to head me off and says that he can get whatever I need.

"I need to move around, and I'm tired of resting. I'll let you know if I need anything."

As I am fixing myself a snack, I'm experiencing a mix of emotions. I am happy to have Gabriel here, but at the same time, I don't know where we stand with each other or how long he will be here. I know that I hurt him, and I don't expect him to just forgive me, quit his job, and move halfway around the world. I know we will have to at least work out some sort of visitation schedule. I think about Mariam and the girls and know that they will be very excited about Jackson. I wonder if Gabriel has told them yet.

I return to the living room and ask, "Have you told Mariam and your sisters about Jackson?"

"Not yet. I still haven't found the right time. I'm sure Mariam will demand some answers. She tried to call a few days ago, and when I didn't answer, she called Amon. He told her that I was out of town on business and would call her when I got back."

I don't press the issue for now. He will call them when he is ready.

It's two in the morning, and I sit in my bed feeding Jackson. I hold his little hand and stroke his silky, smooth skin and think about how amazing he is. I look up to see Gabriel standing just outside the door watching us.

"Why are you up? I thought you were going to get some sleep tonight," I say.

"I heard him cry and tried to go back to sleep, but I felt like I was missing out, and I don't want to miss out on anything else." He says it as a statement of fact and not with any sort of accusation in his voice, but I feel guilty just the same.

"You can come in." I pat the other side of the bed for him to sit down. He's right, I have deprived him of so much already, and he should get to be included as much as he wants.

"I'm sorry I didn't tell you I was pregnant. It was selfish of me to keep this from you." I decide there will not be a perfect time to talk, so now is as good as any other time.

"When I discovered what Ahmad and Aahron were doing, I panicked and was gripped with fear for my…our baby. I let that fear drive me, and it drove me halfway around the world. I should have told you and trusted you. I was wrong, and I'm truly sorry for the pain I've caused you. I don't expect you to forgive me, but I do want you to be a part of Jackson's life. I won't keep him from you ever again."

"I won't lie and tell you I wasn't angry, because I was. I wanted you to hurt like I was hurting. I went to that hospital with every intention of demanding answers and giving you a piece of my mind. But when I walked into that room and saw you, I knew I couldn't hurt you. I still love you, Sarah, in spite of everything." He pauses, and I don't know what to say.

"I am still hurt, but I'm not mad anymore. I let that go when I thought you were going to die. I prayed and asked God to save you. I couldn't imagine my life without you in it, and he needs you, too." He brushes his hand across Jackson's back."

"So where does that leave us? Where do we go from here?" I am relieved that he is not angry at me, but we still have a long way to go.

"I'm going to tell you just like I did on our honeymoon. The ball is in your court. I know what I want, and I think I've made my feelings pretty clear. The only thing I am unsure about is how you feel."

He is right, of course, I have never told him exactly how I feel. I gave him a yes to his question at the hospital, but I have never just come out and told him my feelings for him. "I don't think it is fair that I should be the one to make this decision. I'm the one who hurt you and left. Why should I be the one who makes this decision now?"

"Because you did leave. You have to decide what you want. I can't make this decision for you." Gabriel leans back against the bed.

I know what I want, but I need one more question answered before I make my decision. "Can I ask you a question first?" He indicates that I can. "When did you start praying?"

"Not long after my accident and Aahron's confession. I was confused and needed some guidance when I remembered that day on our honeymoon. I remembered you were troubled and asked to find a church. I can still see you sitting in that pew and praying. You had such a peace when you were done, and then, well, you know the rest." Gabriel folds his hands in his lap as he continues. "I needed that same kind of peace, so I found that same church and went inside."

"Did you find what you were looking for?" I ask.

"Yes, and so much more." I can tell he wants to say more as he sits there collecting his thoughts, so I wait.

"When you were bleeding the other day, I was scared and thinking I might lose you. I prayed, and God showed me that forgiving you was more important than holding on to my anger. That's when I completely forgave you. He also used that situation to help me start building a relationship with your brother. We aren't quite friends, but I don't think he hates me anymore." I smile at him, relieved that he and Ty have come to some kind of understanding.

Gabriel looks at me as he finishes, "I don't understand exactly how, but I do know that prayer changes your perspective."

"Yes, Gabriel, it does." I take a steadying breath. "I love you, Gabriel. I have for a long time, and I regret not telling you sooner. I want to be a part of your life, and I'll go wherever I have to, to do that."

I lean toward Gabriel, and he meets me halfway, and we kiss until Jackson protests that we are squishing him. We shift apart, and Gabriel runs his hand through my hair as he moves it behind my ear.

"We don't have to decide that right now. We have time. But there is something I would like to do right now." He flashes me a grin.

"Now?" I say, "It's two thirty in the morning."

He nods his head and pulls out his phone. "Let's call Mariam and my sisters. I want to tell them about Jackson. It's nine thirty in the morning there and the weekend. They should all be home."

Gabriel decides to video chat with them so that they can see Jackson. I run my hands through my hair and smooth it down the best I can.

I tell Gabriel to show only his face first as he is dialing her number. He agrees. After a few rings, Mariam comes into focus. It is clear that she is happy to hear from him.

"Are you back from your trip?" Before he can answer, she asks, "Where did you go?"

He jokes with her and tells her to slow down and let him answer. He tells her to go get the girls before he answers any questions. She starts to worry, and he just tells her he has good news and wants them all there for it. Mariam calls the girls into the kitchen with her. They each voice their greetings to Gabriel. He tells Mariam, "To answer your first question, no I am not back yet. As to where I am, I will let you see for yourself." Gabriel leans into me and puts my face in the frame with his.

Mariam gives a shout when she sees me. "Does this mean what I think it means?" she asks.

I answer this time. "Yes, it does." She starts to scold me for leaving, but Gabriel cuts her off. "We had another reason for calling." With that, I lift Jackson into the frame, and they are stunned into silence. Jasmina gives an excited cry and proudly says, "I'm an aunt!"

Gabriel and I both laugh. Mariam is struggling to make a make a coherent sentence.

"Gabriel? Sarah? Is that—" It's one of the few times I've seen her at a loss for words. She just stares at the screen trying to come to terms with what she is seeing.

Gabriel confirms what she is asking. "Yes, Mariam. We want you to meet our son, Jackson Gabriel."

"A boy." Mariam starts to cry, but I think they are tears of joy. She congratulates Gabriel on his son. Me, I get a stern talking to for running away and not telling anyone about the baby. I remind her of why I ran, but she is not quite ready to accept my reasoning or fully forgive me. She tells me we could have worked something out. Gabriel thankfully redirects the conversation and asks his sisters what they think of their nephew. They are both excited and want to know when we are bringing him home. Gabriel tells them he is too little to travel right now, but that we will bring him for a visit as soon as we can.

Mariam is full of questions, and we tell them about the past few days. We also tell them that we don't have all the details worked out, but that we will call often so that they can see Jackson. Gabriel tells her that I need my rest and that he will call again tomorrow evening.

I get up and place Jackson in his crib and climb back into bed next to Gabriel. He pulls me in for another kiss, this time with nothing between us. I'm exhilarated and overjoyed to have him back where he belongs. We settle into the bed, and Gabriel pulls me into his arms where I fall asleep thanking God for answered prayers.

ABOUT THE AUTHOR

Celeste Walsh is a wife and mother of three grown men and a beautiful daughter-in-law. She works as a nurse and enjoys reading, playing tennis, and cooking. She grew up in Southwest Louisiana, where she currently resides with her husband Jim.

Printed in the USA
CPSIA information can be obtained
at www.ICGtesting.com
LVHW091557211223
766989LV00038B/170

9 798888 325933